I0627626

TRADING DARKNESS

A DARK FAIRYTALE FANTASY NOVEL

LISA HOFMANN

Trading Darkness
- A Dark Fairytale Fantasy Novel -

Text copyright © 2017 by Lisa Hofmann
Cover design: Artscandare Book Cover Design

ISBN 978-3-946618-05-8

Published by Elisabeth Hofmann Verlag, Netphen, Germany

This book is, as always, dedicated to my husband and children, who never seem to doubt that there is truth at the heart of every fairytale.

Lisa Hofmann, June 2017

Prologue

Wildenburg, AD 1650.

Agnes wasn't sure she could stand up, so she crawled across the cold floor on all fours, favoring her left elbow to drag herself through the darkness and the dirt to the other side of the barn. There, she collapsed on her side and curled up, slowly pulling her knees to her chest as well as she could manage. She prayed for unconsciousness, but there was too much pain.

The previous day had begun as her days always had up until then. She'd started a fire in the hearth, milked the goat her family shared with their next-door neighbor, and made breakfast for the children. They had just sat down at the table when the soldiers came.

The three men took her straight to the castle, and the bailiff had questioned her. When she hadn't given him the information he wanted, he had her taken to the tower and thrown into a cell with a dozen other women from the area. She knew four or five of them, but not very well. Most of them were from Wildenburg, and she was from Oakwood.

Some had been there a week, others only a day or two, but they'd all been to the dungeon, where the councilmen and the executioner met on a daily basis now to interrogate anyone suspected of witchcraft and Devil worship.

Not more than an hour passed before the hangman came for her, and she'd realized the evidence against her had to be overwhelming. She'd briefly wondered which of the women in the tower had testified against her, but this had to be some sort of misunderstanding. They must have gotten her name wrong, or maybe the girl had been terrified and just accused the first person she could think of who wasn't a friend or a relative.

The executioner had shown her the torture instruments, one rusty tool after the other, and explained what they did. But she still hadn't believed he'd really use them on her.

Their sons had played together in his back yard last winter, when she'd been at his house to buy an elixir for her youngest daughter's severe cough. His own little girl had sat on her lap while she'd described her child's symptoms to his wife so she could mix the medicine.

Of course he had to show her the instruments to appease the councilmen, she'd told herself, and she tried to reason with the high and mighty gentlemen. She addressed them directly since they were all familiar with her husband, one of their nobleman's most trusted and reliable messengers, but they hadn't listened to a word she said.

They didn't send her back to the cell, as she'd assumed they would. They got straight down to business, and the executioner broke all the fingers of her right hand, starting with the pinky. He took his sweet time about it so she could have a good hard think about her situation in between one digit and the next, but she doubted if confessing would do anything to improve it.

She passed out by the time he got to the pointer, but he revived her with smelling salts so she wouldn't miss the grand finale when he crushed her thumb. After that, he asked if she was ready to confess, but she refused.

She wasn't free from sin, but she was no Devil worshiper. They had to let her go if she remained steadfast and told the truth, didn't they? Her reputation was ruined, but her broken fingers would heal, and she'd live.

The executioner had sighed and folded his arms across his massive chest, waiting for further instructions from the councilmen. Irritated at her obstinacy, they'd seemed at a loss, and finally ordered the hangman's apprentice to take her back to the tower.

She'd thought it was over then, and that she'd soon be released.

She'd been wrong.

The next morning – *this* morning, though it seemed like a lifetime ago – she'd been brought back to the dungeon, and her heart had sunk, but she still hadn't lost hope. Since reasoning hadn't worked the previous day, she opted for silence. She couldn't say anything stupid they might use against her if she didn't speak.

Furious, the bailiff stopped asking questions and outright accused her of fornicating with the Devil. He ordered her to name the other men and women in her coven so he could pray for her soul and theirs.

When she remained silent even then, more out of shock than defiance, the executioner tore off her dress and underclothes, and chained her to a wooden board that sat against the wall at an angle. There, he stripped the skin off her legs with a rusty iron claw, going about his task even more slowly than he had when he'd broken her fingers. She'd screamed and screamed, but she hadn't caved.

This was when the council had decided another few hours in the overfilled tower prison wouldn't change her mind if the claws hadn't. They whispered quietly among themselves, shaking their heads and casting her glances. Eventually, they all agreed that more drastic measures were called for, considering the gravity of the accusations against her.

The bishop had visited Wildenburg a few days before Michaelmas in late September. He'd received complaints about unchristian conduct, drunkenness, quarrelling among neighbors, and violence, and he'd declared that this valley was positively *teeming* with sin.

He'd consulted with the duke, and then instructed the local priest to support the bailiff any way he could to ensure Christian order was restored so they would all survive the coming year without surrendering their ideals. After two years of poor harvests, and with stores almost used up, they were in for a hard winter.

The priest, a young man fully in his element, had come to the conclusion something evil was afoot. He'd stated there had to be a witch among them, and Bailiff Heistermann embraced the idea unreservedly. He proclaimed he wouldn't stop until he found out who was corrupting the god-fearing souls of the parish, even if he had to question every man, woman, and child in Wildenburg and Oakwood.

Agnes wasn't sure if the bishop knew it was the executioner who was doing the questioning now, but perhaps Heistermann thought he had found his prime suspect. Perhaps the councilmen *hoped* he had. They wouldn't bat an eye at the thought of sacrificing her to his cause, guilty or not, if it meant he'd stop looking. He was taking up their time and spending their money, and things had gotten way out of hand.

The hangman pulled her to her feet, bound her hands behind her back, and with the help of his apprentice, he heaved her onto the Spanish donkey. Straddling the tented sawhorse-like apparatus, she'd immediately felt the jagged metal edge of the upper rim slicing deep into her crotch. Her blood had trickled down the sloping sides of the wooden beast in rivulets. Then he'd tied weights to her feet, and the agony became too much.

At the top of her voice, she'd admitted to adultery, practicing black magic, and fornicating with the Devil. When Heistermann declared she'd also been accused of cursing an infant in its mother's womb and causing the cold spell in spring that destroyed this year's fruit harvest, she'd screamed it was all true, just so the executioner would take her off the donkey.

The council's secretary noted down every word she said into a huge leather-bound journal. The overwrought little man had repeatedly drawn air as he was writing. Heistermann had worn an expression that constantly kept shifting between smugness and feigned indignation.

He was a cruel man, and he obviously loved his vocation. He had enjoyed every moment of seeing her squirm. His greedy leer on her naked broken body had betrayed the joy he found in watching her suffer, and despite her agony, she'd wanted to scratch his beady little eyes out. She supposed she wasn't alone in that.

In total, the tower at Wildenburg Castle probably held thirty people from the surrounding villages in its three prison cells by now, all accused of witchery. Agnes had no idea how the hangman would deal with all of them, how many of those journals the secretary would go through over the coming weeks, and how often Heistermann was going to wet his pants for excitement over the things that went on down here in this hellish dungeon.

When all the grisly details of her case had been recorded and all the writing and witnessing was done, Heistermann had his soldiers take her to the empty barn near Flower Hill, where she now cowered on the floor, living out her final hours.

The barn was located halfway between Wildenburg and Oakwood. Right next to it was the hanging tree, where they strung up murderers. Just a few yards away from the tree was the site where they burned witches. She was neither a witch nor a murderer, but she knew she'd die there one way or the other the following day.

A drunkard with an ax stood guard outside. She thought she knew the man and considered asking him for a drink of water, but she couldn't be sure, so she didn't dare.

How many more women would they bring here during the night? She hadn't revealed any names to Heistermann today, but *someone* was bound to have. A few of the younger girls in the tower might believe they could save themselves if they did. One of them had named her.

The barn lay in complete darkness. Black clouds hid the moon away. Agnes trembled with cold despite the shift they'd put back on her before they'd dragged her from the torture chamber. Straw covered the packed dirt floor where she rested, but it did little to provide warmth.

A pile of last year's spoiled hay reeked of mold and mildew at the other end of the building. It would provide more protection from the night's chill if she could make it there, but Agnes wasn't sure she could. She wanted to be strong, but she was in so much pain, she didn't know if she had it in her anymore.

At least the children would be all right. Her husband had reluctantly agreed to get them out of the village and as far away as he could when Bernhard's men had come for her. She hoped Peter had managed to keep his promise instead of wasting everyone's time trying to persuade Bernhard to have her released.

Peter was so convinced of his liege lord's integrity, it sickened her. Their nobleman had never done anything for them, and he never would. He was a coward, and he would certainly not stand up to Heistermann, when Heistermann was telling people he was on a mission to save the entire fiefdom and all its Christian souls by destroying the enemies of Christ.

Bernhard of Blackvale never meddled in matters like these. He didn't attend the interrogations, and he didn't even come to the executions. He sent his juvenile sons to be present at the burnings on Flower Hill because he didn't have the stomach for it.

The empire had been at war for the better part of three decades now, and for eighteen of those years,

Bernhard's own farmers and crofters had been defending *his* lands with pitchforks, shovels, and their bare hands. Things would have been so much easier if they'd just surrendered the barren, loamy fields and rocky hillsides to the Swedish king, but they'd fought for Blackvale tooth and nail, and this was how he repaid them.

The man didn't have an ounce of honor in his bloated body, and Peter was nothing but a fool, loyal to a fault to Blackvale because Bernhard had taken him in after the first wave of witch trials had left him orphaned. He'd given him shelter, let him work in his stables, and later sent him on the most insane suicide missions behind enemy lines as his messenger.

If Peter had indeed done as she'd asked, he might have taken the children to his brother's house a few miles upriver, but Agnes knew that wouldn't be far enough. She didn't want him to see her like this, but if only she could talk to him now, she'd tell him to take them a hundred miles away from here and to never, *ever* come back.

Peter had been in Bernhard's employ for so long, if his wife wasn't safe, then *no one* would be. In light of her confession, Heistermann would claim the little ones were changelings, and he'd have them all burned at the stake right along with her if he got ahold of them.

A heavy rain set in, then thunder, and the sound of water dripping in through the roof filled the silence. Lightning flashed and lit up the barn through the cracks in the brittle wooden walls. Ozone hung in the air.

The door opened. Agnes expected another woman to be tossed in with her, perhaps the pitiful creature the hangman had tortured right after her. Instead, a cloaked figure entered.

Agnes' heart pounded. She scrambled away from the looming shape, opening every cut on her legs and feet as she did. A raging storm of raw agony pulsed through her lower body with her every movement, but the hooded figure kept coming after her until it towered right above her, black as night, and so tall, it reached right to the rafters.

She collapsed on her side and shimmied up against the wall, closing her eyes and covering her head with her arms. There was nowhere left to go. What would be, would be.

After a moment's silence, the creature bent down to her and sniffed. "I smell death."

She couldn't see its face. Perhaps it had none.

"Tell me, Agnes Smith, are you ready to die?"

She shook uncontrollably. She'd barely shed a tear in the castle dungeon because she hadn't wanted to give Heistermann the satisfaction of seeing her cry, but now a wild torrent of fear, pain, and grief traced lines in the blood and grime coating her cheeks.

The creature bent closer, releasing a cool breath

in her face. It smelled like an early morning wood fire in the fog.

"I said: are you ready to die?"

She licked her parched lips and hugged her knees tighter to her. Was she? No. Despite everything, she wasn't. She wanted to live – at least long enough to say goodbye to the children, and to tell Peter to get them the hell away from this place, even if she had to crawl to her brother-in-law's house to do it.

And, if she still had a day or two after that, she'd find a way to kill Heistermann.

And Bernhard of Blackvale.

And his entire cursed brood.

They were the plague this place needed ridding of, not the wise women or the so-called witches.

They were the scum of the earth who didn't lose a night's sleep over their own people's suffering, and who wouldn't lift a finger to come to anyone's aid if it didn't directly benefit them.

"I can't hear you, Agnes Smith."

"No," she whispered. "I don't want to die."

The being straightened. "I thought not. Humans are *never* ready for death."

She awkwardly wiped her eyes and squinted up at the fiend without seeing more than before. It seemed to be made of darkness.

"There's still *one* thing I need to do," she muttered, though she didn't believe her personal fate or that of her family would be of interest to the Reaper of Souls, or whatever manner of being this creature was.

The creature hummed, as though considering what she'd said.

A spark of hope ignited inside her, and she added, "It's not for me."

"Well, then maybe we can strike a bargain, you and I, Missus Smith. What say you?"

She got the distinct notion that this creature wasn't intent on harming her. Not just yet. Since she had absolutely nothing left to lose, she slowly nodded. She wasn't a Devil worshiper, but she was at a point in her life where she'd pray to any sort of demon that could present her with a way to improve her children's chances of escaping the flames.

"I'm listening," she said, her voice barely above a whisper.

The being chuckled hoarsely. "I know you are. I would like to give you a gift." It paused, perhaps waiting to see if she'd refuse the mere prospect of taking something handed to her by a dark spirit. When she didn't, it continued. "I'd like to give you *time* because I know that's what you need most. I'll give you your freedom for just as long as it will take you to do that *one* thing you still have to do before you leave this world."

She perked up. "And what is it you'd ask of me in return?" Nothing was ever free in this world, and certainly not *time* when yours had run out. She would never have thought how valuable a single day – or even a single hour – could be.

The creature tilted its head. Despite her fear and her dread, Agnes wished she could see its eyes.

"Your soul," it said simply, as though this was a minor, inconsequential thing she had no use for and wouldn't be missing.

She swallowed hard. Why would anyone want *her* soul? It was far from pure. God and the Devil might be at odds over it when she passed on. She'd been meaning to repent in between the hardships of the war and the daily struggles of getting by in these times, but she hadn't had a chance to make good on the intent yet.

She hadn't done *most* of the things she'd confessed to, but she'd done a few others she wasn't proud of. She'd committed adultery. She'd lied. She'd stolen.

Four of her six children weren't Peter's. She'd sworn him on her mother's grave they were when he'd voiced his doubts. Being Peter, he hadn't even argued.

For years now, she'd been bedding his brother whenever Peter's back was turned, jumping at every opportunity. And the worst part? She'd enjoyed playing her games with him, and Peter knew it, but for some reason, he accepted it. Until the birth of her last child.

The midwife had washed the stillborn infant, wrapped the little girl in a blanket, and put her in Agnes' arms.

Peter had cried for the baby, and he'd looked at her and said, "It's God's punishment. For my weakness."

Nothing had been the same after that. Life was fragile in Oakwood, and love was difficult to find, but she'd spent years and years hurting the one man who'd cared for her. Clearly the sum of her transgressions was more than enough to justify a fear of what was to come when she stepped in front of her maker.

Cautiously, she propped herself up on her elbow. "Are you the Reaper or the Devil?"

Again, the creature gave a throaty cackle, as though the mere thought was completely absurd.

"No, child, certainly not. The Reaper you're thinking of and the Devil you seem to be so familiar with can only claim the souls of the dead. *I* collect the souls and the memories of the living before they pass on... before all their... *hunger*... is lost. I come from a world between worlds, and I gather the... let's say *driving forces* and recollections of the ill-treated, and those yearning for vengeance. People like you. You have every reason to be angry. Your Lord Blackvale is treating your entire family unjustly at this moment, isn't he?"

Her eyes widened. "My children…" she stuttered, chest closing up. "What do you know of my children?"

"I know your husband did not bring them to safety. He is still at Blackvale, trying to convince Bernhard to let you go and end these trials. Heistermann isn't at all happy about that. His men will soon be underway to fetch your children so Peter Smith will shut his mouth. The charges against him and all six of them are already written up."

Agnes began crawling toward the door, teeth clenched against the pain. How she hated Peter… weak, stubborn Peter. "I have to warn them."

The creature hummed again almost amusedly as she labored to keep moving, tearing the scabs off wounds that were barely closing.

"You'll never make it to the road like that," it said, sighing.

She knew the being was right. Not on her hands and knees. She'd need a horse, but she couldn't get up on one, much less sit on it.

The creature closed the door in front of her nose. "Unless…"

She looked up, ready to agree to anything. "Take whatever you need from me. Take my soul. It's all yours if you just let me go to warn my children."

If the driving force of her soul was worth the trouble of coming here to collect, surely the price she was asking was fair.

The creature took down its hood, and another bolt of lightning lit up the barn. Agnes saw not one face, but many; young men, old women, children, some smiling, some marked by illness, some hopeful, others screaming – and finally her own, only much younger than she was now. Bright, vibrant eyes and a cherry smile met her desperate glance.

"You have the whole night, Agnes."

She was about to demand a means of getting her there, but then…

Something gave.

Something changed.

The messy, swollen pulp beneath her waistline mended, and her broken fingers straightened. The flesh on her legs healed.

She rose and leveled her shoulders. "The whole night?"

The being nodded. "Use it wisely. Few are given this kind of chance."

One

The Demon

Oakwood, AD 1670.

The heavy double-winged doors of the church crashed back on their hinges. A blast of icy wind brought in a swirling mass of dead leaves, dust, gravel, and shreds of the tattered family standard of Blackvale.

Someone – a nobleperson by the looks of them – stood outside in the yard, elegantly clothed in dark silk and velvet, but unfamiliar to the churchgoers, with the hood of their mantle so far down over their face.

The churning mess that had entered the church eddied and whirled like a shapeless tornado. Bits of sand and grit pelted the parishioners as it passed them, hurtling up the aisle.

When it reached the sanctuary, it consolidated, forming the contours of the hooded figure outside, but so tall that it towered five feet above the priest. The clergyman's eyes bulged in terror, but before he could do anything or even scream, the *thing* lifted him up off his feet and threw him against the wall behind the altar. There, he slid to the floor and lay still, unconscious.

People panicked. Those closest to the back of the building clambered for the only exit as the cloaked figure watched, unmoving. Sir Gregory of Blackvale wasn't sure whether it would be safer inside or out, but then the figure stretched out its arm, balled its hand, and abruptly drew its closed fist toward its chest. The doors of the church slammed shut just as suddenly as they'd opened.

Squinting at the *thing* that had materialized in front of the altar, Gregory and his brother, the Duke of Blackvale, drew their swords and lunged forward to protect their families. Their wives and children still occupied the first row of pews.

The apparition made of storm, dirt, and twigs fell apart just before their blades sliced through the air. It reassembled a few feet away, becoming almost tangible again.

The brothers advanced, hoping to corner it. It had to have a weakness they could use to their advantage. There wasn't a doubt in Gregory's mind they'd have to kill it. If it *could* be killed.

One step ahead of them, the projection – or whatever it was – repeated its trick and disbanded once more in a swirl of autumn leaves, silver magic, and dust.

Gregory shot his brother a glance, but Anton was as confused as he. They could only try to keep it moving until they could think of something more effective. Neither of them had encountered an enemy like this before.

But the being repeated its strategy every time the men came after it. It taunted them and made fools of them as they wore themselves out, hacking and chopping at its incorporeal form, but Gregory realized this too late. Panting, the brothers stopped chasing it, and tried to position themselves between the spinning entity and their wives and children.

A honey-sweet chuckle echoed through the house of worship, rising in pitch and volume until it turned into a screeching, screaming laugh of victory meant to shame them.

The sound forced every living soul in the church to its knees. People huddled between the pews and in the church's corners, clutching their loved ones and pressing their hands to their ears. Gregory's vision blurred, and horrible images danced before his eyes. On the edge of panic, he was barely able to breathe knowing he couldn't protect his daughters against something that didn't exist within the laws of nature.

When the laughter finally ceased, the being manifested in the sanctuary. It settled into the same solid shape as before, resembling the figure out in the churchyard.

"Anton!" it called out in a pleasant voice, neither male nor female. "Duke Anton! Come forward!"

Icy fingers reached into Anton's heart. Gregory knew because he felt them curling around the beating muscle inside his own chest, taking hold, and slowly squeezing just hard enough to give him a glimpse of his twin's death.

Each of the brothers had their own reasons to fear death. No matter how much they'd donated to the church, or how often the clergyman had forgiven them for their sins over the past years, they had done things no man should have to do. Heaven was for the brave, the untainted, and the clear of conscience.

If God was watching them now, He'd see the sons of Blackvale cowering on the stone floor, unable to defend the people they'd sworn to protect, and He'd be ashamed for them both. So would their father. They'd been born to greatness, the old man had always claimed, but the heir he'd appointed to be his successor wasn't *great* any more than Bernhard himself had been. Sweat poured down Anton's temples. He didn't have a plan, and he was afraid.

The commoners' wails died down to whimpers. They'd probably all been convinced this would be their end. The good people of Oakwood, unwavering and firm in their belief, had likely thought the Lord was going to abandon them, as He had during the Thirty Years' War and throughout the difficult years since.

Now that the noise and the chaos had ceased, and the demon had *named* someone, they had hope that they might be spared. It was their nobleman the monster had come for.

The creature seemed to relish Anton's disgrace and humiliation in front of his people. It pointed a bone-like finger at him as he might have done at a servant.

"You!" it boomed. "You owe me a life."

Then everything became clear. This was no ghost. This was the Century Demon.

The older parishioners remembered the stories word for word. The younger ones had heard whispers of them. Gregory and Anton had spent their lives hoping they weren't true.

When they'd been boys and impossible to tell apart, the brothers' grandmother had told them this day would come in their lifetime. She'd also assured them their unanimity and their resourcefulness would save them, just as the family's unanimity had always prepared their father's ground for him, all through the war and the witch trials. She'd said there wasn't a difficulty they wouldn't manage if they stood by one another – they were born to *greatness*, after all.

Growing up, Gregory had assumed the old woman had added a lot of bells and whistles onto an old legend to teach them the lesson behind it and prepare them for hard times. She'd certainly been one of the most knowledgeable people of local history in all the land, but some of her tales had just seemed too tall to be true, and the lessons behind them too abstract. To Gregory, the story about the Century Demon had always fallen under that category.

He believed in God and the Devil, heaven and hell, and a lot of things in between, but he'd never *truly* believed in demons or black magic. Witchery was something the commoners had come up with to explain their own misfortunes, and demons were old wives' stories meant to keep children from wandering too far from home. Or they had been. Until today.

Now he had to come to terms with the fact that it was all true. The Century Demon was real, and both he and Anton knew what that meant.

He felt sick as he went to stand beside his brother. Anton gave him a small nod of acknowledgement before he moved forward. Gregory wanted to follow, but Anton stopped him with a motion of his hand.

"Don't," he whispered. "This is my burden."

The duke took another few steps and fixed his gaze to the demon. "No," he said in a loud, firm voice.

The word registered with Gregory like a punch in the gut, and he gripped the hilt of his sword so tightly, it hurt. He said a quick prayer and prepared to fight, but to his shock, Anton sheathed his own sword, unbuckled the belt, and let it slide from his hip. It clattered to the floor at his feet.

Gregory was the older of them, but Sir Bernhard had chosen to leave his privileges and the fief to the first twin who'd give him a grandson. Anton had always been more interested in the ladies, and more popular with them too, so the race had been decided before it had even begun, and the title had gone to Anton.

Steadfast, brave Anton, the brother who'd never be *great*, because he was the brother who was about to get them all killed.

Irritation overlaid Gregory's sense of helplessness. What did the fool think he was doing? Did Anton assume he could reason with the beast, or was he determined to die a coward's death? He might at least have let them buy the women and children some time to get away.

Again, the creature laughed, and the sound reverberated painfully in Gregory's ears.

"No?" the demon boomed. "You're telling me *no*?"

"I am," Anton replied. "*I* have no contract with *you*."

The demon roared in outrage, and with a flick of its stick fingers, it launched a hurricane at them. Thunder rose, lightning flashed, and the whole building shook, as though its foundations were disintegrating, and the ground beneath it could open up at any moment and swallow the entire stronghold and everyone in it.

Cracks appeared in the walls. Plaster crumbled from the high arched ceiling and showered them with debris. The tall stained-glass windows shattered.

Millions of razor-sharp shards hailed down on them. People screamed. Men and women shielded their children with their bodies.

Gregory tried to find his wife and daughters in the turmoil, but he was too far away to be of any use to them. Glass fragments cut deep into the skin of his arms and hands, and he could only try to protect his eyes until it was over.

When the lead frames were empty and the bombardment ended, the metal-studded doors of the church exploded outward, leaving a gaping hole in the wall. Wood scattered all across the small courtyard.

Gregory looked up and saw that the apparition in the church was gone, but the Century Demon was standing outside, where he had first glimpsed it, cloak billowing, face concealed beneath its hood.

"You *will* give me what's mine," it said. "The contract comes with the title, and it will *never* expire until the last heir of Blackvale has perished."

The creature let that information sink in for a moment, but Anton shook his head as he exited the building through the empty door frame. Gregory thought he must have gone mad, but he stayed right behind his brother, motioning the commoners to remain where they were.

"I will give you *nothing*!" Anton loudly repeated, voice unwavering.

The demon flicked its fingers and sent another blast of wind at him, nothing like the last one, but strong enough to make him stumble. Anton went down on all fours.

"You *will* choose a child from your own blood," the demon said, "and you *will* give me that child by first light tomorrow, or I will raze this place to the ground and take a hundred families from the villages in its place."

Then the being vanished, and an eerie silence engulfed the community. People started emerging from the church, dazed.

Gregory spat out a mouthful of bile, trying to look as composed as he could, but no one was paying him any attention. They were all staring at Anton.

Anton had five children, and his wife had not survived the birth of their youngest. Gregory knew the love he felt for each and every one of his sons and daughters. They were his greatest treasure. It would have been kinder to Anton to hack off his right arm than to force him to pick one of his children and sacrifice it to the demon.

Gregory couldn't say what he'd do in his brother's place. He'd spent years resenting his father for leaving Blackvale to Anton, but now it dawned on him – morbidly – that the fates had been in his favor after all. If his father had left his lands to Gregory instead of his brother, the demon would now be demanding a child of him instead.

That evening, after they'd sent everyone home, Anton stood by the fireplace in his Great Hall, hands folded behind his back and shoulders far too straight. His empty eyes stared into space. He wasn't watching the flames in the hearth, and he didn't feel their heat.

Gregory's heart was heavy with Anton's misery. He wasn't indifferent to his twin's fate, and he never would be. They shared too many genes and too much history. They had their differences, but neither of them was uncaring toward the other, or cold toward others in general. The commoners were wrong when they spoke about the Blackvales that way. Responsibility just forced hard choices, and hard choices required debate.

They were both family men. Their father had favored his brother, and Gregory had always thought Anton was the luckier of them both for it. Now he knew how wrong he'd been.

One child to save the entire fiefdom from a creature that couldn't be killed, but the demon wouldn't return for another hundred years. Things could be very different by then. Situations changed. But right now?

It was one life for a thousand.

That didn't sound unreasonable – not unless it was your own child the monster was after.

Gregory put his hand on his brother's shoulder. He let it linger there longer than he intended, but Anton did not respond. He wasn't going to talk to him about the choice he would have to make tonight, and Gregory couldn't force him to.

He turned to leave. He had to go home to his own loved ones. Theresia would be waiting up for him, and he had some explaining to do. She loved Anton's children almost as much as her own, and she wouldn't take it well. She was Hermann Heistermann's daughter, but she was one of the most compassionate souls he knew.

Heistermann had kept her away from the horrors of the witch trials in his time. She had no idea of the repulsive things her father had done, or what Gregory had done in his name and on Bernhard's orders. Somehow, the men in Theresia's life had managed to spare her good, innocent heart that way, but if Anton didn't do as the demon demanded, their own girls wouldn't be safe anymore, and a world of pain was going to come to their own home.

He was grateful the twins would be in their beds when he got back, hopefully sound asleep. At least he wouldn't have to answer their questions tonight, and it would all be over when they awoke in the morning. He and Theresia would tell them later. But just what *would* they tell them? He didn't know.

How could he explain to those little girls that their family was cursed? How could he explain to them that a long-forgotten ancestor of theirs had somehow managed to enrage a creature so powerful, it could keep coming back to haunt their children's children for all eternity?

He'd almost reached the door when Anton finally spoke, his voice a testament to the broken soul within the once proud man.

"What would you do, brother?"

Gregory was tempted to pretend he hadn't heard and keep walking. He didn't have the answer to that, or *any* answer at all.

He thought of his beautiful little Maria with her gorgeous head of dark curls that bounced around her shoulders whenever she came running to greet him after an absence. She smelled of hay and fresh flowers, and she was never loud or disrespectful.

And there was clever little Louisa, bright as the sun and smarter than any of them. She had her nose forever stuck in a book, and her fingertips were permanently black from the ink on the quill he'd given her for her last birthday.

These two were the light of his life, and he could imagine the darkness that surrounded the duke right now at the prospect of losing one of his own girls.

Gregory would give neither of his children away. God help him, he'd rather kill himself than hand either of them over. A life without them wouldn't be a life worth living. But he was just the duke's brother, and he could afford to theorize and be sentimental. Anton couldn't.

He took a deep breath. "I'd remember my duty to my people," he lied without looking back at the other man, and left.

Life was cruel, he thought as he took his horse's reins from the squire who met him at the front entrance. His hands trembled, and his spine felt weak. He had trouble getting into the saddle. The squire had to help him up.

He didn't thank the man, and he didn't talk to the guards at either of the gates he passed through. All he wanted was to go home.

He drove his mare as hard as he could, and the sound of the animal's hooves on the wooden bridge echoed across the moat and reverberated in the valley like thunder. Gregory was glad when he'd finally cleared the castle grounds.

Avoiding the field roads despite the profound darkness of the new-moon night, he decided to take the shortcut through the forest. These woods had never spooked him before after dark, but the shadows that seemed to move between the trees tonight had him in constant alarm. He had to force himself to slow down so he wouldn't get himself killed. He wanted to reach Wildenburg in one piece and lock out the nightmare that would be roaming these lands until it got what it was after.

Anton had spoken to the people who'd been in the church today. He was good at that kind of thing, but he hadn't been able to convince them they were safe.

Who could blame them? The priest had nursed his wounds and, in front of everyone, immediately begun ranting and raving about how Anton should never have forced Heistermann to leave. He'd claimed they were all doomed, and it was Anton's fault.

As far as Gregory was concerned, getting rid of Heistermann was the best decision his brother had ever made. He couldn't have helped them today. Having a few people executed because their neighbors claimed they were practicing witchcraft was one thing – trying to deal with a demon quite another.

Witches weren't even real, but the Century Demon was, and they'd witnessed what it was capable of. It had truly chosen its moment. The church was always well filled on Sundays, and everyone who'd been there and seen the creature was afraid. They were probably spreading the news to the villages and every farmhouse between one hamlet and the next at this very moment.

The guards Anton had ordered to accompany Gregory's family back to Wildenburg Castle earlier were still on watch at the outer gate. He hesitated briefly before dismissing them, but resolved that he had no right to hold them here. Anton would need them more than he did.

As the soldiers headed off toward the road, he instructed one of his own men to fetch reinforcements. He didn't expect trouble, but it was better to be safe than sorry. Then he directed his horse up the steep path leading to the modest stronghold's inner wall.

One of his stableboys met him behind the keep, ready to take the animal off his hands, but he refused and sent the lad to bed. Not wanting to face Theresia just yet, he set about tending to the mare himself, unable to get the images of his nieces' and nephews' faces out of his head as he unsaddled her. All but one of the children were older than Maria and Louisa, and they were all in good health, save for the youngest.

Which child would it be? The oldest boy, because he was the strongest and would go without question if his father asked him to? Or the youngest, because he was sickly and might not reach adulthood? Or would Anton pick one of the girls?

Lost inside himself, he didn't hear Theresia entering the stable behind him, wrapped in her woolen shawl. He jumped when she called his name.

"I'm sorry, I didn't mean to frighten you."

"You didn't. I'm just tired."

He stared at her for a while and traced the cuts on her face and hands lightly with his fingertips. None of them were deep enough to leave visible scars.

Tenderly cupping her cheeks in his hands, he kissed her deeply, thankful for the warmth of her embrace, and for her very presence in his life. It was a miracle they hadn't all been killed in the church as the glass had rained down on them. Louisa was the only one who'd likely keep something back just beneath the hairline above her left temple. She'd bled and bled, but headwounds were inclined to, as well he knew.

"Just let me finish up here," he said, and made haste to rub the horse down, while Theresia fetched water for the animal.

After that, they went inside the castle, bolted the doors, and climbed the stairs leading to the second floor.

Gregory took the time to look in on his daughters. He needed to see them in their beds.

Pulling the covers around Maria's tiny form more snugly, he vowed to remember this day if ever she tried his patience.

He gently pushed back the locks from sweet Louisa's brow to see how the gash was doing, and quietly promised her he'd never chide her for scribbling on the table again.

When he finally fell asleep next to Theresia, it was no more than a fitful, exhausting slumber, not unlike when he'd dozed through a night and a day of a high fever as a child. In his dreams, he was running through the darkness of the forest with his daughters in his arms. Shadows rose all around them, and silvery shards rained down on them, but they were not made of glass. They were made from the Century Demon's magic. It was after them, and there was no place to go, and nowhere to hide.

Sometime just after dawn, he could hear bells tolling from afar. The north winds carried the sound all the way from Blackvale's belfry. He jumped out of bed and threw open the windows. Peering out, he could hardly believe his eyes when he saw the heavy black smoke churning above the treetops in the distance.

Fire at the castle! He had to saddle the horse and hurry out there to help.

But then something caught his eye. Just below on the winding path that led up to the small fortress, a figure moved out of the woods. His heart stopped. He wanted to close the shutters and make believe this wasn't happening, but it was too late. The demon had seen him. He felt its stare, and the iciness in its voice as it whispered his name. A second later, it was in his yard, and then, suddenly, at his door. In another instant, it was standing right in front of him in his bedroom, revealing one of its many faces to him.

Paling and shaking his head, he backed away.

"No," he stammered, and cast a quick glance at his wife, who was fast asleep and unnaturally still.

The demon smiled, baring rows of pin-sharp teeth that stood in stark contrast to the angelic beauty of its face – a face Gregory knew well, because he'd sent the woman it had belong to to her death many, many years ago.

"Don't worry about her," the demon reassured him. For a moment, Gregory wasn't sure whether the creature meant his wife, or the witch whose face it wore.

"Why are you here?"

"Did you not see the smoke?"

His chest grew tight. Cold sweat beaded on his brow, and the realization sank in. "What have you done?"

"Oh, but I didn't have to do anything," the creature cut him off.

"Your brother did that all by himself. He chose not to choose, and he set fire to his legacy –*your* legacy. Such a foolish thing to do."

"Is he dead?" Gregory whispered.

"He is *now*. He thought he could fool me, and that I wouldn't find him out on the Mountain Road as he tried to flee. Such a cowardly soul, your dear brother. But the men in this family never were very brave, or very smart."

Gregory felt the blood leaving his head and his world began to spin in and out of focus. Tears trailed down his cheeks as he tried to steady himself against the foot of his bed.

The demon drew closer without making a sound. He could feel its cold breath on his skin. Its darkness and its black nothingness seeped through every fiber of his night clothes, chilling him to the bone.

"He did try to bargain for his children's lives," the demon continued, "I'll leave him that. But in the end, he didn't have anything to offer that might have been of interest to me. Nothing he would have given of his own free will."

Gregory couldn't stop the sobs that were shaking him, and it was all he could do to hold himself on his feet in his anguish and his sorrow.

The demon leaned in to him. "Your brother *chose* not to *choose*. He ran. He paid the price. And, since I hate losing out, that would make *you* the new duke who has to *choose*."

"No," he cried out, but then pressed a hand to his mouth.

He hadn't thought about the girls in the next room, and right on cue, Louisa appeared in the open doorway, followed by her sister. His cry had roused them both.

Faster than Gregory could have anticipated, the demon was at the girls' side and picked them both up, balancing one on each hip. Strangely, neither of them was afraid. They smiled up at the being, chortling and giggling as though they were having the time of their lives with a beloved relative they hadn't seen in a while.

Seven years old, and so good and trusting, he thought, devastated as he observed them. They were so very unaware of the misery to come.

He hardly dared to move; his feet felt leaden, like they were rooted to the ground, and time seemed to stop.

"*Choose*," the demon commanded, but its voice was only in his head. The girls couldn't hear it.

Gregory's knees gave out. "No…"

"Do it now, or I will not leave anyone alive. I will not leave one stone upon the other, not one soul unbroken – and then I will destroy you anyway, so *choose!*"

Two

Darkness

The new duke was alone and surrounded by darkness.

He reached out, blindly trying to feel his way around the cold, silent void, but the space around him seemed infinitely wide and open.

In it, there was nothing to touch but emptiness, nothing to hear except for the rattling of his own breath in his lungs, and nothing to see except for the specters created by his heart's worst fears. There was nothing to even tell him which way was up because the ground beneath his bare feet felt like it was shifting continuously.

He stumbled and fell.

When he got up, he dragged himself onward without the slightest clue which direction he'd been going. He was bone-weary, and the next time he fell, he tumbled into what could have been a deep crater, hitting his head, breaking his legs, breaking his arms, and breaking his will.

Lying flat on his back, he decided he could go no further. His strength was spent, and he was nothing in a dying universe of nothingness.

"Why?" he sobbed in his sleep for the thousandth time before he slowly came to, chest tight, nightclothes and sheets drenched with his sour sweat. "*Why?*"

Opening his eyes, he groped around the empty bed for his wife. Of course, she was gone. She was hardly there anymore at all because she spent most every night in the girls' room – in Maria's room – holding vigil, guarding one half of her soul, since the other had been torn away.

One life in return for the safety of a thousand.

It didn't seem too steep a price to pay. Not unless it was your own child the demon was asking for.

One life for an entire fiefdom.

He'd had no other choice. He'd had to do it, but he couldn't blame the girls' mother for hating him for it.

She'd pummeled him with her fists and called him a coward and a murderer, and he'd had nothing to say to his defense. She'd screamed and cried until she'd had nothing left, and looking at her even today, he knew she was still screaming and crying inside every waking moment. He didn't think she'd ever stop.

"Papa?" Maria timidly poked her head in the door.

He sat up, forcing himself to smile at her. "Good morning, my darling. Have you slept well?"

She shook her head, quaking with sadness, and he spread his arms. She flung herself at his chest, tears clouding up dark-rimmed eyes.

"That dream again?" he asked, shivering. She nodded, crying silently into his shoulder as he held her, rocking her gently. He knew the nightmare that was troubling her because it was the same as the one that plagued him.

"It's all right," he lied, mumbling into her hair. "It'll go away, you'll see. I promise. I know it's hard, but you'll have to give it time."

"But Louisa *is* coming back, isn't she?"

"No, love, she isn't. She can't. She's gone."

She was, wasn't she?

He'd watched the creature that had taken her vanishing in a cloud of gray mist, holding her in its arms. Louisa hadn't cried. She hadn't made a single sound, but she'd refused to let go of Maria's hand, and Maria had fiercely held on to her until she'd disappeared. His heart had broken then, but it had been Maria's shrieks that had awoken the girls' mother.

The scene replayed in his head over and over, and he kept asking himself if he hadn't overlooked something, if there had really been nothing he could have done differently. Anton had tried to run, but he hadn't gotten very far despite his head start. Gregory was certain that if he hadn't given the demon what it had demanded of him, he would have lost both children and his wife, and countless others would have died.

What could he have done?

He'd gone to collect his brother's body, and he'd wept like a child when he'd found him lying by the roadside. He'd brought him home, and lain him and his children to rest in the family crypt, and he grieved for them. He often went there to talk to his brother, alternately telling him that he understood why he'd done what he had, and how much he loathed him for it. It got easier as time passed, but slowly. Dealing with the searing raw pain of losing Louisa didn't. Perhaps it wasn't meant to.

All he had left of the elder of his twin girls was the image of watching her go. There was no body to lay in the earth, no stone with her name on it, and he couldn't even bring himself to say her name out loud. She was a ghost that haunted his every waking minute, and his own helplessness tormented him by night so he never found peace. Maybe this was his just punishment for surrendering her.

Another thing kept eating away at him relentlessly: he'd been sure the demon would take her life, initially, making some sort of blood sacrifice of her to his false gods, but the longer he thought about it, the less certain he was of that.

It's what his wife needed to believe, and it's what he'd told Maria for a fact, but he hadn't seen the child die, so it wasn't necessarily the truth.

There was a weak pulse of hope inside of him that she might be alive somewhere, on one hand, but the thought of what she might be going through made him wish that wasn't so. There was no way of telling what that monster was doing to her, and how she might suffer at its hands, so perhaps his little Louisa would be better off dead, and this was what he should be praying for.

Whatever he chose to believe or hope for, he'd never have closure. Deep down inside, none of them would, and his other daughter's question had just confirmed that.

Hugging Maria to him, he kissed her forehead, and his lip touched a tender bulge just above her left temple. He'd never noticed it there before, and then he recalled the gash on Louisa's head after the church windows had shattered. Brushing Maria's dark curls aside now, he drew breath as he took note of the shape and position of it, and his chest closed up for a moment.

"Papa, why did you give Louisa away?"

He let his head fall back against the wooden bedstead, wiping a hand over his stubbly chin. "We've been over this, dear…"

"No," she cut him off persistently, "I mean why did you give *Louisa* to that demon and not *me?*"

He'd realized she'd ask, one day. He'd just never thought that day would come so soon.

Why *had* he taken Maria from the creature's arms, and not Louisa?

He remembered feeling the seconds slipping away, seeping through his fingers like sand, and the demon had grown impatient. He'd felt its agitation. He recalled looking back and forth between his beloved daughters' faces, his heart pounding in his throat, feeling completely incapable of any decision.

"One life to save the entire fiefdom," the demon had reminded him eventually.

"Mercy!" he'd stammered. "Have you no pity?"

"Pity?" the being had laughed, and he'd gotten the idea this demon knew nothing of pity because it had absolutely no concept of compassion.

Sometimes, evil was born, and not made.

"Choose!"

And then, he had.

He'd grabbed the child less hard to please, less difficult to comfort, and less inclined to worry, and he'd done so thinking of the days and months and years that would follow. Misery loved dark places, and his daughters were like the sun and the moon; both were beautiful, brave, and true in their own time, but only one of them would be left to him, and if he *had* to choose, then he'd choose the sun. He'd choose Maria because Louisa was the moon. He'd choose the happier, more forgiving nature over the more perceptive and judicious girl.

The sun knew no darkness, and it would always heal, illuminating and warming the earth, while the moon would hide during the day. Its scars were visible and would never mend, not in a sheer eternity of nights. If she'd lived to grow up, Louisa might have been the stronger of the both of them, but without Maria's light she'd never have been able to shine, just as the moon wouldn't if it wasn't for the sun. Misery wouldn't find dark places in Maria.

Shifting her about so he could look her straight in the eyes, he noticed his wife standing in the doorway, pale and drawn as she leaned against the frame with her arms folded too tightly across her chest. It was as though she was holding onto herself lest she'd fall apart. She didn't look like she'd slept, and he was sure she hadn't eaten.

Maria didn't know she was there, but whatever he said now, it had to be something both mother and daughter could work with, or none of them would ever be able to look the other in the eyes again. Not with this between them.

Maria had just turned seven, and she'd live to see her eighth birthday only because he'd made the decision he had. They'd *all* live because he had done what he'd needed to do. Right now and for the years to come, it was a question of how they'd cope with it, how *Maria* would deal with being the twin who'd lived because he'd thought she'd have a better chance of surviving the aftermath.

"I didn't choose one of you over the other," he said finally. "I loved Louisa every bit as much as I love you, and I'll never forgive myself, but I had to let one of you go so the other would live, and that was her."

He hadn't chosen to give Louisa to the demon. He'd taken Maria from its arms in order to save her, and that was the best he could have done.

Wasn't it?

The child was alone and surrounded by darkness.

She reached out, blindly trying to feel her way around the cold, silent void, but there was nothing in the seemingly infinite space around her.

There was nothing to touch but emptiness after she'd let go of her sister's hand, nothing to hear except for the sound of her own rapid breathing. The image of her father's face disappearing in the distance had burned itself into her mind, and there was nothing but blackness besides. She couldn't tell which way was up because the ground beneath her bare feet felt like it was shifting continuously.

Unsure if it was safe to walk for fear of stumbling or colliding with a wall, she carefully moved onward nonetheless. Putting one foot in front of the other again and again, she began mumbling a rhyme her mother had taught her when the path seemed too long or too steep.

One
and two
and three
and four

and five
and six
and seven
and eight
the sun
the rain
and a woodsman's cane
and forwards
backwards
one step to the side
and one
and two…

Standing still wouldn't help her. Standing still wouldn't get her home.

and three
and four…

And then she tripped and fell.

"Mama?" she sobbed, her voice as tiny and thin as the girl herself. "Mama?"

"She's not here, darling."

The voice was kind and soothing, but the little one hunkered down, hugging her knees. She made herself as small as she could because there was nowhere to hide.

"Mama…" she whimpered in a tiny voice, hoping no one would hear but her mama. She was so lost, and she needed her mama so badly.

"She's not coming, dearest," the voice said again.

The girl couldn't say from where it came. It seemed to be all around and nowhere at the same time, bouncing off walls that weren't there.

"I want to go home," she murmured, crying softly.

She wasn't a cry baby, not like her sister who'd bawl her eyes out over a bruised knee, but everything was so very wrong right now. She didn't know where she was or how she'd gotten here, and there was no light, only blackness. She'd heard of blind people not being able to see, but she didn't think she was blind. It was this place, this *terrible* place.

"You *can't* go home, my pretty," the friendly voice replied patiently. "Your mama doesn't *want* you to come home because your papa doesn't want you there anymore."

That couldn't be true.

Her papa always held his arms wide open whenever he came through their front door at night to join them for supper. He'd laugh and call out her name when she squealed in delight at the sight of him, dancing and twirling toward him on the tips of her toes. He'd say she was his little dove, and he'd ask her if she'd nothing better to do than become prettier by the minute when he wasn't there. He was good to her, and she'd never heard an unkind word from him. He loved her, and she loved him. That was why this couldn't be.

"I want my papa." She was trembling from the cold, though her face was hot and wet from the tears that leaked down her cheeks in haphazard runnels, dripping from her nose and chin.

"No, dear. I'm so, *so* sorry. He gave you away so he could be the new duke. That was more important to him than you are. He had to choose between you and your sister, and he kept your sister because he loved her more."

The girl closed her eyes and listened to the sound of her own sniveling, caught inside herself and heaving. This simply *couldn't* be right… could it? Her papa would never, *ever* have sent her away, she told herself. Not for anything. He'd never have sent *either of them* away. But, maybe he *did* love her sister more.

She was his little dove, but he always called her sister his little *princess*.

He loved her, but perhaps he really *did* love her sister *more*, and if he was a duke now, then her sister would be a real princess, and she… she would be nothing more than a dove.

Princesses were better than doves.

Her head was spinning and her tummy hurt, so she lay down on her side, a tight ball of arms and legs. She was exhausted, and she thought of her sister, who would be feeling what she was feeling, too, princess or not. She always did.

"I want Maria," she wept, "my Maria…"

"No, love… I'm sorry, but she has to forget you now, and you have to forget her. It's not her fault they didn't want you. One day you'll understand that, because one day, she'll need you. You *will* see her again, but not *today*. Not for a while."

"Maria…"

"Hush now, my sweet…"

All at once, Louisa felt a strange presence next to her, but she didn't have the strength to fight against it, and so she just huddled into herself even more tightly. Surprisingly, the presence didn't seem entirely repulsive or vile – it emitted a calm solace, but such was its magic, and Louisa knew nothing of magic. Not yet.

Tender arms curled around the little girl and lifted her up off the floor, cradling her like a baby against the illusion of a warm, soft, young body. Louisa thought she could smell strawberries and sunshine, and she felt safe as she drifted off.

"You're lucky you've got me now, darling," the demon murmured, breathing some of its magic into the sleeping child.

One dose had been enough to bring her here, and this second little waft would ease the pain of human loss sufficiently to make the coming days a bit more bearable. The child would be useless if its soul was broken, or if it died. Time stood still for no one, not even here.

"I'm going to take such good care of you," it crooned softly, watching the girl stir in her deep, unnatural sleep. "And when you're all grown up, you're going to repay me for that tenfold."

Three

The Wishmaster

Heavy snow clouds hung low in the sky and muffled the snorting sounds Gregory's mare made as he dismounted and tethered her reins loosely to a branch in the small natural clearing. Winter was now truly upon them, and he was freezing, but he'd ridden a good ten miles into the remotest part of the woods to be out of earshot of any farmer or traveler who might laugh at him if he overheard what the new duke of Blackvale was about to do.

"Rambert Longsword, I summon thee!" he cried out, cringing as the words left his lips.

Gregory could have sworn he was being watched, and he spun around hectically, searching for any sign of movement in the undergrowth. There was none, as far as he could tell, but he wasn't sure what to expect. Maybe there *was* nothing to expect, and he was lying to himself as he'd been lying to everyone else over the months that had passed.

Having tried to find solace in prayer, he'd discovered his heart wasn't in it. He could derive no comfort from the words, and he'd been meaning to talk to the priest about that, but he couldn't even bring himself to go to church anymore. It didn't seem… *safe*. Not for him, and not for his family. His brother was dead, his nieces and nephews all gone, the castle was a burnt-out ruin, and his marriage was in shambles. God was so difficult to see through all that at this moment.

Between one thing and another, he'd recently been finding himself at the library of Blackvale Abbey whenever he had an hour to spare, trying to figure out what on earth had made him think to go and spend it there. Then, he remembered that Louisa had, for some unfathomable reason, loved that dusty dark place.

Seven-year-olds and stuffy old books didn't really seem to go together, but Louisa had forever been badgering his wife to take Maria and her there. They'd gone as often as possible, but Maria had soon gotten bored with all the *'sitting around and being quiet'*, as she'd put it, and she'd usually preferred to stay home with the nursemaid after the first few times, playing with her dolls and *helping* with the chores around the house. That had been quite all right with Louisa, because Louisa hadn't been interested in dolls or cooking; she'd been all for storytelling and painting. Funny how his girls had looked so much alike while having so little in common.

The last book Louisa had looked at, so his wife had told him, was about the legends of the woodlands. Wildenburg and the surrounding areas were a place of many myths and legends; the forest here was old and unexplored, and folklore told of an ancient magic that resided deep within its heart.

Louisa hadn't been able to read too well yet at that point. She'd been trying hard to learn and become better at sounding letters and words, so he'd been surprised when his wife had shown him the huge volume she'd been tackling.

Theresia had told him the girl had been more looking at the pictures than trying to decipher the slanted, compact blocks of handwritten script after a while, but Gregory was impressed all the same. He'd begun to leaf through the tales Louisa had found most fascinating, and he'd quickly come to appreciate why she'd been so captivated. Tales of magic were always fascinating to children and people who didn't know any better.

The stories Louisa had asked her mother to help her read told of an immortal Wishmaster who had the power to change destiny. Gregory had devoured the tome from cover to cover just to have something to occupy his mind and keep it from straying toward his aching core.

At first, it had been a mere means of reviving details he might have missed out on in his daughter's life, a way to be close to the child he'd lost without feeling the pain, but it had rapidly become a growing obsession powered by the niggling feeling there was something to be learned from the stories about the creature that had held so much appeal for his daughter.

He'd searched for and found other books with stories of what he assumed would be the same being, and he'd had his advocate bring him everything he could find on the subject matter from throughout the kingdom over the last weeks.

He'd discovered that the Wishmaster went by many names, but the name he found most often was Rambert Longsword. It was one of two names he himself remembered from early childhood evenings with his grandparents by the hearth; Rambert Longsword and Rumpelstiltskin, the imp who'd taught a miller's daughter to spin gold from straw. The winter nights he'd sat with his grandmother had gone by barely noticed with wondrous tales like these, but the recollections he still had of them seemed more like a fading dream now than a reality.

The old woman with the crinkly face and ashen hair had been nearly blind by the time he was seven, and while sewing had been beyond her during the last years before she'd suddenly become too ill to leave her bed, she'd still been able to spin wool and knit. She'd produced soft stockings, mittens, scarves, and hats for Anton and him, and they'd been glad of every piece in the long winters of their childhood.

He'd helped her with the wheel and the spool, and he'd wound threads to balls and unraveled them for her when she needed them, relishing the warmth and light of the fire, and listening to her stories of days gone by.

His brother had often teased him for it, but he knew now it was the nature of siblings to feel a need to dissociate themselves from one another. Especially when they bore such a striking resemblance. That had nothing to do with rivalry or stubbornness – Gregory thought it was perhaps the Creator's means of ensuring that at least one of them would be equipped to survive the dog days.

He couldn't remember ever having helped his mama with the task she'd taken over from her mother-in-law when the aged Lady of Blackvale had passed away. Other things had held his attention in the years after they'd laid her to rest beside his grandfather in the crypt that now held both his parents and Anton, too. Boys grew into young men who had other concerns than family history and superstition. Right now, though, he found that the more he read, the better he could remember some of what would otherwise have been lost to him.

The descriptions of magical Wishmasters varied in the books and scrolls he acquired, depending on how long ago the account had been written and by whom. Some clergymen tended to interpret the oral histories handed down from one generation to the next with spiritually founded reasoning, while the worldly scribes often rendered their depictions more leaning toward the common man's fears.

The oldest stories told of a bent, aged wizard who'd walked unrecognized among the peasantry. He'd granted the poorest of the poor a single wish if they took him in for the night and shared their meal with him.

A greedy nobleman once heard of this. He disguised himself as a crofter and went to live in a shack on the edge of the forest, hoping the wizard would knock on his door. The wizard never came, but the beggars of Wildenburg and Blackvale ate one good meal a day from there on in.

The tales that spoke of Rambert Longsword told of a warrior king who'd found a way to travel to the Underworld so he could strike a bargain with the Devil over the prophesy of a soothsayer.

A wise woman had foreseen the death of Rambert's only son in battle, and he wasn't prepared to accept that fate for his boy. She hadn't been able to tell him when the battle would take place or how exactly the lad would die, and so the king offered the Devil his soul in return for a protective enchantment that would shield his son against any man-made weapon for all the days of his life. Confident nothing could harm him, Rambert had the best smiths in the land make a sword, a shield, a dagger, and some armor for his son, and he took him to war with him as soon as he'd come of age. On the eve of their first contact with the enemy, however, the boy fell off his horse and broke his neck. The king was devastated.

While his wife, oblivious to what had transpired, prayed for her son and husband, an angel appeared to her. He warned her that the Devil would come to claim what was his that very night.

She begged him to tell her if there was any way of saving her son, and the angel took pity on her. He cut out a piece of his own heart and placed it in Rambert's chest while he slept, and when the Devil came for him, he found he couldn't take the knight into the darkness with him because of the light that pulsed inside of him.

Rambert lived to a great old age, and when the human part of his heart would no longer beat, the Devil still couldn't take him to the Underworld, and realized he never would. He was so furious, he replaced the human half of Rambert's heart with a share of his own. That way, the warrior king could not die, and he'd see neither heaven nor hell for all of eternity.

Legend had it Rambert grew tired of watching God and the Devil play their never-ending game at some point over the centuries of his extraordinary long life. He acquired a knowledge of a magic that was neither dark nor light so he could throw a wrench in the works every now and then. Having come to understand what desperation was, he learned to grant wishes to those in despair if their wishes had to do with a child's fatal illness or imminent death. It was his aim to prevent other fathers from ever being tempted to strike another bargain with the Beelzebub ever again, to keep them from being damned to an existence like his. He'd had to watch *all* of his loved ones die as time went by, and that was a curse no one should have to bear.

There were quite a few similar stories, but others were different entirely.

One in particular that he'd had his scribe take down from one of the wise women on the outer borders of his fiefdom told of a powerful magician who'd caught the attention of a fairy queen. The fairy queen stopped time itself to offer her love the chance of spending the span of his mortal years with her. For that, she'd employed a dark magic and willingly paid the price of losing her own immortality for the iniquity.

When he refused her in favor of returning to his human wife and daughter, she altered the spell she'd cast to curse him to a loveless millennium of walking this earth. The dark magic she'd used touched upon his heart and tainted it, and he became cruel and merciless. He could neither love nor be loved, and the curse could only be broken if he learned to love a fairy that could find it in her to love him back. Since he could no longer trust himself to be around his family, he left them, in the end, and swore revenge. He began to make hunt for fairies, seeking them out and slaughtering them wherever he could find them. He wiped out an entire race, which was why fairies were said to be extinct, but he never found the queen, and he never found redemption.

Other chronicles portrayed a huge, ugly elven man with a magical sword forged from fairy silver. He'd offered his services to a human king whose army had been all but destroyed by his enemies from the North. The elven asked for nothing in return but a song from the princess, and the king promised him that. Single-handedly, he won the doomed battle for the king, but the princess refused to sing for him at the feast held in his honor afterward. The king was furious, and he had her thrown into a tower, sealing the windows and doors until she'd see sense, though the elven man didn't insist on his prize. He held no grudge and returned to his home.

When the elven came back by chance many years later, he discovered that the tower was still there, and so was the princess, forgotten by all. She was an old woman by then. He set her free, and she sang for him. When she'd finished, he asked her why she'd refused after he'd won her father's war for him. She answered that she hadn't thought her voice would please a being as beautiful as he.

Hearing this saddened him. He cast the blade of his sword into the earth at her feet, and all of nature about was momentarily illuminated in a golden glow. The maples that had until then worn a dirty brown in fall turned golden, and that was to be their autumn color for all time from then on. The old crone's hair turned back to the rich, honey shade of blonde it had been when the elven man had last seen her, and the folds and wrinkles disappeared from her face. She was young again, while the elven man turned to dust. He'd lived more than half of his three hundred years already, and his golden ashes dispersed on the gentle breeze. They settled on the delicate petals of the tiny white daisies native to Wildenburg and glistened golden in the morning dew so brightly, the princess' eyes filled with tears. One drop after the other fell from her cheeks and upon the blooms. They sealed the color, and from that time, the flowers were known as gold coins.

Gregory supposed this was likely the most far-fetched of all the stories, but, oddly enough, it was the most widely-known, perhaps because it served to explain a part of their world. The notion that a flower so widespread and common as a gold coin could have such a story made a simple thing seem precious, somehow, and early October's maples would surely remind anyone who'd heard this tale of their origins.

The tale that had truly captured his interest was that of the king who'd tried to strike a deal with the Devil. Rambert's heart was made of both light and darkness, and he had the power to grant wishes. Gregory had no idea how the angel's light half could have tolerated the Devil's dark contribution, and how any amount of darkness within a heart could bring forth a magic that wasn't equally dark. A tainted heart had to be incapable of conveying anything good or at least impartial.

Who'd have thought there could even be such a thing as a magic that wasn't clearly defined? That aside, he'd been raised to believe that all magic had to be dark because God did not rely on magic. God worked *miracles*. Gregory had never seen proof of such a thing, but he'd *believed* in miracles all of his life, just as he'd believed in the darkness there actually *was* proof of.

Whatever else these tales suggested, the premise they all shared was that the Wishmaster was an ancient Immortal. As such, he had to have knowledge and powers beyond imagining. If the tale of the king with the split heart was true, Rambert was compelled to heed the Summons of any desperate soul in need if his name was uttered formally three times.

If he still existed, that was.

If he ever had.

But, Gregory was indeed a soul in need who desperately wanted to believe Rambert did exist. He needed to believe in *something* after his belief in God had faltered and failed him.

What he *knew* for a fact and beyond a doubt was that there were dragons in Albany and giants in the Iberian mountains. He'd heard of trolls in Norway, and the bloodsucking Undead in East. And, very recently and most significantly, he himself had seen a demon, and it had stolen his daughter.

There was a lot of darkness in this world all right, but there was also light, and every shade of gray that lay between the two, so why shouldn't this Wishmaster be just as real as any of the other magical creatures in the realm, and why should it be wrong to summon him and ask him to use a magic that was neither good nor evil to restore faith within himself, real faith? Why shouldn't Rambert be just as real as any good man who'd had to make gruesome decisions?

"Rambert Longsword, I summon thee!" That was twice.

For the umpteenth time, Gregory wondered what the Immortal would demand in exchange for the information he wanted. Gold? Silver? Wildenburg Castle? Or even Blackvale Castle – what there was of it presently? It didn't matter. He'd give anything, he'd pay any price. There was nothing he wouldn't do to find out if Louisa was still alive, because if she was, perhaps there would be a way to bring her back. If there was the slightest chance of that, he was sure the Wishmaster would know, and he was convinced they'd come to an agreement.

"Rambert Longsword, I summon thee! Wishmaster!" That was three.

Time stood still while he waited, listening, watching.

Nothing.

Nothing but a jay's cawing in the trees and the boiling anger in Gregory's heart.

He should have *known* he wouldn't be heard, he told himself, he should have realized he wasn't important enough in the grand scheme of things to be considered worth the Wishmaster's while.

If he was really out there, he'd probably be laughing at him and at his troubles. Who'd take a man crying over a child sacrificed to save countless others seriously? Children were born and died every day for lesser reasons in these parts, and mothers and fathers moved on.

His brother's advisor had told him to put the unfortunate incidents of late behind him and get on with his life. His treasurer had been nagging him to pay more attention to the pressing issues of state now that he was the ruler of these lands. His best friend had told him he should be grateful for the daughter the demon had *not* taken, that his wife was still young, and they'd have other children.

He was sure that all of these people meant well, but he couldn't just 'get on with his life', he just *couldn't*, because the uncertainty of *not knowing* what had become of his Louisa was slowly driving him insane.

He'd come here hoping to strike a deal, *any* deal, and he could have coped with it if the Wishmaster had told him his daughter was dead and there was nothing to be done about that, but he could feel his insides churning and twisting at the thought of simply not being heard. He was so angry at the Immortal for ignoring him, he was ready to kill.

"Wishmaster!" he ranted, drawing his sword, threatening the thin air and the trees around him. "Wishmaster! I want to talk to you! I summon you! You *will* hear me!"

Again, nothing.

Nothing but his own ravings.

It took a while for him to realize that an impoverished-looking peasant had arrived to the little clearing. The man was visibly frightened at the sight of him, eyes wide, clutching a staff in one hand and the strap he'd fastened to the bale of hay he was carrying on his back tightly in the other.

"What are you gaping at?" Gregory spat.

The lame man briefly pondered his options, darting his glance about wildly as though he was looking for the nearest hole in the earth capable of hiding him away from his liege lord's wrath.

"I'm sorry, I thought I heard someone calling for help," he stammered, staring at the sword in the duke's hand. "I was mistaken, Your Lordship, and I'll just be on my way."

Gregory watched him slowly backing away to hobble off to wherever it was he'd come from, but then reconsidered letting him go. The man recognized him, and the last thing he needed right now was rumors. Anyone who'd seen him here would think he'd lost his mind, and even if he *was* losing his mind, this wasn't what he'd want his wife and remaining child to hear from the mouths of their subjects one fine day in spring when all of this was over with.

"Peasant!" he called after him, and the man stopped in his tracks. "You know who I am, don't you."

It was more a statement than a question, and the peasant nodded, slowly turning around to face him. He bravely fixed his eyes to his regent's.

"Aye, Your Lordship. You're the master of Wildenburg, and you're the new duke of Blackvale who's rebuilding that fine castle. And, you're a man who's lost half his family to a demon in one night."

Gregory was momentarily stunned by the forthright manner of the scruffy, crippled crofter opposite him. There was something odd about him, something that didn't quite fit in with his image of the local riffraff roaming the countryside in search of a day's worth of wages or meals for their labor. His face seemed vaguely familiar, but the poor all looked alike in these parts. Inbreeding did that. He didn't know what to make of the fellow, but tried to tell himself not to read too much into it.

"You'll tell no one you've seen me here today, or I'll come find you and break the other leg," he finally ordered, pointing his sword at him. *"No one."*

Again, the man nodded, but he seemed to relax.

"Of course not, my liege. I wouldn't dream of it."

Gregory was still irritated as he waved him off in a curt dismissal, particularly by the dry undercurrent in the man's tone of voice, but he could hardly slay him for that. He probably *should*, but it wouldn't be right.

"If Your Lordship please," the peasant began then, unexpectedly lingering, "I know my place, and I'll beg your forgiveness before I forward an unwarranted and unasked for piece of advice, from one father who's grieved to another…"

The duke startled, shocked at the fool's presumptuousness. He wasn't going to stand here and listen to the rabble offering him words of guidance. Drawing himself up to his full height warningly, he gripped the hilt of his sword so tightly, his fingers hurt, but the village idiot didn't seem to take note and babbled on with a new-found fearlessness as if there had been some bizarre shift in their standing and his life meant nothing to him.

"If you're going to summon the Wishmaster," he suggested, brazenly flourishing a twirling finger at him, "you should know you'll need to call him by his *real* name."

The haggard man paused, waiting for a reaction that Gregory couldn't muster while still processing the coherencies without feasible outcome.

"By that, I mean the name his father gave him," he reiterated eventually, rolling his eyes, "*before* he traded his soul. His father loved him, you know, just like he loved his own children in turn. No demon would have made him choose, *Blackvale*, because *he* wasn't afraid for himself, and because magic is all about the price you're willing to pay for it. If you can't man up and handle that, you don't have any business trying to do business with the Devil or any other kind of dealmaker."

At that, Gregory launched himself at the considerably shorter featherweight, who might have moved aside but didn't.

Snarling, he grabbed him by the grimy collar of his threadbare cloak and lifted him up off the ground so that he was standing on the tips of his toes. Gregory wasn't aware of his own strength, and he barely registered what his rage was making of him as he drew blood with the blade he was holding to the crofter's throat. The man was a cripple, and he was unarmed, but Gregory didn't care if he killed him then and there.

"I think I'll need to teach you some manners, and a thing or two about *fear* so you'll remember your place!" he barked as he pressed his blade's edge harder against tender, breaking, bleeding skin.

Surprisingly, the peasant who should have been paling in terror by now was actually *grinning* at him. He'd dropped his staff to grasp Gregory's wrists lest he strangle him with his own cloak, and tufts of hay were spilling onto the ground from the bale on his back, but he was grinning like a madman, barely able to contain himself.

This both confused and infuriated Gregory even further, and he could hardly see beyond the moment.

"Who do you think you are?" he bellowed, his blade slicing even deeper into the tender flesh before shoving the man to the ground and kicking him in the stomach and ribs repeatedly where he lay.

Instead of begging for his life, however, the crofter burst out in shameless fits of hysterical laughter. It was as though the predicament he found himself in was the most hilarious thing that had ever happened to him.

"Oh," he howled, half-heartedly scrambling away, "you really have no idea, do you? You're a man of means by no means, your memory is miserable, and you're not very imaginative!"

Gregory would have stabbed the arrogant dim-wit in the heart, but suddenly he found himself alone, and his blade plunged into nothingness. Bewildered, he looked about until he realized someone, or *something* was standing right behind him. The presence he felt, however, was hardly that of a man.

Turning cautiously, he found himself gazing into the dangerous, gleaming eyes of a being that was both human and unhuman at the same time. It moved too fast to be anything but a fiend as it backed away from him just enough to be out of reach of his sword, baring a mouthful of black rotting teeth in a twisted smirk.

For a second or two, Gregory could have sworn he was looking at a walking corpse: sickly, wilted grayish skin over the fouling flesh, and an air of death long overdue.

To him, that proved the creature's adversity to nature beyond a doubt. It had to be evil, because it wasn't with God's permission that the dead wandered the earth. There was nothing remotely resembling *light* magic here.

But then he thought of the demon who had taken his daughter, and he remembered the lesson he'd learned about appearances; things weren't always what they seemed, and it was easy to confuse black and white when you were living in the gray areas in between. He was the one with the sword, and he'd been ready to murder a pauper for an outburst of insolence. He'd killed with a passion during the war, and he'd carried out Heistermann's orders without question for years afterward, but he'd changed. He'd sworn off the killing because he'd grown weary of remembering all the faces of the people who'd died at his hands during those terrible times.

He was still gaping when he felt the electrical charge in the air, and the surge of it coursing through his sword's metal made him drop it. Chiding himself for losing his weapon as he rubbed his hand, he swiftly bent down to retrieve the blade, but, to his astonishment, it had dissolved in a puddle of steaming acid. His jaw clenched. Taking a deep breath and writing his sword off, he accepted what this meant and straightened to face the consequences of what he'd brought upon himself.

"I take it *you're* the Wishmaster."

The creature huffed a laugh and stalked around him, hands folded behind his back, scrutinizing him. "Well, you're a bit slow, but you caught on in the end after all, didn't you?"

Gregory stood his ground. He managed to keep his temper as well as his tongue in check, but he knew he wouldn't stand a chance if the Wishmaster decided to end his life on the spot.

Dying didn't worry him much because leaving this world might finally put an end to the misery that had taken charge of him. He just didn't want to die begging. He wasn't looking for humiliation or pain, and a creature that had the ability to turn metal into acid could certainly cause both. Or worse. Heistermann had taught him valuable lessons about human frailty, and he was sure he was in for some follow-ups today.

"I do think I need to teach *you* some manners, *Your Lordship*," the magic wielder hissed, pointing a finger in his direction that brought him down on all fours and immobilized him.

Gregory groaned, and he wanted to close his eyes, but he couldn't. He fully expected pain, but none came, and the Wishmaster continued talking in a tone as if to make light conversation.

"*Much* better, don't you think?" he said, glowering down at Gregory. "It's *respectful* to kneel in the presence of your betters, and I like *respectful*. Now, when you've practiced *respectful* for another bit by yourself over the next days and weeks like a good boy, and when you *really* remember how to behave in the presence of people you wish to beg favors from, you might want to learn how to address those people properly as well."

The Wishmaster leisurely hunkered down next to him, resting his arms on his knees so his hands were dangling.

"*If* indeed you can manage to do that, you call upon me again, and I'll *think* about whether or not I'd be interested in helping you, depending on what you've got to offer me in return. Do you understand that?"

Gregory wanted to nod, but he found he couldn't so much as tilt his head.

The Immortal laughed, clapping his hands all the same. "Wonderful! I'm glad I got that across."

Then, he vanished, and Gregory collapsed onto the ground, face first.

When he finally found himself able to take command of his hands and legs again, he got up and brushed the dirt off of himself. He supposed he'd messed up pretty thoroughly. Unless, of course, he could find out Rambert's real name and offer him a deal he couldn't refuse – it couldn't be that hard, since he already had a whole collection of alternatives.

Four

Something to Believe In

The demon knelt in front of the child, taking her delicate, milky hands in its bone-like claws. The girl looked it firmly in the eyes. She saw what she chose to see, what she *had* to see, and none of the coldness that resided there within.

The demon smiled.

So pliable, it thought, so trusting.

The Underworld was a dark place, and yet Louisa had learned to *see* because seeing was believing. All humans needed something to believe in. The demon loved that about them. The strong ones seemed capable of finding even the most minute pinpoints of light in the darkness to guide their souls toward what they hoped would be salvation. The being knew this, because it had only ever been worth its while to bargain with the strong ones, those with an ability to focus. The weak ones always withered before their time. Such was evolution, such was the survival of the fittest. Very entertaining to watch.

Clearly, Louisa had excellent survival instincts, and her soul would endure for a long, long time, should she choose to seal the pact in the years to come, if there was time. A decision like this could only be made by free will, and it would be a while yet, before Louisa knew what that even meant.

"Are you ready, dear?"

"Yes."

Of course she was. The demon was pleased. Louisa had been such a good choice. Her father would never know just *how* good a choice, the blundering fool.

"Can you remember what we talked about?"

The child nodded. "Yes."

"And you promise to be good?"

"Yes."

The demon smiled again, and the girl smiled back this time. "Then come."

Louisa wrapped her arms around the demon's neck, and the being stood up, lifting her along with it. Then, they both vanished in a swirl of gray mist.

Particles danced and whirled, brilliant lights and images of places flashed in and out of perspective, and time broke to pieces only to reassemble in another pattern. When reality settled back into colors and shapes, the child looked about, and her eyes adjusted to the dusty gloom of the Great Hall they found themselves in.

Tall stone walls surrounded them, built to last, and paneled with dark wood to the height of a grown man's waist. Above that, they were adorned with rich heavy tapestries depicting the kind of hunting scenes men of standing seemed to have such an affinity for, and portraits of what the demon supposed might be past generations of noblemen and their families. The renditions were greatly exaggerated, making the people thereupon seem more grand and beautiful in their time than they could possibly have been.

All of the men looked down at them severely through grave and piercing eyes, and all of the pudgy dough-faced women wistfully looked away.

Above them, a huge wrought iron and glass chandelier hung from a chain from the dark cased ceiling. The glass elements clinked slightly every now and then in an almost unnoticeable draft, and the demon observed Louisa looking up at them, perhaps imagining herself touching them. Cautiously probing the girl's mind, it found fragmented recollections of the glass marbles the girl had played with, once upon a time... somewhere... The flash of memory was there and gone in an instant.

The demon put her down, but sensed a tense anxiety about her even after the images of another life had vanished. The child was reluctant to stand on its own, as though its weight was too much to bear. The demon worried for a moment, but then told itself Louisa was still young. She would need a world of reassurance for years to come yet. The prospect of having to be the one to provide this to her was irksome, but Louisa was only human, after all, and humans were such needy creatures.

"It's all right, you just hold on to me," it told her, gently squeezing her hand, and the fleeting seconds of uncertainty passed by without consequence like a sigh on the breeze as Louisa finally relaxed.

The child would get over the fleeting memories of the life left behind, and she would get used to traveling by magic, just as she'd gotten used to darkness, the demon was sure. She was a fast learner. She had a natural proclivity for both magic and darkness, and the look on her face now was a mixture of curiosity and satisfaction. Things couldn't be going much better, considering, and the demon was determined not to lose this particular child.

It was plain to see Louisa was destined to firmly embrace both the character and quality of its magic because her heart had taken to it so naturally. All humans needed a place to keep their heart, and they were inclined to trust in what they were most familiar with. The demon's world was soon going to be what Louisa knew best. By and large, she'd already accepted her fate without even knowing it, and a few short years from now, she would know nothing else. By then, nothing else would matter anymore.

"Stay close to me, darling, and you'll be invisible."

"The evil sorcerer won't see us?"

"No, I promise. We'll be perfectly safe. I wish I could have spared you this, but you'll need to get to know him a little so you'll know how to defeat him, one day."

"He's an evil monster."

"That's right. He's the reason you are where you are – he's the reason why we're both where we are."

"I hate him."

The demon glanced sideways at the girl. "Hate is not good because it can cloud your judgment."

Louisa's cheeks flushed, and she looked at her feet. Her mother had been trying to teach her not to speak out of place. Especially of things such as evil or hate. It wasn't becoming, and it wasn't right because darkness lived where shadows fell.

The demon found this rather amusing. Humans always tended to speak out of place, whatever they'd been taught, even if the words that formed in their minds didn't leave their mouths.

"Don't worry about it. I understand because I hate him, too."

Five

The Eye of the Storm

Maria was busy gathering fireflies in a jar while the adults were enjoying their last meal of the day in the neat little gazebo her aunt had only had built the year before she'd been killed. She'd had it built for temperate evenings such as these, evenings with the family. Miraculously, the fire had left it completely untouched.

Watching his daughter, Gregory consciously reminded himself once again of how Louisa and all of his nieces and nephews should have been here. He should have been talking and laughing with his brother, discussing affairs of state and the price of wheat, and the children should have been playing games on the lawn in the last of the evening sun without a care in the world.

Chasing the tiny pinpoints of light, Maria seemed oblivious to the throbbing memory he was trying to defeat by confronting it head on. He'd imagined it would get easier, but it didn't.

They were well into summer now and the crops stood high in the fields, but winter hadn't released its icy grip on the duke's heart. He simply couldn't bring himself to appreciate what remained, though he kept telling himself what remained to him was more than what most people had to begin with. He was aware of what was important at present, and well capable of keeping up appearances, but inside, he felt as dead as the people he'd buried in the tomb he could see from where he was sitting. The food on his plate remained untouched.

He was barely listening to his wife's eager assurances to the clergyman opposite him that they were going to build the long-awaited chapel in honor of Saint Nicholas on the hillside pass to the east of Wildenburg. He wasn't taken by the idea of having yet another chapel built, no matter how far the mountain farmers had to walk to get to church or how urgently the merchants using the pass were in need of a place of quiet reflection before descending upon them with their novelties and vanities. Unspoken thoughts of having Saint Sebastian's Church in Oakwood demolished were bouncing around in his head whenever he passed the building, and that was something he'd much rather have addressed. It *had* been desecrated, after all.

He hardly took in his treasurer's ramblings about the foreseeable increase in the year's tax yield due to the surprisingly good harvest they were expecting. This would be the first good, healthy harvest in decades. The man was garbling on about how fortunate they'd been with mild spring weather and moderately warm summer months, but Gregory knew what really lay at the bottom of the wishing-well.

This year, they had simply so far been spared the vicious raids they'd been consistently subjected to since his Bernhard's passing.

A number of marauding knights from Triumph, their northern neighbor, had each led small, versatile troops onto Wildenburg territories around harvesting time. They'd moved fast and systematically looted and ransacked the secluded farms located too far out of the way for Blackvale to protect. Triumph had denied all knowledge, and so far, the matter hadn't been taken to the Electoral Prince. Anton had, against his counselor's advice, always claimed they'd solve the problem themselves.

Burning and pillaging was a grueling tactic that generally went ahead of war, but views and politics changed, sometimes. Especially, when rivaling rulers contracted physical diseases brought on by greed – Ergotism, for example.

Gregory involuntarily smiled when he thought of the name the locals had for the illness that had put an end to the attacks: Saint Anthony's Fire. It sounded so God-sent. William of Triumph had probably contracted it from eating flour made from the fungus-infested rye his knights had stolen from Wildenburg fields. Triumph's next plight had come upon him while he'd lain ill – half of the small town that nestled at the foot of Triumph Castle had burned down in one night, almost thirty houses. No one knew who'd set the fire, but fact was, William would have other concerns for a time than expanding his influence southward.

Almost ironic, how fate had now apparently swayed in their favor after it had chosen to grab away so much of what had been dear to his soul. Aside from that, neither the agreeable weather nor the eerie peace were particularly comforting because both seemed so temporary, so improbable. It was all too quiet in the fiefdom, and while everyone else was counting their blessings and congratulating each other on how lucky they were, he felt as though he was caught right in the eye of the storm.

Things were slowly going back to something close to normal for everyone else, but that was really only appearances, Gregory believed.

Leaning back in his chair as he continued watching Maria from where he sat with his glass of sweet red wine in his hand, Gregory couldn't say his daughter struck him as being unhappy. But, she did have that far-away look about her again that told him she was lost in rumination even as she followed the tiny blinking lights about the garden near the pavilion. She wasn't necessarily thinking about Louisa, but her musings were certainly of a different, more serious nature than they'd been a year ago.

Recently, she'd been spending a large part of her time with things that hadn't held much interest for her before, and he'd been really worried, while his wife had been doing her best to overlook that. He was glad to see her out here with them now, having a little fun.

To his mind, children shouldn't be spending their days cooped up in dark places, poring over books and slates while the sun was shining outside – or while there were fireflies to be caught. Life was short, and youth but a brief experience. He'd been trying to tell his wife that, but she seemed rather pleased to observe Maria finally expressing a keen interest in learning to read. He didn't like to argue with the girl's mother, least of all about her child-rearing methods. She'd long since let him know they were none of his concern. Not anymore.

He didn't hear his squire approaching as he emptied his glass, half-listening to the conversation his treasurer was having with the clergyman about financing the wretched new chapel while the knight next to him babbled on and on about some trivial land issue or other at the same time. He startled when the boy bent down to whisper to him, and he had to acknowledge that he'd gotten far too jumpy.

"Sire, the list of names from Silesia has arrived."

Rising instantly, he excused himself from the table, anxious to open the message he'd been waiting for. His wife cast him a quizzical glance, but he just smiled at her. He'd been doing a lot of that lately, too.

"Nothing to concern yourself with, my love," he assured her, bidding her to stay with their guests. "Just some business that needs my attention."

She hesitated, but then decided to let it go. He was

certain she knew he kept secrets from her, but they didn't talk much as they walked on eggshells in circles around one another. They both did what they could to hold it together, each of them in their own way – each of them smiling.

The list from the Silesia was short, as it turned out. There was only one name on it, and he just hoped it was the one he'd been looking for. Rewarding the envoy with a few coppers before instructing him to go to the kitchens for a good meal, he reread the scrap of parchment, trying to memorize the strange sequence of letters.

"Papa, what's that?"

Startling for the second time that evening, he spun around to find Maria looking up at him.

"Oh, nothing, dear, nothing for you to worry about."

Fumbling with the parchment as he folded it over on itself, he tried to keep it from her and put it away, but she reached for it, taking it from his hands before he could object without emphasizing its importance.

Her eyes roamed across the untidy script. "That's not right," she told him, and he was shocked.

"What isn't right, sweetheart?"

He hunkered down to get a better look at her and reclaimed the vellum, wondering if he'd missed something. She couldn't possibly know. He'd been so careful. And yet, her summer-sky blue eyes told him differently. He'd overlooked many things, and she knew something he didn't about matters she should never have been aware of.

"This isn't the name you've been looking for."

"Whatever do you mean, my Maria?"

He was irritated. He'd never talked to her or his wife or his advisors or *anyone* about the Wishmaster, *never*. The only person he'd spoken to were the squire and the envoy, and as far as they were concerned, they were helping him with the compilation of a history of local legends. Both were young and ambitious, but also loyal and well paid for their services and silence. He trusted them.

It was hard to keep calm, but he told himself that maybe Maria was just confused. Or he was. Or they both were.

"This says *Eisenhans*," she went on, however, as though she was explaining one of her drawings to him, "and he was the sorcerer Merlin turned into a sparrow when he was looking for the Hat of... the Hat of... I don't remember. But Eisenhans is not the Wishmaster. Ricdon is."

Gregory thought he needed air. His chest felt strangely tight again. That just couldn't be. The name *Ricdon* was nothing but a placeholder, a term for an evil or mischievous spirit that could take on various shapes, but he'd never heard or read of even one who could grant wishes.

"How do you know this? And how do you know I've been trying to find out the Wishmaster's name?"

She blushed, looking down at her feet, and he gave her time. Finally, when she returned her gaze to his, she took a deep breath. "Louisa told me. She tells me lots of things."

Six

Treasures

Being able to watch the Wishmaster so audaciously in his own lair without him knowing they were there struck the child as both imprudent and unwise. Maybe he couldn't see them, but what if he *felt* their presence in the old castle as much as she could feel his?

She wondered why her companion didn't just reveal itself to him and fight. Surely a demon as powerful as this could go up against a little man with rotten teeth and bad skin… She'd learned that no weapon built by man could destroy him, but there had to be a magic potion or a spell, or *something* the demon could do to get its revenge. Louisa couldn't imagine why the creature thought it would need *her* to defeat Ricdon.

She watched him intently as he sat at his workbench, manipulating a sizeable diamond into the setting of a ring he'd yet to enchant. Her lip curled upward in disgust. The ring was as breathtaking as Ricdon was hideous.

He dressed like a nobleman craving for recognition, but brocade vests and shiny leather boots couldn't hide the decay that lay beneath. The foulness that had eaten its way into his very core wafted out from him so intensely that it turned her stomach. Or at least she imagined it did.

Perhaps Ricdon just appeared so monstrous to her because he stood in such stark contrast to the few but exquisite things of beauty he surrounded himself with. That, and she wasn't used to ugliness anymore. The Underworld knew only the beauty of the darkness, and in darkness there was no contrast.

Above ground, everything seemed so radically invasive to her senses. The demon had warned her about this; her sharpened perception was now showing her colors she hadn't noticed before when she'd spent all of her days looking at them. Even the sky seemed bluer to her now than it would appear to any other human being, and her eyes were challenged with rearranging the different shades of ultramarine, azure, and cobalt about in tiny dots and patches so that she felt as if she was looking at them through a kaleidoscope. It was best to just not linger in the daylight, and she wished she didn't have to linger here, wasting her time watching him.

When Ricdon wasn't working on the enticing, precious charms he created for his various clients and their various purposes, he was sewing magical threads into dresses and cloaks that looked like they could belong to kings or queens and murmuring incantations over them. When he wasn't doing that, he was brewing harmful concoctions for witches or women who would have liked to be witches. When he wasn't sewing, enchanting or brewing, he was scribbling notes into a brown leather journal that seemed strangely out of place with him; fingers and hands and many, many years had worn the plain binding thin, eroding any kind of decorative patterns that might once have crept along its edges or adorned some manner of crest or emblem.

The journal was the one thing she found remotely interesting about him. She couldn't study it more closely because he never left it lying about as he did so many other things. He shrank it and kept it in a pocket of his vest when he wasn't writing in it or rereading his own words. A few mumbled syllables in a language she didn't yet understand, and it shrank to a fraction of its true size every time he closed it. She asked herself what secrets it would hold that he could never bring himself to part with it, not even in sleep.

Ricdon did not sleep.

This was a peculiarity he and the demon shared.

At night, he'd wander the empty, quiet rooms of Falconaer, aimlessly and almost forlorn, just as the demon wandered from one chamber to the next in its endless labyrinth beneath the earth. He'd walk the halls above the earth, and the demon those below – both of them alone.

Louisa knew all about being alone, but she didn't feel sorry for either one of them. Their kind of self-inflicted loneliness was a chosen one, and young in years as she was, she understood that.

The demon was alone because it was waiting, as it had been for so many years. It was waiting with one aim to be fulfilled, and after its one goal had been achieved, Louisa was sure her guardian would be granted redemption and peace forevermore. A wrong that could be righted by any means would erase all the other wrongs that had been committed for the sake of justice.

The demon was firmly convinced the justice it was looking for was finally within reach, and justice didn't require pity. It stipulated dedication and demanded completion, and Louisa admired the clearness and the integrity with which the demon viewed its existence only to that purpose – and hers.

She didn't know if Ricdon had any kind of goal beyond making others as miserable as he himself seemed to be. Integrity was no trait she would have attributed to him, and he wasn't looking for justice. His magic was harmful to anyone who sought him out, in the end, and all of his doing immoral.

He seemed to hate the world around him enough to want to destroy it, mocking mankind by masking betrayal and fraudulence with charity so cleverly, the souls he toyed with might still marvel at the splendor of his craft even as they fell to their knees and begged for deliverance. He had shaming the desperate down to an art.

No, Ricdon did not deserve pity for his loneliness.

He was, however, far more dangerous than the

demon because he disguised his malice with gold and fabrics of velvet and silk. He professed a worthy cause behind his deeds, but he never acted selflessly, and whatever kept him awake at night, the girl doubted it had to do with matters of conscience.

When Ricdon finished polishing the diamond ring, he placed it on a blood-red cushion in a box the color of onyx, and rose from his upholstered chair. Louisa backed away as quietly as she'd trained herself to do. The soles of her feet were less than a whisper on the soft carpet as he turned and looked right through her on his way out of the room.

Following him down the hall and up the stairs, she saw him fumbling with the keyring he'd detached from his belt. At first, she'd thought he possessed several different rings, but over time, she'd discovered it was an object that could vary, depending on the use he intended it for.

The ring as such was always the same. Its fastening was fashioned to resemble the head of a serpent biting its tail, and twisted bands of gold shaped its body.

The keys dangling from the ring matched its design. Their shafts were formed from twisted gold, and their bows looked much like its fastening. There was one for each door in the castle, but sometimes other keys would appear in between the matching ones. They were a mad mix of old and new, big and small, slender and chunky, and the demon had told

Louisa they opened gates and entranceways elsewhere, in places where Ricdon had no business being.

He stopped in front of a door she'd never seen open before in the year she'd been coming to Falconaer. Louisa noticed him unlocking it with one of the keys that didn't belong with the others. He had to turn it several times alternatingly in both directions before it would allow him to enter, and she tried to memorize the sequence, curious as to why this particular door would open with a rusty old iron key instead of one of the golden serpents, and why the lock seemed so stubborn.

Entering the room in his wake, she realized they'd left Falconaer. They'd stepped through the door right into another dimension. With what she'd learned of reality beyond the narrow horizons of humankind, she didn't flinch at the thought. What did surprise her was that they were standing in a peasant's kitchen. The low ceiling sagged where the old timber framework was failing, and mold clung to the walls.

Ricdon flung back the moth-eaten curtains and opened two of the small front windows to let in the light and the cool morning air, but Louisa didn't feel the breeze that ruffled his hair – or *it* couldn't feel *her*.

The chunky oaken shelves beneath the windows held nothing but dust. They'd been stripped of everything that might have been of value ages ago.

Only a ratty doll lay face-down on the bottom board of the one nearest the door. It lacked its arms. Ricdon bent, picked it up, and set it straight a few times, but it kept slumping over. Eventually, he abandoned it in favor of wandering around to look at some of the other broken odds and ends strewn haphazardly around the room. A banged up oil lamp on the rickety table. The pieces of an earthenware plate on the floor. A wooden cross on the ledge above the fireplace.

Louisa walked with him through the room to the rear end of the house, where two small beds stood end to end with a heavy chest between them. Ricdon stared at it for a while before he knelt and slowly raised the lid. It creaked. Carefully, he poked around the raggedy old clothing inside. He took out a shawl that nearly fell apart in his hands, a pair of lad's breeches torn at the knees, a crumbling slate that may have been used for learning the alphabet, a small shoe, and finally a little figure, amateurishly carved from soapstone. The tiny horse held his attention like nothing else. He turned it over in his hands almost reverently. Sitting back on his calves, he took a handkerchief from his pocket to rub at the dirt that had settled on it.

All at once, Louisa could feel the demon at her side, and she startled. She'd been so absorbed, she had no idea how long it had been there. It didn't speak into her mind, and she accepted its silence.

Quietly staying where she was, Louisa observed

the way the half-man, half-monster frantically scoured at the unsightly piece. She couldn't make sense of it. The trinket seemed as completely misplaced in his hands as the doorway to this room was misplaced in his castle.

"What's he doing?" she whispered to the demon's mind after a while.

"Remembering," it replied, its mien unreadable. "Remembering the life and children he abandoned here once upon a time."

Louisa's heart skipped a beat. She was about to ask for the story behind this, because it was one the demon hadn't told her yet, but suddenly, as if he'd been pulled from his musings by an unexpected noise, the Wishmaster's head jerked up, and he threw the little figure back into the chest along with the handkerchief. Closing the lid with a thump, he vanished. The window closed, the curtains drew, and the door banged shut.

Louisa glanced up at the demon in bewilderment. "What's going on?"

"He's been called," it told her. "He's bound by magic to heed… certain Calls, whether he wants to or not, and this is one Call he does not want to heed… but he *must*."

Louisa wanted to know more, but the demon shook its head and took her hand in its own so they could travel, a satisfied look on its kind face. "Enough for today. Enough."

Seven

Anything

The duke drew a lungful of air. "Eisenhans, I summon thee!" He felt ridiculous. "Eisenhans!"

He waited for a moment, observing a jay hopping about in the lower branches of a beech tree nearby. He couldn't feel his toes, and his throat hurt, so he raised the fur collar of his cloak and stomped his feet to encourage the circulation. He'd dressed for a winter's day on this unusually sunny September morning, but he was still cold despite the climbing temperatures. He was always cold since that day in the chapel when he'd first felt the demon's breath on his skin.

"Eisenhans!"

That was three.

Anxiously, he scanned the brush for any kind of movement as he'd so often done on this very spot over the better part of the year. Digging his hands deep into the lining of his cloak, his fingers found the parchment concealed inside the hidden pocket. Written on one side of the vellum was the name he'd just called out. It was the result of the last lengthy trip he'd sent his envoy on – to no avail once again, it seemed.

He took ahold of it without pulling it forth, and folded it this way and that, barely resisting the urge to look at it again just to make sure he'd pronounced the name correctly. He knew he had, it wasn't that difficult, but the sorcerer wasn't answering his Summons because it simply wasn't the name he'd been looking for.

The young man he was paying hadn't tried hard enough. Perhaps he hadn't spoken to the right people.

Gregory knew he should have gone himself.

No. That wasn't right. None of this was. His place was here. It had to end.

The Wishmaster hadn't heard him, and he wasn't coming. It took Gregory a while to accept that, and when he was finally ready, he straightened and turned to leave the little clearing back the way he'd come.

He'd had this part of the forest declared forbidden to the commoners so no one would see him making a fool of himself. No one knew he was here, not even his wife. If she did, how would she see him now, he asked himself, and what would she do? Perhaps she'd be so shocked, she'd leave him, and she'd be right to. Or perhaps she'd pity him, and he'd be the one to end their marriage so she wouldn't have to.

What *had* he been doing out here but wasting his time and hers?

If it felt, looked, and sounded like a fool, it had to *be* a fool, he thought bitterly.

The sorcerer – or whatever he was – had heard him very well the first time he'd come to this place because he'd heard the broken desperation in his voice and in his heart. Gregory was sure he could hear him now every bit as clearly, but he obviously wasn't coming. Perhaps he'd been watching him all along and laughing at his wretchedness.

The Wishmaster hadn't answered to any of the names he'd offered, and there had to have been close to a hundred by now. Gregory was fairly sure he could try a hundred more, and still he wouldn't come.

It had to end now, he told himself again, his fist clenching around the parchment as he walked away from the place where the Wishmaster had had him on his knees, humiliated him, and lied to him. There wasn't a doubt left in Gregory's mind the sorcerer *had* lied to him. There probably *was* no other name than that which the Fallen Knight had been given by the men who'd fought and died in his services. Longsword was a devil as much as the demon that had stolen his child, and it had probably never been his intention to strike a bargain with a fool.

Again, Gregory's fingers curled around the already torn and scrunched up ball of parchment. This time, it felt hot in his hand, and it weighed like a stone. He stopped in his tracks just a few paces from the tree line where he'd tethered his horse to one of the hazels, and he brought forth the scrap of vellum.

Smoothing its creases, he turned it about until the

other name he'd written on it to humor Maria became visible. Despite himself, he still couldn't rule out he might have been wrong to disregard what she'd told him the night before.

She'd spelled *Ricdon* out for him, and he'd taken it down letter by letter with all the earnestness he would have bestowed on the debates of his councilmen. The minute she'd been out the door, he'd dismissed the idea that she could know something he hadn't been able to find out in a whole year of research.

He'd *wanted* to dismiss it.

He'd been convinced she was either making it up or confused. She had to be.

However, unlikely as it might appear, there was a chance she could be right. At least about the name. *Of course* she hadn't learned it from her sister. Children easily mistook dreams and fantasies for reality. He understood her so well. He'd had a twin brother and lost him, and both Anton and Louisa were still with him in his dreams, too.

No, she could have picked it up somewhere, or found a mention of it at the library. He might have overlooked it in one of the books Louisa had been so fond of. Children had an eye for details most adults were blind to, so it wasn't *entirely* unreasonable, was it...?

He couldn't say which notion he'd find worse, though: the one where his Maria should be aware of a name that could summon an evil sorcerer, or the idea that she believed she could talk to her twin, her sister who was likely dead by now, whether or not he wanted to admit it to himself. But whatever else, Maria claimed to know differently, and he didn't have any more proof for one assumption than he did for the other.

Not knowing was what he couldn't live with *at all*, and that was why he stood here now. Again. That was why he always kept coming back.

He stared at the other name on the parchment, penned in his own almost illegible scrawl, and then decided he had nothing to lose.

"Ricdon!"

He was met with silence, but what had he expected? He'd only called once.

"Ricdon!" he yelled again at the top of his voice, and an eerie chill in the air sent shivers down his spine.

At that moment, he knew Maria had been right. Rambert Longsword was Ricdon, though why the sorcerer would have claimed his father had given him such a name was beyond Gregory. No man would really name a beloved son *Ricdon*. Or would he…?

Improbable, but not impossible.

"Ricdon!"

"Yes, yes, I know," the Wishmaster cut him off curtly, making him jump when he appeared out of nowhere right behind him. It was like he'd been expecting Gregory and growing impatient as he'd waited. "I summon thee, I call to thee, I command thee, and so on and so forth. You've been yelling every version of this at me for a year now."

"You're here." Gregory took another deep breath, two parts relieved and one part terrified for himself, and for his daughter – or for both of them.

"Obviously. *You* are becoming… irksome." He rubbed his chin, as though he had to think about it for a moment. "And just so you know: you still haven't got it right, but it's close enough. Out of curiosity, how did you arrive at *Ricdon*?"

Gregory didn't know how to answer that. He didn't want to. Finally, he stammered, "That's beside the point. I did, and we have to talk."

Quirking an eyebrow in amusement, Ricdon folded his arms across his chest. "All right then, I'm listening."

"You know why I'm here."

"I know your story. Half the empire knows your story. But you'll have to be more specific, *Your Lordship*. What is it you want of *me*?"

"I want her back."

The Wishmaster couldn't hide his astonishment. *"What?"*

For the first time, Gregory saw something on his face that wasn't related to conceit.

"Good Lord! She's dead, man! Dead is dead, and

even *I* can't bring back the dead. Were you not aware of that?"

"I know no one can bring back the dead, but I'm not sure she really is." Gregory looked him in the eye, difficult as it was to hold his burning gaze. "If she *is* dead, I want to bury her. I want to lay her to rest and mourn her. I want to put flowers in her tomb and I want her mother and her sister to be able to say their goodbyes."

His chest felt far too tight and he realized his voice was on the verge of cracking, but he plowed on nonetheless. "And… if Louisa is *not* dead, I want her back. From one father who's lost a child to another, *please!* I want her back, and I'd do *anything* to make that happen."

Pausing to regain himself on grounds that swayed beneath his feet, he was aware he'd exposed himself in all of his weakness. He ordered himself to get it together, but the ache that burned inside his heart was fueled by so many things he'd never said out loud, it threatened to consume him. The tightness in his chest became almost unbearable, and cold sweat beaded on his sallow brow.

When the Wishmaster slowly turned away, Gregory was convinced he'd abandon him again. A new dimension of rippling panic arose for one stumbling, faltering heartbeat, crushing down on his gut, but the sorcerer quietly remained where he was. He just stood there with his back to Gregory, his head bowed and unmoving as if to grant the Fool of Blackvale a moment of mercy to himself, and Gregory was absurdly grateful. He was far too busy with the basic labors of continued breathing to notice that the words he'd spoken seemed to have awoken the sorcerer's very own demons.

After Gregory had somewhat managed to steady himself, he wiped his face on his handkerchief, cleared his throat, and moved to stand beside the Wishmaster. The realistic prospect of being turned down was something to be dealt with when it became a fact. The sorcerer was still here, so there was hope.

"Well?"

Refocusing his attention, Ricdon's gaze met his eyes. "I can't," he said softly, and when Gregory drew air to cut him off, he raised an assuasive hand, but not his voice.

"I'm Immortal in this world, and I can't follow a demon or any other being to the Underworld, or to any other world, for that matter. I can make sheep sprout wings and take flight, turn pigs into worms and teach them to sing. I can brew potions that will put entire kingdoms to sleep for a hundred years, and I can weave the moon's rays into the fabrics of heaven. I can do a lot of things, but I can't go *above* or *below* the world we live in. I can't cross dimensions. Not even for a child."

Gregory wanted to sit, but there was nowhere to do so except on the ground. His search had been for nothing. All the time, money, and the manpower he'd invested, and he was never going to find out what had become of his daughter.

But then, as though Ricdon's mind had suddenly done an unexpected leap, the Wishmaster seemed to remember something. He conjured a small mirror in his hand, the glass no bigger than the bowl of a spoon. Its surface was milky until he rubbed it with his thumb, blowing on it lightly. Gregory found himself hanging on a thread yet again as the sorcerer grinned up at him when the glass cleared.

"But I do know how you can get certainty, at least."

Gregory's jaw dropped as he watched as Ricdon made an image of Maria appear in the looking-glass. He'd never seen anything like this before, and he didn't care what nature of magic produced the moving pictures – light or dark – if there was a chance they'd be helpful, then the end would justify the means.

Sweet little Maria was sitting on the floor of her room at the castle, drawing. A closer look told Gregory she was sketching the image of two smiling, identical children with their arms around each other on a summer meadow out in the sun. He knew this rendering well because he had dozens like it. Maria supplied them almost on a daily basis.

"That's *Maria*," he stated unnecessarily. He'd hoped it would be Louisa, of course.

The Wishmaster ignored him.

"They had so much more in common than their eyes and their hair," he mumbled as the image faded out to make way for another, a much older one that showed both girls playing together. Gregory couldn't take his eyes off them.

"You see, blood will always find back to itself," Ricdon continued, shifting his gaze from the glass to Gregory, "and I know a woman who can help you use its properties to find out whether your child is still alive or not. For a price, of course, but I gather you'd be willing to pay."

Gregory was. He didn't even ask what that price would be because it didn't matter. He couldn't live like this anymore, and if that price was his life, he'd give it gladly just to have peace. He'd gladly give *anything* for peace.

"How can I find this woman and what do I have to do?"

Eight

Hopes

Gregory had never much liked traveling by carriage. He hated the days of gloomy confinement and being tossed about in the back of some uncomfortable, damp wooden box on wheels, no matter how elegantly his cartwright had painted it.

The smell of moldy timber and rusty iron nails and hinges made him wonder if this was how lying in his own sarcophagus would be when death came calling for him. Only then, of course, the roads he'd be traveling to his final resting place wouldn't be quite as bumpy and muddy as the hollow ways and forest paths to Winterfield Castle.

A rotting, rolling sarcophagus for the rotting, rolling Fool of Blackvale, a taunting voice in his head whispered. It had the same husky, earthy quality as that of the demon, he thought, and it made him shiver.

Forcing a smile across at his wife, he discovered she seemed genuinely excited to be going on this trip with him. A pinch of real enthusiasm lay in her voice as she told him for the third time about the town market as she remembered it from before they'd met, and the bales of woven cloth she intended to buy there.

The tense anxiety that had become a consistent feature about her face over the past year had already faded into something he found less painful to observe. It was reassuring to think this visit could at least serve to take her mind off the things that were tormenting her. She had no idea why they were really going.

Maria had fallen asleep with her head on Theresia's lap, and the slender hand that had been stroking their daughter's chestnut-colored hair now rested on the child's waist as she continued speaking quietly of the ingredients she'd need for fabric dyes, and the old childhood friends she hoped to see at Harald's court. In truth, he wasn't really listening to what she was saying very intently, but simply enjoying the melody of her voice like a piece of good music.

Studying his daughter's porcelain form between nods of agreement and hums in what he hoped would be all the right places, he recalled the trip they'd made to an old friend's wedding in early summer the previous year. Maria was good as gold for all of her outbursts of ill temper and crankiness when they'd made their way south to Bartholemburg, one of their only true allies. Bitterly, he recalled how she'd made him wish Louisa had been an only child at the time, yelling the words at her before he'd been able to stop himself. It was hard to imagine the situation that had led to his overreaction at this moment, and he felt more ashamed for it now than he had then.

He'd gotten his wish just months after the trip, only it was Louisa they'd lost.

He hadn't meant the words. The Lord knew he hadn't, but things happened while they could. Looking back, perhaps this one angry, helpless utterance had been the initial spark, the beginning of all of his troubles. Perhaps careless statements like these were what woke darkness and attracted it. If the Good Lord heard your every thought and saw what was in your heart, the Devil surely did, too.

Darkness thrived in gloomy places.

Gloomy as the sarcophagus you'll lay your daughter's dead body in if you ever find her, the demon in his head murmured, *or any piece of her.*

He needed light, and he pushed back the sliding window to let it in. A chilly draft reminded him of why they'd kept it shut, but the cold felt kinder than the darkness had.

Maria stirred in her sleep as she dreamt whatever dreams little girls dreamt, and he swore she'd never walk in the shadows he cast ever again. He bit down hard on the inside of his cheek so the pain would jog his memory, should she for any reason start niggling and pestering them when she awoke. But, she wouldn't, he was sure. He was the responsible adult here, and he was in control of himself and of his thoughts. She was his child, and she was good as gold.

Not that any amount of goodness or gold could save her if darkness became aware of the light that shines within. Just a tiny pinpoint of luminosity would suffice to advertise her presence in a whole ocean of blackness. And... goodness is so frail and sinkable...

He felt sick, and he found it difficult to fill his lungs and keep a clear vision. Pressing the heels of his hands to his temples, he pushed his head all the way out of the window opening. The air made him feel better.

"Are you all right?" Theresia inquired behind him, and he closed his eyes.

"Just fine," he lied.

Get it together, man!

Settling back in his seat, he ignored the questioning look in Theresia's eyes by training his own on the girl again and fixing what he hoped would be another pleasant smile to his lips.

He was so glad Maria was becoming more sensible. The less cause she gave him to lose himself in the dismal thoughts that occupied his mind, the better. One year could make such a difference in a child. Aside from that, they were *all* trying very hard to be kind and careful with one another. The effort they were making seemed almost believable. It felt almost like they were a family again.

Almost.

Whispers, be gone, he begged.

He had to concentrate on what darkness had left him with, or he'd go insane. The tightness in his chest had returned, and he tried to make himself relax so he'd get through this spell as he'd gotten through all the others.

Breathe he told himself, *just breathe.*

The woods were beautiful at this time of the year when it wasn't raining, he realized as the coach rattled onward, and he wished he'd taken a horse and rode alongside.

By late afternoon, the next inn where they were to make halt came into sight between the fiery golden beech trees and the bare white trunks of the birches that had already cast their blanket of hues upon the earth. It promised to be a warm and friendly place. Most of the inns where they'd stayed so far had been. He was glad he'd sent an envoy ahead to announce them.

The burly innkeeper served them a hearty meal by the fire. They laughed and joked while they ate, and the evening melted away easily. Entertaining Maria with games and stories didn't pose a problem to Gregory now that their feet were back on solid ground and he could move about; he had a lot of sweet memories from his own childhood to draw on, and they came in handy whenever the occasion arose. He became aware of the way Theresia watched them, and it drove away the darkness even as night descended.

Again, they somehow managed to get around talking about Louisa, avoiding the awkward silences that had become so dominant whenever they'd been in a room together. And again, Maria was good as gold and permitted Theresia to take her to the room next door to theirs and tuck her in when it became late.

He poured them some fruity red wine and waited for her. She shut the door so softly, he hardly heard the latch fall into place, and when he looked up at her, he thought he saw something akin to contentment on her face. He hadn't seen that expression since they'd lost their daughter...

... because of the darkness he'd attracted and the choices he'd made... Whispers, be silent!

... and he couldn't take his eyes off her as she slowly, deliberately closed the distance between them. She took the glass he offered her, and her finger brushed lightly against his own.

She was as beautiful as the day he'd married her; so much more so without the black shroud of anguish she'd been wearing. The humble furnishings of the room and the candlelight contrasted that remarkably.

The picture he always found in his mind when he closed his eyes and tried to imagine her wasn't made of skin and flesh, a dress and the perfume she wore; it was formed from the beauty that resided beneath those corporal things in her soul. It was a flower that would never wilt as the flesh might. That didn't mean the flesh wasn't desirable even still, on the contrary. Over the years, he'd discovered it just magically smoothed the creases around her mouth, brightened her eyes, and carried his longing further than youthful infatuation could have done. He'd been an inexperienced boy when he'd first taken her to his bed, but everything they'd learned, they'd taught each other. He'd never betrayed her; she'd been more than enough. She had been – and still was – beautiful in every way.

An almost startling wave of yearning washed over him as she tentatively entwined her fingers with his, stepping closer, so close he thought she might hear his heart beating when she kissed his lips. He hadn't been aware of how hungry he'd been for her touch, and when she put her wine glass down on the window sill next to him he wanted to immerse himself in her warmth, determined to give her what she needed from him tonight and every night she might choose to invite him to.

The kind of love they'd once shared would never return because it had fallen from a great height and shattered, but he would do whatever it took to make sure she knew he still wanted her. He wanted her to feel how much he needed her, because he'd never been good with words. She knew that. He wanted to tell her he'd do whatever he could to make her happy, and that he wanted to be the husband she deserved, if he could, and for as long as he could, but he couldn't speak. All he could do was hope that she knew this, too.

It took every bit of restraint he had to undress her slowly, tracing patterns on her body with his tongue and the tips of his fingers, and it was almost impossible to let her touch and caress him in the same way. Returning her kisses and making love to her without losing control demanded an amount of discipline he hadn't believed himself capable of, but he wanted her to come undone beneath him before he did. He wanted her to love what he could give her because he was awed she'd still want him to give her *anything* after all that had happened. This was what normality had meant for them *before*, and he wanted a return to that normality – for her. She deserved it.

He hadn't expected this to happen when he'd asked her to come with him, but it had. Lying with her afterward as he watched her sleep, he would have given anything to know what she was dreaming of. Good things, he hoped, not the kind of nightmares that plagued him. He hadn't told her why they were really going to Winterfield, and with any luck, she wouldn't find out if this trip didn't bring about the success he hoped for. His little chat with Ricdon had left a bitter aftertaste, but also straws to clutch at.

The official reason for their visit to Winterfield was a diplomatic one. Duke Harald of Winterfield was a distant cousin of Gregory's, and Gregory had always been meaning to rekindle the good trade relations they'd maintained before Bernhard had passed away.

His brother's ambassador hadn't displayed much of a talent for renegotiating terms and conditions when things had become tight during the difficult years, and *all* of the years under Anton had been difficult. Gregory had loved his brother, but most of his councilmen hadn't been particularly good at what they'd done, and Blackvale's ambassador to Winterfield had surpassed them all.

Gregory was certain the man's natural arrogance had left a harrowing impression with Harald's advisors. They would certainly not have been tempted to take a chance on the utopian promises he'd been making and not keeping all over the empire. He'd managed to sever all diplomatic ties not only to Winterfield, but to a number of their other neighbors also, isolating Anton in the space of a mere five years so thoroughly, there hadn't seemed to be any going back.

Anton, the stronger brother of them both, had been too weak to crawl out from under the barrel he'd trapped himself beneath, and things had gone steadily from bad to worse. The former duke of Blackvale hadn't even been able to guarantee for safe roads and passage anymore in the end. He'd lost the fealty of several of the knights along the main trading route and the river that wound its way through the narrow valley, and they'd stopped protecting it. Regaining their loyalty had been an uphill struggle, and Gregory had had to learn to swallow his pride, but arrogance was something Blackvale simply couldn't afford anymore.

Harald might not be inclined to trust again so easily, but Gregory knew him as a man who didn't bear grudges. Harald was better than that, and he understood himself as a businessman – as Gregory did. Wars weren't won on the battlefield. They were won long before the first soldier lay dead, slain by the choices you made and the people you chose to make them with.

For Theresia, the hope of repairing severed bonds and negotiating new agreements for the sake of Maria's future alone would have seemed a logical enough reason for undertaking the trip. She hadn't asked any further, or inquired why he didn't insist on going alone, fearing for their safety, as he so often did.

He buried his nose in her hair as he listened to the even breaths that testified to her untroubled sleep, a sleep she would not have afforded herself if he'd told her the real reason they were going to Winterfield. He could never have explained the outcome of his little chat with Ricdon to her, or the bargain he'd struck with the Wishmaster for the information he'd gotten, so he hadn't even tried, and he would have taken Maria along whether Theresia had come with him or not. Life took unexpected turns, and woe unto those who couldn't adapt to new circumstances, even if they demanded a strong stomach and a will to make sacrifices.

He didn't think he'd get any more rest tonight than he'd had any other night since he'd lost Louisa, but settled for watching Theresia sleep, and that was enough, perhaps more than he deserved.

Nine

Smalltalk

The ballroom was ablaze with glistening silvers and the rich, dark red that was a part of the Winterfield family standard. What seemed like miles and miles of fabric impressively carried the theme across the hall; drapes and tapestries, and even the tableware was in silver and red beneath wide loops of the same material that decorated the high vaulted ceiling.

Celeste had spared no expense.

The sheer ocean of people in attendance amazed Gregory. The buzz of their talk and their laughter filled his ears and blocked out everything else. For a few minutes, he actually enjoyed the sensation.

He'd seen a few of Celeste's dinners and banquets in his time, and he recalled what dazzling occasions she'd made of them even and *especially* when the Thirty Years' War had finally come to this part of the Holy Roman Empire. This banquet would be no exception, and it was held in honor of the Duke and Duchess of Blackvale – meaning Theresia and him, not Bernhard, and not Anton. He was no longer the fifth wheel, the appendage, the poor relative left in charge of Wildenburg.

Silver platters and fine porcelain dishes laden with the most exquisite foods sat on a table at the far end of the hall. They'd been prepared by cooks who'd learned their craft rather than just acquired a few kitchen skills, and the smells of herbs, pepper, and other exotic spices wafted across the room to remind Gregory of when his father had still been able to acquire and afford them.

Dark-skinned musicians readied their instruments and soon began playing a tune Gregory wasn't familiar with. Some of Celeste's guests applauded in genuine delight and started dancing to the music, while others were content to watch the show, their sideways glances in constant comment of the dancers' efforts at grace.

Winterfield was still the same Wonderland it had always been, Gregory decided. The names and the faces may have changed over the years, but the kind of people Celeste liked to surround herself with hadn't.

The good side of this was that very few of the guests present here would be concerned with his troubles, which was just fine by him. Theresia and Maria didn't need anyone rubbing salt in the wound that had only just started closing. None of them needed commiserations or pity from strangers who had no idea of what they'd been through. They'd both had enough of the well-meant condolences and speculations as to what had *really* happened in Oakwood.

Those who'd seen the demon never spoke of it,

and those who hadn't didn't want to believe in it. Those who'd only heard the rumors surrounding the Blackvales' misfortune believed in many things, ranging from intrigues and family disputes to conflicts with William of Triumph. Gregory had held his silence throughout.

Not inclined to move along and mingle just yet, he stood near the door and looked around more attentively for his host, grateful for the glass of wine one of the servers had brought him. He couldn't see her anywhere, but Celeste had a thing for grand entrances, and he supposed this just hadn't happened yet. What did happen eventually was that his wife and daughter arrived, and their beauty took his breath away.

They'd had barrels of fun dressing up in their finest gowns and shoes, trying on this and that, and fussing about their hair, but he hadn't expected the result to be this fetching when he'd left their rooms. He realized how impatient he still tended to be with Theresia and he could have kicked himself for it. The mere sight of her with her hair piled in loose curls upon her head, emphasizing the curve of her neck and the grace with which she moved, and the flowing, silky golden gown caressing her slender, perfect body in all the right places would have been worth *any* wait. She'd never have worn this dress at home, but things were different here. Very different.

Maria wore a dress made to match her mother's

exactly. The necklace to go with it was one of two he'd had made for both his daughters just weeks before Louisa had...

Just weeks before you *gave Louisa away,* the demon's voice boomed just then, ripping through the happy moment.

Emptying his glass in one swig, he told himself it wasn't real. It was only in his head, and it didn't speak the truth. This wasn't how it had been. No. He hadn't just given Louisa away.

But arguing with a voice that wasn't attached to anyone corporally didn't make sense, and he knew it. He had to put it out of his mind. He couldn't keep thinking of Louisa every time he looked at her sister tonight – or any other night, for that matter. It wasn't fair to either of them, and he needed to keep his wits about him now more than ever. He had an agenda, and by God, he was going to come through on every last item on his list.

Making himself smile at the child who'd survived, he winked down at her, and she winked back. Her eyes shone the way they tended to whenever she was truly happy, and he wanted her to be. This was how he wanted to see her. For all of its irrelevancy and the tastelessly forthright statement behind it, the exaggerated pomp all around them had to be costing Harald a fortune, but little girls with a love for pretty dresses and music knew nothing of these things. He hoped she wouldn't grow up too quickly and find out.

Wishing he could capture the moment's wonder on her face in a painting, he watched her bob up and down on the balls of her feet in anticipation as she scanned the room for the other children she'd met at the stables earlier that day. They'd been playing together while Harald had shown him the fine steed he'd newly acquired. Answering her questioning glance with a nod when she'd located them, he released her to join her new friends, her chestnut-colored locks bouncing about her shoulders as she skipped off.

How pretty his little girl was, he thought, observing her amid the other children, and how lucky he was to have her. Exchanging an affectionate glance with Theresia, he knew she, too, couldn't wait to socialize. He gave her hand a brief squeeze and then motioned her to go.

Waving for a servant to bring him more wine, he wished from the bottom of his heart it could always be like this for Theresia and Maria – for all three of them. He wanted to offer his family a whole week full of Sundays every week for rest of their lives, but he was by no means as well situated as his cousin seemed to be. Not that he begrudged Harald his good fortune, but he couldn't help but wonder just how the man did it.

They'd be going home in a few days, and he sincerely hoped Ricdon was right and he'd have the answer to the question that was haunting him by then so he could move on and reclaim his own fate. He hated the thought of ending up as the millstone around Theresia's neck, or Maria's, or losing his titles and becoming anyone's indebted dependent, in the end.

A man had to be able to provide for his family and at least maintain what he'd inherited, if he couldn't add to it. He had to be someone they'd be proud of, someone who made the most of his chances and wasn't always too distracted or too tired to handle the things that needed his attention. They seemed to be doing so well, and they deserved better than what he was giving them. He wasn't sure he'd survive the winter if he didn't resolve his issues. He mightn't even if he did, depending on what that answer would be, but he was here, and he was going to do his best. For the daughter he'd sacrificed.

You mean the one you gave up without a fight, shaking from fear, nearly wetting yourself...

"What a delightful child," Celeste told him from behind, startling him.

He froze up for a second and almost dropped his glass.

A maid refilled it for him a third time. He immediately downed half of it before turning, and tried to relax. The alcohol was slowly taking effect, abrading the edge off the anxiety that had become his constant companion, and his lips curved upward automatically as he faced her.

"Thank you, Milady. She makes us very happy."

Celeste barely looked a day older than when last he'd seen her, not a worry-line or crinkle about her eyes.

"Children always make their parents happy."

He believed she was convinced of that. She was a proud woman, radiating a rare kind of quiet confidence, and she was used to having people listen to her when she spoke. He noticed that she did not drink; she was holding a glass of her own, and it was still full. She struck him as a frighteningly clear-minded personality who'd probably consider it wise to keep it that way, especially on a night such as this.

"I haven't had the pleasure of meeting Steffen yet." He knew Celeste's son was roughly five or six years older than Maria. He'd attended the boy's christening, but he hadn't seen him since.

She shook her head and gave a small laugh. "No, unfortunately he's been taken ill. Nothing to worry about, though, just the measles. I'm afraid we've got a bit of an epidemic here, but most of us have had to go through that at some stage, haven't we?"

"And we parents *always* worry."

She hesitated before answering. "We do."

She seemed uncomfortable, and he wondered whether it was the nature of the topic in general, or the fact that she had to assume he might be thinking of Louisa. It didn't matter, he supposed. Now was as good a time as any to forward his request because he didn't know when he'd get a chance to talk to her like this again. This was as much of a private conversation as they'd ever have because he'd never get her alone.

"Actually, I've been speaking with a mutual friend of ours about a parent's worries only recently," he told her.

The idea briefly appeared to alarm her, though the emotion was there and gone from her face in an instant. He would have missed it, had he not been observing her so closely.

"Really?" she inquired, her voice a little too high in pitch. "And who would this *mutual friend* be?"

He took another drink of his wine. Tasting it for the first time rather than just gulping it down, he found it sour and gritty. He didn't feel like finishing it.

"A man whose name is hard to guess." He paused to let that sink in, but he couldn't tell whether it meant anything to her. "He was sure you could help me because he thinks you may have a way of giving me certainty as to whether the child that was taken from me is dead or alive."

Celeste drew air, shifting her slight weight from one leg to the other as though her back was hurting. Looking down at her glass, she didn't answer right away, but decided to take a small sip of her wine after all.

"Our mutual friend is very assuming."

"He thought you'd know at least one good reason

why you should do this for me... as a – what did he call it? – *a form of redress*, I think he said."

Producing the parchment he'd been given by Ricdon from an inside pocket of his cloak, he wondered for the umpteenth time what was written on it. He'd kept his promise not to break the seal, but he'd spent the last weeks speculating about the manner of relations between Celeste of Winterfield and Ricdon. Whatever connected them, it had to be something she didn't like to remember.

She unfolded the vellum, but she'd barely begun to read before her eyes widened to equal parts in astonishment and disbelief. Her fingers closed spastically around the letter, clawing, creasing, and crumpling the paper before she threw it back at him disgustedly for lack of anywhere else to put it.

Darting a glance around to see if anyone had witnessed their exchange, she emptied her glass in one go and set it down on a passing servant's tray, picking up a new one immediately. There was nothing left of her naturally graceful poise as she fixed her quaking, wavering gaze to Gregory's.

He had the impression he'd struck a nerve.

"What on earth did you promise him in return for his advice?" Her lips were no more than a thin line.

He didn't think she really wanted to know. "That's between our friend and me."

And that was where it would have to stay. He'd worry about it when the time came. Who could tell where they'd all be twenty years from now?

Celeste's lips thinned even further than he'd thought possible. Gregory could guess she'd thoroughly amended any favorable opinion she might have had of him.

"I'm not sure you have any idea what you've gotten yourself into," she said, her voice low and pleasant, but there was a coldness in her eyes he wouldn't have attributed to her before this evening.

"And I don't think you have any idea what I've already been through," he replied, leaning in to her slightly, "or what means I'd be prepared to employ to find out what's become of my daughter."

He wanted to make certain she was aware he meant it.

"I don't doubt our friend has equipped you well."

Her hand trembled, and the glass she held along with it. She was visibly irritated by the fact when she became aware of it. Seemingly willing it to stop, she straightened her back, and looked around for her husband.

Harald was talking to some people at the other end of the room, but he caught her glance as though someone had jabbed him fiercely in the ribs with their elbow, and he excused himself, starting out across the hall toward them right away. Gregory couldn't think what to expect.

"You know, Maria mentioned she's been learning to read," Celeste told him just before Harald had reached them. "Why don't you bring her to my private study tomorrow morning? I'm sure I have some books that might catch her fancy."

Harald demonstratively took Celeste's hand and raised it to his lips, brushing her knuckles lightly with his mouth. "What can I do for you, my love?" he inquired, pouring some of the warmth she was so observably lacking back into her smile with his own.

"I'm a little tired, darling. Would you mind accompanying me to my quarters so I can rest?"

Harald looked a little bewildered, but Gregory was sure Celeste had him completely and utterly under her heel. His cousin was a good man, but he'd married a woman with secrets.

"Of course," Harald replied. "As you wish."

Celeste hooked her arm under her husband's, and Gregory gave a little bow as the couple walked away.

He didn't notice that his wife had returned to his side, and he wasn't conscious of his own strained mien.

Touching his shoulder affectionately, she brought him back to her. "Are you all right?"

Looking at her, he cupped her cheek in his hand and pressed a kiss to her lips. "Yes," he lied. "Having a wonderful time."

Ten

Blood

Celeste stood at the window of her private sitting room, but she wasn't looking out. She'd lain awake half the night, cursing the stars and the fates and every saint she could think of. After tossing and turning for hours before dawn had finally put her out of her misery, she'd drifted off, but she hadn't found rest. She'd dreamt of events she hadn't thought about in over a decade, and she'd been tormented by the muddled recollections of someone she'd been trying awfully hard to forget.

Harald had breezed in earlier, anxiously concerned. She'd sent him away, telling him she was feeling much better because that was what he'd needed to hear so he wouldn't worry when he rode out.

He did his rounds of the nearby villages most mornings before he began conducting his business, and she encouraged it because it kept him grounded and helped him to sort his thoughts. It also took him away from the castle and out of her hair for a while during the day.

Of course, she was far from *much better*, and she doubted she'd even be bordering on *fine* anytime soon, but she could hardly talk to Harald about that.

Who'd have guessed she'd end up losing sleep over Gregory of Blackvale, of all the insignificant people on this earth?

The letter Blackvale had waved under her nose had torn open an old wound that had festered for far too long. She'd been afraid it would never heal when she'd inflicted it upon herself. She understood now that it hadn't. Helplessness wasn't a reaction she was accustomed to offering, but seeing the parchment and realizing whose hand had penned the words upon it had awoken a deep-rooted anguish that shouldn't still be throbbing the way it did. Not after all these years.

Blackvale had caught her off guard, and she couldn't tell how much he really knew. What if he'd somehow opened the message without breaking the seal? What if he'd learned what was behind it? And, what *exactly* had Ricdon told him of the workings of the magic she possessed? Enough to give her away if she tried to fool him?

Four wobbly, top-heavy stacks of books sat on the table next to her. They looked like they'd never been read, and for all she was aware, they hadn't. Steffen wasn't much of a bookworm. One of the younger, inexperienced stewards had brought them in, and she'd purposely left them just the way he'd piled them.

The mirror she'd be needing today lay there in the chaos. It balanced hazardously on the topmost tome titled *Small Mammals of Winterfield.*

The looking-glass was old, ugly, and extremely valuable, and she'd gone to great lengths to acquire it. She'd never regretted having added it to her sizeable collection because it had proven its worth every single time it had shattered.

There were many kinds of magic mirrors in her collection. Some revealed the future, while others shed light on the past. A few presented things as they *might* have been, and there were ones that worked with a counterpart as a means of communication between people in different places. There were mirrors that could show you a loved one's dreams, and mirrors that would let you steal a glance at their truths.

Very rarely did one happen upon a mirror with the power to reveal a person's whereabouts, no matter where they were in this world. If they were alive and merely lost, the mirror would show them. It would show landmarks and peculiarities so they could be located with a little effort.

If that person was dead, the glass would cloud over. After a moment, an ancient forest would appear. Trees and plants the like of which there were none in this world grew abundantly there, blossoming in an array of colors. The forest teemed with insects and animals, pulsing with a life one might not expect in the world of the dead. A flock of sparrows would rise from the branches and fly toward the glass, passing it like through an open window.

Celeste had nearly died of fright when she'd seen this happen without being prepared for it, but now it was barely amusing anymore. Many of them would turn to sand on this side of the mirror once they'd passed the barrier between the worlds, but some would escape if Celeste set them free quickly enough. They seemed able to survive outside of man-made structures. For a while, at least.

The third possibility was that the missing person was neither dead nor alive. If this was the case, little Louisa's voice would join the chorus of lost souls; heard but never seen in the darkness of the world between worlds. There were never images to go with the spirits that resided there, but they wanted to be heard, *needed* to be heard, and Celeste did whenever she touched the cool, clear surface of the looking-glass.

Tipping her finger to the polished reflector, it became liquid, and a thousand whispers rippled outward, reverberating in her head. Celeste had learned there were many more of those lost souls than she would have believed. At first, she'd feared them. After a while, she'd grown used to them, and she'd begun listening to their tales, hoping to learn things that might be useful to her.

Now, Celeste thought quite a few of them might be better off dead than they would be alive if they ever escaped that place. Anywhere had to be better than where they were, but life wasn't an option after a hundred years in the shadows. Listening carefully to the stories of the tortured, she didn't think it... *wise*. They had no idea of the damage they'd taken, or the harm they'd cause if they tried to return to the realm of the living.

Generally, the people sorely missed by their desperate relatives were lost causes. They were dead, and the dead were of no help to anyone trying to make a comfortable living. But, more often than not, the bereft paid the asking-price even for that information. This particularly lucrative business endeavor had, unbeknownst to poor Harald, become a mainstay of the Winterfield family economy.

The witch who'd created the ugly mirror had done so by means of a terrible blood sacrifice. Great achievements always demanded great sacrifices. The old hag had killed her least-loved daughter to find the son she'd favored.

You never got unless you gave.

Thinking back, Celeste remembered how reluctant the witch had been to surrender the looking-glass. But Celeste was used to getting what she wanted. Even if it meant more sacrifices and even if it involved prying her prize from the cold, stiff hands of a man-eating monster.

Forty mercenaries had died to bring her the mirror, but she'd felt no remorse. She never did. Celeste got what others gave – *ten* for every *one* that had been taken from her before she'd met first

Rambert, and then Ricdon.

Many of those who'd come to her to use the mirror had regretted it later, but that was none of her concern.

She felt no pity, and she felt no shame. These emotions were beyond her. Ricdon had kept his part of the contract.

Once she'd been reimbursed for the troubles she went to so others could wallow in their sorrows – find peace, find closure, whatever they needed to do to move on – all she felt was the weight of the gold in her purse, and the satisfaction of owning the beautiful things it would buy.

The surviving girl's blood would reveal what had become of the daughter Gregory of Blackvale had lost. He'd get his answer and he'd have to live with it.

Celeste hoped the mirror would release sparrows for him. She'd never be rid of him if it revealed anything else. He was weak, and for most weak people, there was no living with uncertainties. He'd keep coming back, wanting information if he thought his girl was still out there. He was a liability as it was, and if he became bothersome, she'd be forced to take action.

There was also no rescuing a child from the Century Demon, whether it kept her above ground or below. It couldn't be done, and if Blackvale was intent on trying, he'd take the rest of his family to hell along with him.

She hated Ricdon for putting her in this position. Why couldn't he simply have put on a bit of show and told the man his daughter was dead? The sentimental old fool was still disinclined to lie to the broken-hearted, and he never could recognize the lesser evil. Why did he not learn from his mistakes, and why was she still paying for hers?

She'd tried to summon him during the night, but he hadn't come.

Of course he hadn't.

The last time she'd spoken with Ricdon had been on the day she'd given birth to Steffen. She hadn't seen him since, but she sensed his presence every now and then. He made sure she did.

He'd frozen the midwife and the chambermaid in mid-pace after they'd bathed the newborn child. The two women had turned to statues of themselves; one carrying away the bloodstained sheets, and the other the wash water. Celeste had asked herself if everyone in the castle was suffering the same fate.

The sorcerer had appeared next to her and seated himself on the bed as though he'd had a right to. He'd asked to hold the baby. Reluctantly, she'd let him, watching the otherwise so carefully guarded expression on his face shift from feigned, self-righteous indifference to regret to heartbreak.

She'd known he would not harm her child – nor any other child, for that matter. Deep down, he'd loved her even still, and there wasn't a bone in his body that hadn't been aching from loss because he was more human than most of the people she surrounded herself with nowadays.

He, too, was weak in that respect. Always had been.

She recalled how he'd wished the newborn a happy life in good health, and that he'd never want for anything. After he'd placed the baby back in her arms, he'd pulled the contract they'd made and broken from the lining of his leather coat. A dangerous smile playing about his lips, he'd put it down on the bed in front of her where she could see it.

For the first time since they'd met, she'd been afraid of him. She'd tricked him, and he'd never forgive her.

Steffen wasn't his child. He could have been, but he so *obviously* wasn't. He had Harald's olive skin, and a black shock of curly hair confirmed his lineage beyond a doubt. Celeste didn't know what he would have done if Steffen hadn't displayed so many of Harald's telling features.

Ricdon had told her he knew he had no right to take Steffen, but he was sure Steffen would call for him, one day. Black magic had a way of spreading misery, and when hers had all but devoured Winterfield, he would be back to talk about the price of the acreage, and the position of the former young duke on the estate. With that, he'd left.

She'd always dreaded that day. She'd done her best to shield Steffen from anything even remotely to do with magic, even and especially *her* magic, but she was certain Ricdon would be proven right. Sooner or later, he always was.

She'd tucked the contract safely away so no one would happen upon it before the midwife and the chambermaid had begun stirring. Then, something strange had happened: the parchment kept reappearing in the most unexpected places and at the most inappropriate moments, and she hadn't been able to figure out what to do about it.

She'd tried burning it, but it had been on her breakfast tray the next morning, unscathed.

She'd tried tearing it to tiny pieces and scattering the bits to the wind above the castle moat, but when she'd climbed into bed that night, she'd found it under her pillow, no different to the day Ricdon had drafted it.

She'd dissolved the parchment in acid, but the scroll had been returned to her not an hour later, sitting in Steffen's crib beside the sleeping child.

Only when she'd finally found it in her to read it again did she turn it over in her hand, and the writing on the back became visible. Words meant for her eyes only faded in when her breath brushed the vellum. She blew on the invisible ink again. Astonishment almost stopped her heart when she discovered that the marriage contract she'd signed for the sorcerer was penned upon a parchment pieced together from the love letters that had passed between them.

The words had stirred memories of an impossible hunger. She recalled the dull ache it had left her with even when she'd already been married to Harald as if it was still fresh.

She'd read each one of his poetically phrased notes until she'd gotten to the last, realizing how they touched her soul even with no compassionate heart in her chest. It was entirely ridiculous, debilitating and troublesome, and she'd wanted it to stop. It had taken years to put Ricdon out of her mind, and now that she'd finally managed to strike an agreement with the Electoral Prince's general and found a way to put Steffen on the prince's throne once he'd come of age, he was back and bothering her.

A knock on her door pulled her from her ruminations. She rang for her maid to let Gregory into her suite.

Maria clutched her father's hand far too tightly as she tried to keep up with him, taking two steps for one of his. Celeste sensed their combined anxiety, although she assumed he wouldn't have told her why they were really coming to see her this early in the day.

"Milady," he addressed her formally, and Maria curtseyed as Celeste dismissed the maid.

"I'm so glad you could join me," she sang, bending to caress the little girl's cheek and get a good look at her eyes.

The eyes usually told her what she needed to know about a person, and she was surprised to find how vibrant and bright Maria's sought her own.

So unlike her papa's, she mused, and smiled.

"My, aren't you the perfect little lady?"

Maria beamed.

"I promised your father I'd show you some of the books my own son doesn't read anymore. You can take home as many of them as you please."

Steering Maria toward the table, she was sure the piles of old tomes would be sufficiently unstable to topple no matter which one the child chose to look at first. Gregory must have thought the same thing because he tried to stop her, but Celeste held him back. The child had to be the one to break the mirror because it was her blood that was required. You never knew whether or not the man who'd raised a child as his own was actually its father. Ricdon had been wise to instruct Gregory to bring the girl.

As expected, the first stack started coming apart when Maria reached for one of the leather volumes near the top. She tried her best to keep the books from tumbling to the floor, but in doing so, she caused even more of an imbalance. Between catching hold of one book and pushing back another, she knocked the mirror to the floor, and the glass shattered. Maria immediately reached for the shards. She cut herself on the first one she touched. It was only a shallow wound, but the child cried out and instinctively dropped the shard. Sobbing, she told Celeste how sorry she was for being clumsy.

Celeste couldn't say whether it was the pain that was making Maria's eyes water, or the embarrassment. A cut from these shards hurt more than it should. She'd suffered their angry sting herself. Magic always came with a price.

Taking a handkerchief from the sleeve of her dress, she pressed it to the child's hand, smiling at her reassuringly.

"It's all right, dear. Don't worry about it."

Gregory had already bent to pick up the books. He looked about for something to collect the shards with.

"Don't bother with those," she hastened to tell him.

There was something insistent about her glance, and Gregory's mien told her he'd caught on. She hugged Maria to her as though she'd known and comforted the girl all her life.

The chambermaid reappeared at the door right on cue.

"Please accompany Maria to the kitchens and have her hand bandaged," Celeste told her, encouraging Maria to go with the maid.

Maria's eyes begged her father not to send her away, but Gregory gave her a reassuring smile. "I'll bet there'll be a treat in the kitchen for good girls."

"Very likely," Celeste agreed. "And, I'll

have *all* of these books sent to your room so you can look at them there."

The girl still seemed irritated, but did as she was told.

By the time Celeste returned her attention to the mirror, the shards had fixed themselves back into their place. The cracks were mending, melding together liquidly. In a matter of moments, the splintered surface was smooth and even as it had been before it was broken, save for in one place. Picking the mirror up, she frowned at the chink with the bloody edge near the bottom.

"What is it?" Gregory asked, alarmed at her expression. She corrected herself immediately, handing him the looking-glass so he'd focus on that rather than on her.

"It's nothing at all – you only have to hold it and look at it. The magic won't take long to apply itself."

"Like this?" He seemed unsure, but that wasn't anything Celeste was unfamiliar with. Most people were nervous when they held the mirror. They didn't know what to expect, and it was just as well. The gap, however, was still there. Maria's blood had not seeped in, and Celeste was quite certain it wouldn't. She didn't know what would come next, but it was time to improvise.

"It's simple, really. If your daughter had been alive, she would have appeared by now. The dead never do because their souls have passed into the next world, and that's beyond the mirror's reach."

She couldn't imagine what had gone wrong. She'd done everything precisely as she always had. It *couldn't* be the blood. It had to be something else. Perhaps something – or someone – was interfering with the magic. Perhaps this particular demon was stronger than she'd thought and capable of hiding the child so well, even the mirror couldn't find her.

Celeste didn't come to any practical conclusions, but she had to tell Gregory *something* fast. If she didn't, the fool might end up nailing the transcripts of the document he had in his possession to every tree and post between here and whatever backwater he came from. She didn't want to have to send her mercenaries after him. People with lands and a title were hard to dispose of without attracting attention.

Hastening to reclaim the looking-glass, she decided the situation wasn't to be helped.

"Gregory, I'm so sorry for your loss," she lied, pasting the most concerned expression to her face she could muster. "I really am." She paused, studying him. He was torn between anguish and anger, and she chose to tread lightly. "I'm a mother, too, but I can't begin to imagine what you must be feeling, so I won't pretend to. I've grown so attached to Maria... She's such a delightful personality despite what your family has been through, so please let me know if there is *ever anything* I can do for you. Anything at all."

He looked down at his knees like a whipped dog.

"No…" he mumbled without lifting his gaze to hers. "I got what I came here for. Thank you."

With that, he left, not looking back before he closed the door quietly behind him.

She directed her glance at the mirror once more. The crack was still there, obscuring her reflection. The glass was broken, and that was all there was to it. She wondered if it could be fixed, but maybe a mirror such as this could only be used so often, and the magic was spent. She'd never heard of anything like that in connection with magic mirrors, but the hag who'd died defending it hadn't exactly left instructions.

Then, the glass turned dark, and a noise arose from the depths of blackness behind it. What first sounded like a hoarse cackle turned into a raging roar. Wings flapped, razor-sharp beaks emerged from the looking-glass, and a murder of crows lunged at her face, aiming for her eyes.

She screamed.

Eleven

Pain

The maid dispatched to bandage Maria's hand materialized in the hay loft above the stable a split second ahead of the child next to her. She peered around, and all was as it should be.

The demon shed the maid's form like a ghostly shroud that evaporated the moment it touched the plank wood floor. Louisa's eyes widened at the sight of her twin sister lying motionless on a bed of straw in the corner.

"Go to her," the demon said, replacing wind and leaves with Agnes Smith's face, because this was whose years she was living out, and this was whom Louisa expected to see when she looked at her. Humans were so needy when it came to comfort and familiarity.

The twins' natural likeness never ceased to astound Atiram. Their faces, their hair, their hands, and even how they grew at the same time. It was too good not to make use of once in a while when the occasion arose.

Such a shame that she had no right to the other girl. She would have liked to take Maria to the Underworld with her for a time, but no soul that wasn't given to her in free will could cross the borders between one world and the other. What a waste.

She'd hidden Maria's sleeping body above the stable so no one would happen upon her in the main building while she turned Celeste's magic against her. It hadn't been too difficult to take on the maid's appearance and fetch the child before Gregory arrived at her room, meaning to take Maria to Celeste. He'd taken Louisa to the witch instead, the blundering idiot, and Louisa had performed perfectly.

Celeste hadn't known a lot about the mirror she'd stolen. Black magic always demanded sacrifice, especially when it was used wrongly. Not that Celeste wasn't willing to make sacrifices – just not ones that might impede her own well-being or deny her personal advantages. Humans clung to their earthly existence with all its trimmings in such a pitiful manner.

The restless spirits that guarded the in-between realm did not take well to being awoken without cause. Having traded Louisa for Maria ensured their wrath. Atiram thought they'd have torn both the flesh and the soul to pieces by now, and extracted the information she needed in the process. Having Louisa watch Ricdon had neither gotten the demon the whereabouts of the boy, nor those of the human Rambert was currently impersonating, but she was certain Celeste had revealed all she'd known with her dying breaths. Humans were so afraid of pain.

Louisa sat and watched her sister for a while. "When will she wake up?"

"In a few minutes," the demon answered patiently. "But we'll have to be gone then."

"And I can't speak to her at all?"

Atiram did not reply. Louisa knew the answer already. She was such a questioning creature even still.

"She will be all right, won't she?"

"Yes, dear. Perfectly." Reassurance and more reassurance.

The demon conjured a small knife and was about to inflict a little cut on the Maria's hand, but Louisa grabbed her arm and cried out.

"Nothing to worry about," she told the girl, briefly struggling to keep her human face. "It's just a tiny cut, but if I don't do it, your father will wonder. He may punish your sister for telling lies when she says she doesn't remember cutting herself."

"But she won't remember because it wasn't her…"

"He will ask her never to speak of today to your mother or anyone, and he will never bring up the subject himself again."

Gregory of Blackvale was an oaf begging to be fooled. Today's events would ruin him beyond repair and lay the foundations for the downfall of his house, and many others, in turn.

Louisa sniffed, and wiped her runny nose on her sleeve as Atiram swiftly sliced into the skin of Maria's hand.

"See? It is done," Atiram said. "But just know this: pain is only temporary. Pain is only a small signal that will set off a reaction, depending on how deep it goes. It's not important. What *is* important is this: nothing will remain of it, if you are strong and determined to seek a way of overcoming it." She breathed lightly on the wound to stop the blood flow, just as she had done with Louisa's. "Nothing but a small scar to keep the recollection alive and prevent you from repeating the mistake that led to the injury."

She could see the girl didn't completely grasp the science behind this, but it didn't matter. She'd teach her the magic first, and the science would follow. At least as much as was necessary to distract from the pain they would both have to endure until this was over.

Up until then, she would have to wipe the memory of this little trip from Louisa's mind. Humans were so frail. To them, most kinds of pain became unbearable over time, and she needed the girl's soul intact. She needed her to remain Maria's twin for some years to come, and the only way to safeguard that was to see to it they remained as much alike as possible in the essential things.

Maria stirred. "Louisa?" she mumbled, her eyes still closed and her limbs heavy.

"Come, child," Atiram said as gently as she could, holding out her hand.

Momentarily, Louisa hesitated, but then obeyed. All was as it should be.

Twelve

Regrets

Ricdon stood far back in the crowd that had gathered outside the church. He'd taken on human form to be at Celeste's funeral, choosing the face he'd shown her when they'd first met. She would have hated that, but in the end, she'd hated him, no matter which face he'd worn.

He couldn't see the casket from where he was, but that was all right. He didn't need to. They'd said their goodbyes when she'd made the final payment on Falconaer's promissory note to Leopold II of Trier, ridding him of the last of Rambert's debts on his castle and his lands.

And he'd seen too many burials as it was.

The one he recalled most vividly as he listened to whatever word-fragments from the requiem he could catch was Agnes'. No clergyman had been present to bury his wife, and no one had said a prayer for her soul, or for his four children. No monument marked their grave near the woods on Flower Hill, a little way from where they'd been beheaded and burned. He'd seen the Hanging Oak from where he'd stared into the pit that held the remains of his family. Two diggers had tossed them into a hole in the ground like sacks of flour, together with three other women and a leper the duke's soldiers hadn't wanted to take back to Oakwood for fear of infecting the good citizens.

Ricdon felt Rambert's presence before he could see him, and it irritated him. The once-king, once-immortal didn't usually squander much of his precious time on socializing with him, and he'd chosen a truly bad moment to turn up.

"Still enjoying my life?" he asked quietly when Peter Smith's form moved in beside him.

Peter's body had aged. He'd be almost fifty now, and he looked it. Ricdon wondered how much time the man had left.

Rambert grinned. "Relishing every last moment of it, believe it or not. My back may be bent, but my heart is strong. What about yours?"

Ricdon studied him for a moment. "Unstoppable, as well you are aware. What makes you so brave today as to venture out to haunt me?"

"My, my, you're not still mad at me for keeping my end of the bargain we struck?"

"To the word, I know... But I still say you tricked me."

Rambert *had* saved Peter's children – but only the two Peter had actually fathered. The old king excelled at two things: evasiveness, and taking requests literally. Perhaps this was the only sport eight hundred years of listening to other people's pains had left him with.

Ricdon recalled his last night as Peter Smith well. He'd spent most of it trying to persuade Bernhard to get rid of his witch hunter and stop the madness, but Bernhard hadn't been ready to listen, and he asked himself now if Rambert had known this already beforehand.

Bernhard hadn't understood how Heistermann would have single-handedly managed to plunge Wildenburg into chaos. He'd already been too demented to realize the extent of the damage done because he'd trusted Heistermann more than Peter. A man trying to save his family would say *anything*, after all.

In the end, Heistermann had accused Peter of accessory to murder by harmful magic. He'd convinced Bernhard that Peter was the Devil's bastard, and his witch-wife's accomplice, and that the people of Wildenburg knew this. *Everyone* knew this but he, their duke, because wrongly placed loyalties blinded men for the truth.

Ricdon still heard Heistermann's voice echo in his head. "Trust in God," he'd told Bernhard. "God will rule wisely, so leave it to Him."

Bernhard had drawn air, avoided looking at Peter, and conceded to Heistermann's arguments. He'd had him arrested, and trusted him to God's judgment without even bothering to answer Peter's question as to what God would say to the pain and suffering in the tower of Wildenburg, and how readily men had their friends and families tortured in His name, only on the grounds of a book some sick monk had written, not God. Malleus Maleficarum was not the Bible.

"What comes next?" Peter had shouted as the guards dragged him away, kicking and screaming. "Would you let Heistermann tell you Anton was the Devil's servant, or Gregory, if either of them stopped going along with this?"

"Blasphemer!" Heistermann had yelled after him.

That night, Peter had called Rambert, and the Immortal had come to him, heeding his Call as a father fearing for his children. He'd offered him a deal he couldn't refuse, and they'd traded one darkness for another.

A man who vaguely resembled Peter strangulated himself with his shirt sleeves in the tower during the early morning hours, and when the guards had found him, Peter was declared dead. They'd burned the body along with the rest of the witches who'd been tried during the week so they wouldn't rise on Judgment Day.

The smell of smoldering flesh had hung heavily in the air when *Ricdon* left the area with his two remaining sons. Masking himself with the semblance of a nobleman whose name Rambert had been living under, he'd brought the very young and confused boys straight to Falconaer. Rambert had advised him to place them in the care of the village baker's wife.

She'd treated his children well while he learned to deal with his own new circumstances. By the time he'd come to terms with himself, the children called her *mother*, and the burly man who'd never been able to give her babies of her own *father*.

"And you're still not over this, even after all these years?"

Ricdon wanted to punch Rambert, but he was afraid he'd break the old man's brittle bones, and their bargain along with them, if he even touched him. Their deal would be nullified if he physically raised a hand against him. Ricdon had often wondered if this meant their souls would trade places again – the wording he'd agreed to was that they'd each get back exactly what they'd given. *Exactly* what they'd given…

"Remember yourself," Rambert said. The grin on his face widened, etching time's own contract deep into the parched skin.

Ricdon looked down at the old man. "Oh, I do nothing besides, believe me, though sometimes I have to question what it is I got from *you*."

Rambert studied him for too long. "How are those boys of yours these days?"

Ricdon felt his fists tighten. If Rambert had found him here today, and God only knew how he had, he undoubtedly also knew of his eldest son's death.

He'd given the baker's wife a very generous monthly income to keep Nicholas and Thomas' background a secret and treat them as her own, and she'd kept word.

Nicholas had always been a sickly boy, and his death in their second winter at Falconaer had wounded Ricdon so deeply, he'd avoided looking at Thomas again even in passing over the following years. He'd ensured the boy never lacked anything, but when Thomas had turned seven, he'd had him taken into one of his liegemen's services as the knight's page just so he'd be elsewhere – anywhere but at Falconaer. At fourteen, the boy had become Sir Gernot's squire, and at twenty, he'd left the knight to become head of the Electoral Prince's guard.

Thomas didn't know who had paved his way, and he wouldn't until Ricdon was ready to have him back at Falconaer. He'd prepared all the necessary documents, but he hadn't contacted him yet. He thought he might do that when Thomas intended to marry and start a family, but so far, his son hadn't seemed willing to make any such decision yet.

"All is well and as it should be," Ricdon said from between clenched teeth.

To guarantee his son's future, he'd have to continue on the course Rambert had set and made a part of their deal, and he'd have to keep doing it until Rambert died and finally went to hell, or wherever he was going. He'd have to play his part and heed each and every desperate father's Summons he was alerted to, even if that Summons came from the man who'd aided Heistermann in taking five children from him.

Five children gone, and nothing would bring them back, but *one* lived. To keep that *one* alive and compensate for all he'd lost, Ricdon had sworn he'd take any kind of insult from the old crook.

Rambert's face went blank, but only for a moment. Then, he huffed into the silence and turned away, scanning the crowd. People had begun leaving the church. Gregory of Blackvale appeared in the doorway. Heistermann's daughter walked beside him, their child between them. Their *remaining* child. The irony of it all was astounding.

"Well, you've managed to make a right mess here, haven't you?"

Ricdon folded his arms across his chest. "Not really. I heeded a Calling. This is what I do."

Rambert hummed. He leaned forward on his cane, but his eyes were on Blackvale, who was moving toward them with the mourners heading for the graveyard. "Yes, of course, and people die, when you make mistakes."

Ricdon shrugged, though his insides were churning as he turned to leave. This funeral was definitely over. "They die when they're called. May she rest in peace."

The once-king grabbed his arm. "I'm no fool. I heard the stories, and I'm almost sure you brought this on Celeste."

Ricdon looked at the old man's hand and conjured an army of black beetles that bubbled up beneath his wrinkled palm. Rambert withdrew instantly in disgust. He couldn't fight his human instincts, Ricdon realized, pleased with himself. He might not be able to strike out against Rambert, but he wasn't entirely helpless either.

"I certainly did not. And what's it to you anyway? Will you be missing the dear duchess? Did she give you insights? Mix you potions? Sell you powders? Salves for your arthritis?"

The look on Rambert's face told all. Of course she had. He knew they'd been old acquaintances. Celeste had told him this one night as they'd lain together. What she hadn't told him was that Rambert had been to see her after he and Peter had traded places, and that he'd made Winterfield his home. Was anyone from his other life aware of this? Did Rambert still have enemies? He could have gone anywhere, but he'd settled here, and Ricdon guessed he and Celeste had benefited from each other. Well, the little bastard was on his own now.

"That's not the point…"

"Then what is?"

"You're a fool. You're dabbling in things you don't understand."

Ricdon's patience was wearing dangerously thin. He hated it when people wasted his time. "What *is* your problem, old man? I'll deal with the Century

Demon or whatever other creature is responsible for Celeste's death when I find out exactly what happened. There aren't too many monsters left in this world to choose from, and the Devil doesn't bother to walk this earth anymore because man creates enough monsters to keep everyone busy, so I won't be long looking. If you've got something to tell me, say it, or leave."

From the corner of his eye, he saw how six of Winterfield's soldiers carried Celeste's coffin out of the church. Harald and Laura walked behind them, pale and drawn. Rumor had it there wasn't much inside the casket. The birds hadn't left a whole lot of the duchess. He'd heard that a good two dozen had been feasting on her when her servant had entered the room.

"You have no idea of what you'd be treading loose," Rambert said under his breath.

Ricdon felt his blood boil.

At that moment, the Blackvales passed them a little way ahead of the bulk of the crowd. Gregory's gaze caught on his face, and Ricdon saw a spark of awareness, a sense of recognition. He was somehow sure he'd be hearing from his new best friend again soon. Things were looking dismal for Blackvale.

Renewing contracts with the man whose visit had brought misfortune upon his family was bound to be the farthest thing from Winterfield's mind right at the moment.

That would have to hurt Blackvale just as much as not having gotten information on the whereabouts of his daughter's body. Winterfield was bound to be cursing the day he'd let Gregory into his house, and Blackvale's bags were already packed so he could depart immediately after the funeral to reconnect his little fiefdom to the civilized world someplace else. In Triumph, perhaps, since it was along the way. But Gregory hadn't yet learned to keep his enemies close. Old grudges were not good for new business.

"He's a part of my problem – *our* problem," Rambert said, gesticulating at Blackvale. "Consider *not* heeding his next Call. Stay away from him, no matter what happens."

Ricdon bit down hard on the inside of his cheek to keep from turning his companion into a toad. He decided he'd had enough. "Goodbye."

The old man wouldn't let him pass, and Ricdon's fingers tingled. How he longed to wrap them around his own former neck... The scenario was almost comical to imagine, but it would cost him dearly. Neither his life, nor his immortality were so important, but he had Thomas to think about.

"Listen, I've still got a few years in me," Rambert said, an urgency in his voice Ricdon had never heard from him before. "I wasn't lying when I said I *like* being mortal. Why do you think I went to the trouble of saving your sorry arse from Heistermann if I'd been intent on going back on the deal when my time is near? You *do* know what I've given up."

"Our little agreement stands. I don't doubt the intentions you had twenty years ago, but look at you now! With age comes regret."

Rambert's eyes narrowed. "Regret? Well, you're an expert in that field, aren't you?" He paused for a moment. "I've let go of all of mine. You, on the other hand, my friend, are full of regrets, and you'll have more to add to the pile soon enough if you don't heed my words."

"Then help me understand your confused message. Do you actually know what killed Celeste?"

Rambert was about to speak, but fell silent when the casket was carried by. Winterfield didn't look too good, but what man did when the mother of his child had just been torn from this world. It didn't matter if she'd been a saint or a sinner, rich or poor. Grief always found those left behind and had its way with them.

Rambert took a little flask from his belt and took a swig. Ricdon smelled fruit brandy and recalled how that had always given him heartburn as a young man. Rambert didn't seem bothered by such ailments, or he was past them, and he looked like he needed the warmth.

"The creature that murdered her steals souls to prey on them, and it's safe to say she'd do anything to see you tumble and fall far enough to lose yours."

Ricdon scoffed. "Again: What is it you want of me?"

He couldn't imagine why any soul-gobbler would have it in for *his* lost spirit. There was nothing to be gained from it, because darkness held no life force, and no years worth stealing.

Rambert licked his chapped lips. "Well, I'd say we *are* linked for better or for worse until Peter Smith's calling, aren't we, and I think I have a right to guard my interests. I've lived a bloody long life in damnation, and I have my eyes trained on the horizon now, so I'm really only here to warn you, because I have no intention of going back to... to..." He appeared lost for a word, and finally waved a finger in Ricdon's direction in disgust, as though the mere sight of his former self was making him sick. "... *this*. Stay away from Blackvale, and stay away from anything to do with him."

Ricdon laughed despite himself. That was going to be difficult, considering the price they'd agreed on for the information Gregory had asked of him. It was hard to believe Rambert did not want his magic or his immortality back, but something made him think the old nobleman was telling him the truth.

Perhaps, eternal life wasn't all it was cracked up to be. Standing here proved that once again. One day, perhaps he himself would be hoping to encounter someone desperate enough to swap places with him. Rambert could probably see the light at the end of the tunnel. He'd live out the last of Peter Smith's years and die in his bed, like any other man, while Ricdon knew he'd be attending Thomas' funeral, and his grandchildren's, and their children's after them.

Just then, a young man walked right into him by accident, nearly knocking him over.

"Watch your step, boy," he growled, grabbing the fellow's collar and giving him a shake, perhaps too hard, because he was imagining Rambert in his place. The man hurried to apologize, and fled.

"As I was saying…" Ricdon continued, looking around for Rambert, but Rambert was gone, and he felt the sudden urge to put as many miles between himself and Winterfield as he could.

Thirteen

Wealth

Crumbling, tumble-down Bartholemburg Castle crowned a hilltop half way between Blackvale and Falconaer. Huntsmen made jokes about how winter lasted twice as long here as it did elsewhere, and that wolves were extinct in this part of the country because they couldn't survive on the frozen larvae that burrowed beneath the earth.

Louisa loved the tall, frost-coated pine trees that covered most of the surrounding countryside, and she stood on the battlements of the outer defensive walls for a time just looking at them, despite the biting wind. Eventually, she began asking the demon questions, as was their ritual, or *game* as she saw it, whenever Atiram took her anywhere in the Aboveworld. She liked playing their game. Ten questions were a minimum requirement, but she generally had more, and the demon would answer most of them, because the world was big, and her time in it was always limited.

Louisa asked about the conifers, and why there weren't any beeches or oaks. All of Wildenburg was covered in trees that turned to every shade of fire before they shed their leaves to prepare for their icy sleep in late October.

"They've all been cut, dear one," the demon replied.

"Will they grow back?"

The demon laughed. "No. Not in a hundred years. They need so much longer than pines to mature, and Bartholemburg can't afford valuable trees. Besides, the cones and needles have made the soil sour over the years. Not every kind of timber will grow in meager soil. Trees are much like humans that way. Some will thrive only in the sunlight, but only an exceptional few will do well in less favorable circumstances."

Next, Louisa inquired about the sparse, unkempt farmland, and the demon drew pictures of ground frost in May inside her mind, and how the cold could slay an entire crop of spelt on the fields, before the first wild summer storm ravaged the year's yield of rye, and people went hungry.

Bartholemburg's only real asset was the slate quarry an hour's walk from the village. The able-bodied men toiled there by day, while the women and children worked on the rocky fields for bare survival. More people left Bartholemburg than stayed. Many went to seek their fortunes in growing cities along the Rhine and Mosel, where the sun shone more often, but most of them came back. The demon had no explanation for it.

As they walked across the courtyard, the impression Louisa got from the maids and laborers going about their chores wasn't one of desolation. The red-cheeked cook sat on a stool in the sun and hummed a merry tune as she plucked the hen that would probably be Sunday dinner the next day. One of her helpers, perhaps a daughter or a niece, was scrubbing parsnips beside her and talking quietly to the puppy at her feet. A young man stole a kiss from her in passing on his way to the gate, grinning broadly while she scolded him to his back.

At the stable, Louisa and the demon came across Count Dietmar and his wife and oldest daughter. They were watching one of the hands saddle a small horse for the girl. The child pulled giddily at Dietmar's fingers. He laughed, and swept her up in his arms. Her mother didn't look well. A hacking cough nearly doubled her over and hurt her chest. Louisa thought she should have been in bed instead of out here, but she kept telling her husband she wanted to see this.

"Can this be my horse?" the girl asked.

Her mother cast her as stern a glance as she could manage. "No, dear, a horse is not a pet."

The child pouted. "I never have *anything* of my own."

"Learn to ride it, take care of it every day, and we'll see," the count promised, and sat her on the horse's back. The creature's patience betrayed that it had seen many a winter, and many a rider.

"Will you teach me how to take care of it?"

Dietmar nodded. "Just like my father taught me."

Louisa knew Dietmar. He was a friend of her father's. Her family had attended his wedding. It felt strange to have to conceal herself from him, but she was dead to the Aboveworld, and life had so obviously moved on. She didn't think there was anything left to prove she had ever lived there in the first place. Not even a horse or a pet. Everything she'd owned had also belonged to Maria, and a child who hadn't even been born when she'd last been at Bartholemburg was now learning to ride a horse.

She recalled the day of Dietmar's wedding and lost herself in the memory for a few moments. Her family had been invited, and they'd all shared a drafty room in one of the outbuildings. She remembered how his young bride, now older and struggling with a chest infection on the sidelines, had walked down the short aisle to join him at the altar.

The little chapel where they'd said their vows resided within an apsis some god-fearing ancestor of Dietmar's had added onto the main building of the castle, but it was so small, and Dietmar had invited so many guests, they didn't all fit inside. A good number of them stood in the drafty hall, and they chattered happily all through the ceremony.

Louisa's meager command of Latin had her wishing she could be out in the hall as well, but the priest, a practical man she'd taken a liking to, put in a real effort to keep it short. The celebration afterward, on the other hand, had lasted long into the night.

Maria and she had been sent to bed in due time, but they'd lain awake, listening to the music and merrymaking until the wee hours, planning their own weddings. This was the part she remembered best.

Maria had wrapped a sheet around herself and pretended it was her wedding dress. Louisa recalled carrying her train. The groom had been a broomstick they'd named... What had they named it? Prince Somethingorother... She didn't know anymore, but certainly *Prince*, because Maria had been their father's little princess, and princesses married princes.

Who would Dietmar's little girl marry, one day?

"He's different from your own father, isn't he?" the demon remarked as they watched Dietmar showing the girl how to handle the reins.

Louisa didn't know whether to affirm or deny Atiram's remark. Had Gregory ever played with her or Maria at all? He'd brought them gifts, yes, but she just couldn't remember if he'd ever played with them, or spent the amount of time with them Dietmar was spending with his daughter right now. He'd often been busy. Things might have been different if they'd been boys, she thought, but Dietmar wasn't above teaching his little *girl* to ride today. Louisa's first time on horseback had been under the supervision of a squire, and her mother had taught her most of the other things she knew. Theresia had also been the one to take her and Maria places, not Gregory. Here, things were different. Better, maybe.

She found she'd lost interest in being at Bartholemburg. "Why do you bring me here?"

Atiram smiled. "I want you to get to know the count. He's your father's only friend."

Louisa felt her brow knit. It occurred to her she couldn't name even one other man her father might have called a *friend*. She'd seen many people come and go at Wildenburg, but their visits had usually been about Blackvale. Everything had always been about Blackvale.

"Dietmar never came to see us at Wildenburg," she said.

"Because he was never invited there anymore after your parents fell in love. He had no liking for your mother's father, and Theresia had no love for him, or his new wife. They didn't get along." The demon paused while she worked out the logic. "You know, your father and Dietmar laughed a lot when they were boys together, much like you and your sister."

It was hard to imagine.

"He had Uncle Anton when he was younger, just like I did Maria."

"And your grandfather loved spending more time with your Uncle Anton than he did with your father, just as your father loves Maria more than he did you."

Louisa felt her shoulders stiffen, and her throat hurt when she swallowed. She watched in silence for a time as Dietmar led his daughter's mount.

"He's a good man, isn't he? Dietmar, I mean," she said eventually. "So why are we watching him?"

"I told you: because you need to get to know him. I haven't managed to strike any kind of bargain with him, or his wife, but your sister's life will depend on his willingness to help your family, one day."

Round and round the horse went, carrying Gerlinde on its back, while Dietmar trotted alongside, puffing and panting.

"She's doing beautifully, isn't she?" he called to the stable boy, breathless.

The lad nodded, and the countess clapped her hands in delight, lungs rattling, but she returned her husband's wink.

The demon moved to stand beside the woman.

"What are you doing?" Louisa asked, following.

The demon bent down to her and placed a hand on her cheek before blowing lightly in her face. It was a gesture Louisa had come to know. Atiram did this whenever she was giving her the gift of some of her magic. Little things, sensory things, became clearer and easier that way, sometimes only for a while, sometimes for good. The more complicated crafts, such as cloaking spells, had to be learned and needed practice. She knew many difficult words in an old language now.

"Step closer to the countess and smell the air."

Louisa did. Sour. As she imagined the soil beneath the pines would be. "She's really ill, isn't she?"

Atiram nodded. "So sad. She gave birth to her third child only a few weeks ago."

"Can… can anything be done?"

"No, dear. I don't… *interfere* with fate when I'm not *entitled* to, or unless the dying themselves entitle me."

Louisa didn't understand what that meant, but she didn't ask. She didn't think she would get an answer. The demon did not discuss certain things with her, and going by the tone of Atiram's voice, this could be one of them.

She felt sorry for the countess, but she suspected the demon did not, despite her words.

"I want to leave this place," she said.

Atiram remained silent for a moment, considering her request. Finally, she hummed. "All right, love. I'll take you back, but I'll have to return. I have things to discuss here."

Louisa sniffed and straightened her shoulders as the demon offered her hand. She took it and held on tight, and soon, she found herself back in darkness.

She did not see the demon place a cool hand on the countess' chest later that evening when there was nothing left to discuss. Neither Dietmar nor his wife would do the monster's bidding, even in trade for a life yet unlived. The demon accepted this with regret, but it meant Louisa would be visiting here more often than Atiram had hoped she'd need to. The girl would have to get acquainted with Dietmar. She had to know how to talk to him when the time came to lay the grounds for a war that would destroy Ricdon and thus lay waste to everything Rambert had lived for and built. She didn't like the idea, but this was the hand she'd been dealt.

One final coughing fit shook the feverish young mother. The countess collapsed as her lungs filled with secretion and her stumbling heart stopped fighting for its rhythm.

Unaware of what went on in the Aboveworld as she waited beneath the sour earth, Louisa realized that wealth could not be measured in gold and silver. She'd witnessed it in the form of the happiness that dwelled at Bartholemburg Castle, and she'd learned it didn't depend on gems and the returns of a holding. Happiness was the love a parent had for a child. It was a promise of a chicken dinner, a stolen kiss, a pony ride, a wink between lovers, and the belief in tomorrow.

On her next visit in early spring, she discovered that it was also very withstanding.

Fourteen

Between Worlds

Time passed. It did, whether you were listening for the seasons to change or not.

"Concentrate," the demon said. Louisa held her breath. She focused as hard as she could on the ancient words in her mind. They altered the size of an object, and she held on to the back of the chair in front of her tightly, willing it to shrink. It finally did, scaling down to something a dwarf might feel comfortable using.

Her reward already awaited. A path lit up in the darkness. She followed it without looking back at the demon, taking only two leaps through time for all the many miles the glowing cobblestone road led her away from where she'd been practicing her incantations with Atiram.

A door appeared. It didn't have a handle on the outside, but Louisa knew how to get in just the same. She carefully reached her left hand into the fibers of the wood. When it emerged on the other side of the panel, she felt around and found the iron handle. It opened effortlessly for her, but she had to illuminate the room behind it with the power of her thoughts, because the darkness here was so profound, her eyes had nothing to work with once the path's glow had receded.

Gradually, pieces of furniture became visible.

Hundreds of leather-bound volumes sat gathering dust in chunky shelves from floor to ceiling against every inch of wall space. There were even shelves around and above the door, and some of them appeared to be so old, she thought they might be there since the beginning of time, or at least half an eternity before she'd been born.

Her fingers danced across the dusty, timeworn spines of the books that occupied the shelves she could easily reach, and she deciphered the gold and silver letters that spelled out their titles. She chose one that seemed familiar and pulled it forth. Folk tales had been her favorite stories when... when... when *had* she learned to love them?

A long time ago, a tiny voice in her head whispered.

Ever such a long time ago.

A table with a small oil lamp stood in the corner of the room, and next to it, a comfortable wing chair. With her arms wrapped around herself and her knees pulled up, she settled back on it to read. The words evoked vivid images she had to work hard to remember, since she'd only seen the Underworld, and occasionally Falconaer Castle and Bartholemburg for many years now.

She dreamt with her eyes wide open of trees,

boats, horses, fields, villages – all of that was embedded in tales that came to life on pages and pages of someone else's fantasies, but she found herself gladly chasing shadows of people, places, and things beyond her reach because they produced memories of life as it had been, or as it *could* have been, and upholding that seemed extremely worthwhile, all at once.

Deep down, she'd never stopped feeling a desperate need to recall and hold on to a number of little things from her childhood that had taken on meaning like she wouldn't have guessed they could. They hadn't seemed so important when they'd still been a part of her reality.

One of them was the clean smell of washing on a sagging line in the yard. Another was the taste of her mother's fresh bread and homemade cheese down by the murmuring river where she'd built dams with her sister and bathed in the cool water. Another still was the birds' call to roost at dusk when the day was done and Maria and she were pleasantly tired from playing.

These recollections and others like them were the pictures and feelings she'd shuffle through one after the other whenever she'd finished reading and was settling in to get some sleep, something in the way she would the motions of casting a spell.

She didn't feel justified in complaining or feeling sorry for herself, and that wasn't what this was about; the demon had explained to her the pitiful human need to perform rituals, something no other creature in the world had a use for, and she supposed this was hers. It was the glue that held together the bridge between who she'd been and who she was now, and she felt compelled to maintain it well, even if that would seem pitiful to Atiram. Atiram wasn't detracted by the *little things* that tended to occupy Louisa's thoughts.

She knew she had the demon to thank for so many things; she was strong and healthy, and she couldn't recall even having been ill since she'd arrived, aside from having cut herself deeply once, and from having the measles. The demon took good care of her and provided for her. Atiram had been mother and father to her after her own parents had abandoned her.

The only thing she'd never have as long as she was here was natural light, and that was one of the *little things* she'd always miss because she had no way of telling the time of day or even year, when she hadn't been to Falconaer or Bartholemburg for a while.

The profound darkness of the place where she'd grown up had inevitably become a part of her. It had gradually entwined itself firmly with the fabric of her essence, and the demon encouraged her to embrace it. Without its protection, she was sure, she'd just wither and fade away, and she didn't want that. She wanted to live. The demon told her this was how it had to be if she wanted to return to the light one day, and she did. It was the only way to appreciate all the brilliance of light as such clearly anyhow. Darkness brought forth beauty because it contrasted light, just as noise did silence, and silence brought forth wisdom. Darkness brought forth insight, the creature kept telling her insistently until it made sense, and she accepted it. For a time.

Generally accepting her fate and the way she existed and what she lived for only became questionable again when her body started changing about a year after she'd discovered the library, and she realized just how human she was, despite everything she'd learned.

There were no mirrors in the Underworld, but she'd noticed both the subtle and obvious changes about herself a while before she woke up that morning to find blood in her underwear.

The demon had warned her this might happen at some stage and told her how to deal with it, but it came as a shock nonetheless when it did. The blood proved she was a woman. She'd been a child when her father had traded her in for his title, and now she was old enough to have children herself.

The thought of that caused a landslide within, a whole avalanche of confusion and emotion coming down an already crumbly hillside. It ripped through everything she'd been convinced of for a decade. She had so many questions that made her head spin, and suddenly she didn't think the demon had all the answers anymore. Of course, Atiram had taken her in, been good to her, been patient and more than kind, and she didn't want to repay that with doubt or insubordination, but… she *had* doubts about the most fundamental things, and it was hard to keep them to herself.

In the following year, time began to move forward in a whole new way. She now had a means of counting it off by the month, and she developed a feeling for it. That in itself was good, but it also brought with it an acute sense of shortfall and loss because she was becoming painfully aware of how the weeks were slipping through her fingers, and she grew impatient.

She was torn. She wanted to feel, taste, and hear like other humans did, be *alive* in the world of the living despite being unwanted by her family, and despite the purpose she had yet to fulfill so that both Atiram and she would be avenged. No matter how her parents had treated her, she was curious to at least hear their voices again and glimpse them in daylight before old age, illness, or war took them.

There were times when she wanted to talk to Gregory and ask him why he had chosen Maria over her, why he had loved her more, because she finally needed an explanation for that. She'd tell him she'd forgive him regardless of what he'd say, though, because she knew none of this was his fault, really. It was all on Ricdon.

At other times, she wanted to confront the great Duke and Duchess of Blackvale directly and tell them what a sorry excuse for parents they'd both been because of the choice Gregory had made and her mother's unvoiced approval of it. And then, maybe she'd use her magic on Gregory and make him grovel and beg for her forgiveness if he hadn't asked for it by then. Louisa was conscious of the fact that she'd been much better off than Maria, but still…

Maria.

Most of all, she wanted to see Maria. She *needed* to see Maria, even if she didn't think she could talk to her. They'd never be sisters again, but she needed to see if the child more loved than she had a life worth living so she'd know that what Atiram had planned wouldn't hurt her any more than either of them had been hurt already. She didn't want Maria to suffer. She wouldn't have it.

That being decided, she was fairly sure she'd have to muster up the courage to speak to the demon. If she waited much longer, neither her mother nor father would be around for her to gain an understanding of them, or alternately convince herself of how cowardly and terrible they were and give herself the closure she needed. Ricdon would live forever, or until she brought about his end, but her parents wouldn't.

Although she was quite certain Atiram would say no, she knew she had to ask, or regret it for the rest of her days.

She usually found the demon in one of the doorless rooms within the hive-like central maze, so this was where she went to look. She searched its levels one by one, and each room in turn until she got to one on the lower floor that could only be reached by passing through the stone separating it from the level directly above.

She folded her arms across her chest, grasping her shoulders, and tucked in her chin like a diver before a jump, bracing herself for the drop when her feet started melting through the floor. In her head, she went over what she was going to say when she emerged in the room below, but abruptly stopped thinking when the creature spun around to face her, caught off guard.

Louisa had assumed she'd seen all Atiram's semblances by now, but today she found herself opposite a persona she wasn't familiar with yet. Straightening and dusting herself off absently, she wondered why.

The being's inner identity remained unaltered no matter what mask it chose to adopt, and Louisa could physically feel the faint, almost imperceptible buzz of its essence whenever Atiram was close by, a whiff of old hay and autumn forest, but she was surprised nonetheless. The form she had taken on wasn't the woman Louisa had grown accustomed to seeing most often.

The woman she was faced with now was different, and Louisa had the feeling this was who she really wanted to be, or who she *had* really wanted to be, once upon a time.

The essence in her ocean-blue eyes told of both happiness and pain, hope and love, and the lines around them betrayed memories of every other human emotion Louisa thought she'd ever read about. Her lips must once have been full and fond of smiling, as the crinkles around them showed, but her pale brow was furrowed with worry and anguish beneath her long, but thinning white hair.

"You're different," Louisa remarked quietly, almost immediately wishing she hadn't said that. She didn't really know how to approach the creature.

"*Old,* you mean," Atiram returned amusedly, no more than the tiniest suggestion of a smirk playing around her mouth, and it broke the ice.

"Yes," Louisa admitted, looking at her feet as she released a deep breath she hadn't been aware of holding. Then, she fixed her gaze to the demon's once more, putting aside the reason for her visit. This seemed more important. "Why are you old?"

"Because I'm *getting* old, dear. My time is almost up, though I never got to grow old while I was… almost human."

This was news to Louisa. How could Atiram have been anything even close to human? Demons weren't *made* – they were *born*, were they not?

"Looks can be deceiving, and things aren't always quite as simple as they would appear," the being gently reminded her. "You should know that by now."

Of course she did. Ricdon was immortal, and his wealth and power were almost limitless, and still he took pleasure in making so many innocents suffer by not fulfilling their wishes even though he had the power.

"Getting old is not a bad thing, Louisa," Atiram continued. "Not if you're strong and good at making the kind of choices that will get you what you need to be happy. Nothing is ever unmanageable if you're bold enough to seize the moment, and if you're with someone who is like you and can make you happy. I would have gladly died of old age if I'd remained human, but I had that taken from me."

The demon-turned-woman paused, and Louisa knew that Ricdon had taken away *both* their choices and their happiness, and she hated him for it more by the hour.

Atiram, however, smiled, as though reading her mind. "I'm permitting you to see me like this today so you'll remember what I *would* have looked like, in the hope you'll come back to me of your own free will."

Louisa startled. The old woman sighed, taking a few steps toward her. She offered her hand, and Louisa took it, feeling a quality of human weakness and frailty about it for the very first time. It made her think how little she knew about the being that had raised her, and how much she had yet to learn. Perhaps she wouldn't have enough time left to do so.

"I think you're mature enough to make your own choices now," Atiram told her softly. "I'm granting you the freedom to be with the people who gave you life, even if they didn't love you. I want you to see what's become of them, and how they've fared. They *are* your family. I didn't get to be with *my* family because of Ricdon, but I'm giving you a chance I didn't have because I *do* love you, and I know how important this must be to you. I'm not blind."

"I don't understand…" Louisa objected, suddenly overwhelmed.

"Yes, you do." The crone laboriously straightened her back. "I'm showing you how to get to your father's castle, and I'm leaving it up to you to stay there or come back."

She pulled a small, flat pebble the color of ash from the pocket of her cloak and handed it to Louisa. "And when you're done finding out what you've been lacking, make your decision. I won't hold it against you, whatever you do. You're free. But, should you choose to come back to me, all you have to do is find water and look at your reflection in its surface. If you throw this in and follow," Atiram said, tenderly folding Louisa's fingers over the smooth stone, "it will bring you back to me. Then, and *only* then, will we talk about how we're going to defeat Ricdon and all he stands for."

Fifteen

Home

Louisa's eyes hurt. She squinted at the sudden brightness following her transition into what she thought of as the Aboveworld. A gentle summer breeze tussled her hair, and she breathed in the scent of warm sunlight on grass.

She startled when a flock of sparrows rose in one smooth movement from the apple trees that lined the field road. A hawk gave chase. His shadow passed over her, and she marveled at the bird's speed and grace, but he failed to make prey nonetheless. The sparrows vanished into the forest, and the trees seemed to absorb them as though they'd never existed outside of their branches' protection.

The hawk soared higher and higher in the sky until he finally disappeared from sight, but Louisa didn't doubt he'd be back, because even if she couldn't see him, he would still be watching her from above.

A rye field almost completely covered the narrow valley to her left. It swayed in the wind, as though to beckon to her, tempting her to lose herself in its sanctuary like a sparrow in the woods. She briefly considered it, but she hadn't come here to hide, and she was no longer the little girl who might have tried.

She knew she had to get going, or she'd lose her courage.

The sloping meadows and untended woodlands of Wildenburg were very different to the landscape she sometimes looked down upon from the windows and battlements of Falconaer. It was the untamed countryside that had given her father's fiefdom its name, and she loved the inconsistencies and the jaggedness that shaped this place because she could relate so well to imperfection.

A lump formed in her throat.

Her fingers closed around the hard, smooth pebble in the lining of her cloak. She could just return to the Underworld and forget she'd ever come here. It was that easy – and it was that hard. No. She decided she wasn't going to stand in her own way. She'd never stop asking herself *what if*, if she didn't go through with this.

Mumbling the words of the cloaking spell Atiram had taught her so no one would see her, she stepped out onto the road, and set off for Blackvale. The castle was just a short stroll from where she'd emerged. She wanted, no, she *needed*, time out in the daylight, the blue sky above her, and time to revisit her birthplace and the circumstances that had led to her expulsion from it.

A dog barked at her when she passed the mill. The miller's wife looked around, and then right through Louisa in bewilderment. A giggle escaped

Louisa before she could suppress it.

The woman paled at the disembodied sound. She ran inside the building, slammed the door behind her and bolted it tightly. Louisa could imagine her blocking the shutters and falling to her knees to say a prayer, or whatever people did here to ward off evil.

Several more homesteads lay close by the road she'd chosen. While the people who worked there went about their chores, oblivious to her presence, the grazing livestock was aware of her. She couldn't say why, but perhaps animals were immune to the kind of magic spells Atiram had shared with her, and she asked herself if there were other exceptions.

A pair of geese hissed at her near the river where three women washed clothes, and Louisa found herself running. The situation might have been comical, but all at once, she found herself face to face with a teenaged girl she'd overlooked. She would have bumped into her in another second as she sprinted toward the next curve in the road, and only avoided her by inches.

The mousy girl's eyes widened, even though she could not possibly see her, and she dropped her sack of laundry. A silent scream lodged in her throat.

Louisa was sure the girl would hear her footfalls if she hurried away, so she backed off treading ever so lightly, realizing she had to be more careful; humans believed what they saw, chose to remember what they *thought* they'd seen when it was over, and feared what they did not understand.

Fear, Atiram had taught her, had a way of spreading. It was the true plague of mankind. It was a hawk in the clouds, a lie in the promise, and a ghost in the wind.

The sunlight barely bothered her anymore by the time the topography flattened out, and she repeated to herself that she was not afraid of anything she might discover today. She would never let fear rule her actions, because Atiram had also taught her that the only thing worth fearing was fear itself. A hawk was mortal, a lie was predictable, and *she* was the ghost.

She didn't intend to show herself to anyone but Maria, if she got a chance to talk to her alone at the castle. Louisa had dreamt of speaking with her every day when she'd been younger, and she'd imagined Maria might have heard her thoughts on some level. Her sister had often replied to unspoken questions when they'd been children playing together before fate had separated them, so perhaps she'd been listening all these years, and just forgotten how to answer.

Louisa longed to hold Maria tight. She'd tell her how much she'd missed her, and how glad she was to see her. Maria would know this anyway, of course, but Louisa thought she might be lost for anything else to say out loud now that they were adults. What *could* she tell Maria without breaking the promise she'd given Atiram?

Betraying Atiram because she might not be able to betray Maria was the only *little fear* she allowed herself, and she disliked the gnawing anxiety it caused her as she neared Blackvale. The family standard flew at full mast above the inner gatehouse.

A donkey cart came up from behind her, and she had to move aside so it could pass. Soldiers stopped the cart for inspection. She frightened the animal by accidentally brushing its flank in the narrow passageway while trying to avoid a drunken beggar coming her way. The creature started bucking, and it stomped on the farmer's foot.

He yelped and swore at the animal, but Louisa was sure he'd live, and prudently took herself out of the way to keep from getting kicked. The guards hardly noticed the beggar making off with the poor man's coin pouch because they were laughing so hard at the song and dance, and Louisa had to bite down on her lip to keep from joining in.

Her father's carriage had always been halted here for a quick check, even though Gregory had been Anton's brother. She recalled how he'd jested about this being the plight of the poor relatives from the backwaters. The guards had never laughed at any of his jokes. Not then. They'd been infinitely more grim and intimidating, and they'd kept meticulously to their strict directives.

Louisa remembered how utterly terrified Maria had been of them. She, on the other hand, had habitually stuck her tongue out at the soldiers. Their mother had been cross with her about that and told her off for it more than once, but this hadn't deterred her. To her mind at the time, the soldiers deserved it for scaring Maria. If they'd ever so much as *tried* to put a more pleasant expression on their faces once in a while when they were looking into the coach, she wouldn't have been so afraid, but they never had.

Observing how the guards on duty now helped the ill-fated, hobbling farmer to gather up his wares from the ground led her to believe that some manner of change must have swept through Blackvale's halls. That, or Gregory's rule was lacking authority.

Louisa was certainly past sticking her tongue out at anyone, but by the time she'd tamed all the straying thoughts tumbling around inside her head, she realized she was standing in the middle of the courtyard, facing that *little fear* of hers. It had grown to twice its size over the past half hour, but she was still in control of it.

She took a deep breath and tried to get her bearings as the sights and sounds of the bustling household rushed at her: children played, maids and varlets chattered as they went about their tasks, a horse neighed in the stables, and a smith worked on a hot iron rod, hammering steadily away at it until it looked like it could become a door mounting.

Life here seemed much like it was at Falconaer, but she felt overwhelmed all the same because this was *not* Falconaer. This was her family's home. She'd never lived here because Wildenburg had been her father's inheritance, but she'd spent a lot of time here as a child, and some of her fondest memories had been born within these walls.

Again, a lump formed in her throat, and again, she felt for the pebble. This was too much…

Just as she was about to turn and leave the way she'd come, a comforting aroma wafted across the yard and made her jaw drop. The fragrance defeated and conquered every other sensation assaulting her: it was the smell of freshly baked bread. She melted away at the mere idea of how it would taste, thinking whatever else happened here today, she was going to get some and reward herself with it later on, and cheese, too, if she could find it – just as soon as she'd at least seen Maria, even if she didn't have a chance to talk to her alone.

Looking about, much seemed familiar, though she hardly had any real memory of detail. The exact color of a door or a window frame wasn't important enough to carry across an entire decade.

She was sure a rather large new building with a sundial fixed above its entrance had sprung up between the stables and the forge, but it struck her as odd that some other important part of the complex seemed to be missing as she slowly scanned the enclosure. It took her a while to realize it was the chapel.

The little church was gone, as though it had been blasted completely out of existence. Cobblestones covered the ground in fishbone patterns where the remnants of its foundations would have left their marks, and a young oak grew in an open circle of freshly limed soil where the sanctuary would have stood.

She unconsciously raised a hand to her left temple, where her fingers found the little bulge left over from the day the windows at Saint Sebastian's in Oakwood had shattered, and a shard had cut deep into her skin.

Perhaps her father hadn't rebuilt it after the fire. Or he'd grown tired of Blackvale and Wildenburg's patron saint looking down on him, reminding him of how he'd come to be the master of this house. The craftsman who'd made and fitted the stained-glass windows in Oakwood had used the same motifs for Blackvale Chapel.

Fear was a powerful regent. Maybe the most powerful of them all.

Eventually, she moved on through the inner gatehouse toward the keep. Just as she was making her way across the courtyard, she spotted Maria coming out of the main building's entrance in the company of a maid. The two women were followed by a dark-haired young knight as they descended the stairs.

Maria carried herself with all the grace of a princess. She appeared to be in good health and untroubled in any way as she politely ended the light conversation she'd been having with the maid before they parted ways at the bottom of the stairs.

The maid happily scurried off to the well, where she met with another servant and eagerly began chattering, while Maria made a quick survey of the yard and then took a left turn, around the side of the building. She seemed really happy.

The knight hesitated for a moment, looking a bit lost by himself as she walked away from him.

Louisa's feet felt as though they'd been somehow adhered to the ground, and she needed a few seconds to recover before she could make herself start breathing again and go after her. She had to talk to her. It was now or never. She nearly collided with the young man, since he'd finally made up his mind he was taking the same direction as Maria.

Giving him a little head start, she trailed after him. He peered around, visibly nervous, trying so hard not to attract attention, it was almost funny. Louisa couldn't make sense of it.

A small kitchen garden was located behind the keep. A hedge rimmed one side of the small area, and an ivy-covered wall closed it off at the far end. A clever architect had designed it so its plots faced south, immersed in light throughout the day. Louisa wondered whether she'd just forgotten this was here, or if her mother had created something from nothing after the family had taken over the estate.

The sun smiled down on a wide array of herbs and sprinklings of red poppies and blue lavender. Oddly unable to locate Maria at first sight even though the garden was tiny, and there was really nowhere to go, she kept following the knight. He purposely crossed to the ivy-covered wall and pulled the thick tendrils aside like a curtain to reveal a narrow plank door.

The door didn't have a lock, and the knight didn't think of closing it behind him, so Louisa passed through unhindered in his wake without even noticeably stirring the ivy.

Maria sat on a wooden bench by the water's edge, throwing crumbs to a family of ducks. The young man stood watching her for a moment before she spotted him.

Louisa guessed she had expected him to follow her, but perhaps not so soon. She observed her sister's face light up when her gaze met his eyes.

"Steffen!" she called to him, and Steffen smiled.

Louisa stopped at a distance from the couple, uncertain of what to do. The two had come here to enjoy a private moment that wasn't private anymore because she was here, and she felt awkward and misplaced when Maria reached out for Steffen's hands and drew him close. Their fingers interlaced.

The sparkle in her sister's eyes mirrored perfectly in her suitor's, and when she said his name again, he couldn't restrain himself and leaned down to kiss her tenderly, carefully, letting go of her hands and gently taking her in his arms as she melted into him.

Little Maria had grown into a beautiful young lady, Louisa realized, and she couldn't help but stare at her sister, drinking in the sheer radiance of a stunning woman in love. The expression on Maria's face would have been enough to illuminate the darkest night, but then it struck Louisa like a blow in the gut: she *should* have been insanely happy for her twin, since this – if not exactly *this* – was what she'd been hoping to find. Instead, a confusing, combustive mixture of elation and sadness stirred a nasty ache within, twisting her innards in the most excruciating way. She'd never felt anything like it before, and she was grateful Maria couldn't see her.

She gazed down at her feet for the space of a few heartbeats before making herself consciously look back up at the better sister, the sister who'd gotten *everything*. Why could she not be pleased with what she'd found here? Why could she not share the joy that must be overflowing in her twin's heart?

Maria reluctantly disentangled herself from her knight before things could get any more heated, and Louisa was forced to admit to herself what she'd known all along, deep down: the demon had been right in everything it had told her about her sister and herself, and why her father had chosen Maria over her.

Maria was everything she was not. She was Light, Hope and Love, and all Louisa would ever be was undesirable, unwanted, and unbearable. Perhaps their father had seen this the day they'd been born; alike, but not the same, because destiny was predetermined, and their places in fate's workings were set in stone.

Louisa was sure she could never love anyone as deeply as Maria did; not because she wasn't meant to, but because it was so difficult to love someone, so complicated, and Louisa had been the more complicated of them both, the more bothersome. She'd read in one of the books in her infinite library beneath the earth that neither logical reasoning nor magic had any influence on love. Love thrived on Light, and Maria *was* Light, while all Louisa would ever be was Darkness.

That aside, there simply hadn't been anyone for Louisa to love, never mind fall in love with, and she knew there never would be. To her, romantic love had been no more than an abstract notion formed by the abstract philosophies of authors who didn't have the slightest inkling of the agonizing beauty of it when they'd penned their assumptions. That much certain now.

Maria had every kind of love in her life; her mother and father's, the love of her friends, and the kind her admirer was more than willing to bestow upon her. She would never be lonely, or sad, or cold, while Louisa hadn't even been worthy of the most basic form of caring: their parents'.

She was damned to live in the shadows, in the places and in-between spaces where no form of real love would want to reside. True love was too fragile to endure that. Atiram had taken her in and seen to her, and Louisa knew she had to be thankful for that, because it was all she was going to get, and it would be enough, if the end justified the means. The outcome was all that was important. Overcoming the pain was all that was possible.

And what *had* she been thinking? Wonderful, gorgeous Maria would never want her in her life anyway. Why should she?

Maria didn't need her complicating things and causing a ruckus at this point in her life because she had other things on her mind – really *good* things, things that were *right* for her. They were no longer children. Maria was going to be the next duchess of Blackvale, and she'd have a handsome man at her side to help her make smart decisions and live her life to the fullest.

The only thing Louisa could do for her was compensate for the envy she felt. She had to protect her from Ricdon and make sure he never laid hands on her and took all that away, like he had taken everything away from Atiram. Because he lived, she would never walk beside Maria again, never walk in the *Light*, and always be forced to hide away from love, lest she destroy its delicate fibers, or begrudge her sister it.

Strange, how much clarity a film of tears could bring.

She could hardly breathe, and she slipped her hand into the lining of her cloak once more to touch the pebble. She didn't really want to go back to the Underworld, but she didn't want to stay here anymore either. She'd had enough, and yet, at the same time, she wanted more; more of the sunlight, more of the giddy excitement that emanated from her sister, more of both the beauty and of the agony of this moment.

"Will you be cheering me on, then? At the tournament, I mean?" she heard the knight inquire softly somewhere along the sidelines of her breakdown. His voice wavered a pitch above what she'd have considered normal. It was almost annoying.

Maria smiled up at him shyly and nodded before she mustered the moxie to stand on her toes and pick up where they'd left off a minute ago. Her lips caressed first his cheek and then his mouth, letting him know she'd have eyes for no one else. He couldn't get enough and all but devoured her for it, it seemed to Louisa as he pulled Maria to him. Louisa hated him. Why couldn't the fool have chosen another day for this and stayed wherever it was he'd come from?

Why couldn't *she* just have stayed where she'd come from?

"How dare you!" an angry voice boomed from behind her then.

Louisa startled, spinning around to find herself confronted with her father stomping toward her at high velocity without seeing her. He was different from how she remembered him, much heavier and a lot older than seemed right. How had she not heard him coming? She'd been too busy with herself, she realized. Too busy trying to control feelings she hadn't been aware could hurt so much.

"I'll have you drawn and quartered!" Gregory yelled, and Louisa thought poor Steffen would wet himself.

Louisa sidestepped to avoid getting bowled over by the burly, red-faced man as he passed her. A sickly sour odor wafted out from him, and she wondered if he'd been ill.

She felt unbalanced, as though the ground had suddenly become swampy beneath her feet, and all the words she'd collected in her head had gone. Everything she'd imagined she might say to him vanished, as thoroughly erased from existence as the little castle chapel.

"Get away from my daughter," Gregory ordered the younger man harshly when he'd reached the couple.

Steffen did as he was told, paling as he backed away so abruptly, he almost fell into the moat. Gregory positioned himself between him and Maria.

"Father–" Maria began, and Steffen babbled in an attempt to apologize, but Gregory tilted his head and raised one eyebrow at her, and her mouth clamped shut.

Seemingly satisfied that he'd admonished, embarrassed, and intimidated his daughter's suitor well enough to safeguard her honor, Gregory snapped his fingers at the squire who'd finally caught up with him, and instructed the breathless servant to fetch his wife.

Theresia must already have been on her way because she was there before Louisa could finish considering whether she was still willing and able to brave the storm, or rather make a break for it, toss the pebble into the moat and dive after it and be done with this horrible day.

She'd been so unprepared for the waves of nausea that overwhelmed her when she breathed in the scent of roses and fresh reeds as Theresia passed her by, she didn't think she'd stay afloat in her present reality, never mind make it to the bottom of the moat and pass through into the Underworld. The fragrance stirred awake some of her very earliest childhood memories, and they had a physical effect on her.

She'd wanted to see Gregory, and she'd wanted to see her mother, yes, but after having already found she couldn't deal with Maria, her parents' presence proved even more difficult to bear, and she wasn't as strong as she'd thought she'd be. She couldn't explain why, but she was empty and drained as she watched Theresia putting her arm around Maria's shoulder. She was in way over her head.

"Come on, let's see about that dress you're planning on wearing to the ball after the tournament," Theresia told Maria, firmly leading her away from the men.

Maria didn't look too happy leaving Steffen alone with her father, but she wasn't asked and didn't have a say in the matter.

"You need to be more respectful, boy," Gregory told Steffen, jabbing a finger at his chest while at the same time ordering his squire away so they could have a little talk. He was still furious.

Louisa had to make a quick decision, and rather than stand there and watch her father take a bite out of her sister's companion, she set off after Maria and Theresia, hurrying to catch up and keep stride with Maria on the other side of her mother. She was fairly sure this wasn't the best idea she'd had today, but she did it anyway. She could part ways with them anytime, she told herself.

"You need to be more careful, young lady," Theresia advised Maria when they were out of earshot of Gregory and Steffen. Maria blushed.

"Mother, I didn't mean to…"

"No, stop," Theresia cut her off softly. The older woman smiled nonchalantly and hooked her arm under Maria's. "Don't get me wrong. It may come as a surprise, but I do remember what it's like to be young, and I'm not saying *don't see him*. I'm just saying *be a little more discreet*, dear."

Maria didn't reply right away, but Louisa saw the strain going out of her expression, and the corners of her mouth curved upward, as did the corners of Louisa's. Maybe she'd stay around a little longer after all, so she could have a peek at that dress Theresia had mentioned, at least.

"You know," the older woman said then, "sometimes I'm glad you're an only child. I don't know how I would have dealt with two of your kind."

Louisa stopped in her tracks. She gasped. A flood of hot tears spilled down her cheeks, and she lowered her gaze as her fingers closed painfully firmly about the pebble. She didn't want to define the form of misery that was slowly burning a hole in her heart, and all she knew was that it had to stop. Ordering herself to turn around and put one foot in front of the other right now, she accepted that she'd made a terrible mistake in coming back.

The gatehouse wasn't far. She could just walk right off the little drawbridge once she'd tossed the pebble into the water. She only had to get there and dive after it.

One
and two
and three
and four
and five
and six
and seven
and eight
the sun
the rain
and a woodsman's cane
and forwards
backwards
one step to the side
and one
and two...

Standing still wouldn't help her. Standing still wouldn't get her home.

... and three
and four...

And then she stumbled and fell, going down on all fours just as she'd reached the drawbridge. She did not take notice of the knight who'd appeared at the other end of the bridge, but he saw her. His horse was weary after the long ride to Blackvale, and he would have dismounted here anyway, but he nearly fell over himself when he observed what happened next.

The pebble fell from her hand and skipped into the water. Her reflection was distorted by the ripples that formed and spread outward from it, multiplying with the heavy raindrops that began tumbling from the heavens above. She crawled toward the edge of the wooden bridge and commanded herself to finally stop crying.

The knight had almost reached her, but something kept him from calling out to get her attention. No one else paid her any heed, as though she was invisible to them, and this realization seemed to spark something within the young man. His eyes widened for a moment before settling back on Louisa.

"Atiram…" she whispered in a tiny voice, hoping no one would hear her, only the demon – but *someone* did, and the man took another hesitant step toward her, but dared go no farther.

She was so lost. She needed Atiram.

"I'm here, dearest," a gentle voice told her.

She couldn't say from where it came. It seemed to be all around and nowhere at the same time, bouncing off walls that weren't there. Atiram was inside her head. Perhaps she always was.

"I want to come back, please," she murmured.

"Then let me take you," the demon said.

Louisa took a deep breath and slid head first into the cool water. She felt the pull of the Underworld. There was nothing here for her. There never had been.

The knight rushed at her, fearing for her. He tried to grab her, but he was too late. Sprawling flat on his belly, all he could catch ahold of was her boot.

Beneath the water surface, Louisa felt something was wrong. Something was holding her back. She turned and tried to free her foot from what she thought might be a tangle of plants, but released a lot of air in surprise when she saw the man coming at her. She sensed something familiar about him, *dangerously* familiar, but then everything went so quickly, she didn't have time to think about it.

She pulled him down with her another few feet, trying to pry his hands off her, but he didn't seem angry or shocked. What she did see in his kind face when she stopped struggling long enough to look at him was worry. Plain and simple.

He thought he was saving her as he drew her close, and oh, how she wanted to be saved by him, but *no one* could save her. The touch of his hands on her skin burned almost as much as her lungs did. A well-aimed knee in the groin, one last push, and he let go of her, leaving her to vanish in the dark tunnel the pebble had driven into the mud at the bottom of the moat. She was going home.

Sixteen

The Milksop

When he thought the ladies were out of earshot, Gregory struck Steffen smartly across the face. That boy had a lot to learn, and by God, he was going to teach him. He'd have to, if Maria had made up her mind to love him.

Gregory had spent the past year hoping Maria's childish infatuation with the fool would pass, and she'd consent to marry the man he picked for her, but that obviously hadn't happened. He'd considered ordering her to comply with his wishes, because he only wanted what was best for her, but Theresia's arguments against making arrangements Maria wouldn't like had a lot in common with his own contemplations about married life. You could certainly *learn* to love someone, like Anton had, but true love was by far more valuable.

He himself had married Hermann Heistermann's daughter for love. His father hadn't been that interested in who he loved or married, because he'd already named Anton as his successor, but even if he had, Gregory thought he still would have married Theresia. He'd never had eyes for anyone else.

This was probably why he'd done the things he had, done whatever Hermann had required of him during the years of the witch trials. Looking back, he remembered distinctly that they hadn't had even one secret rendezvous. They'd never have dared. Theresia had been much too scared of her father... and perhaps also of him, in a way. He hadn't wanted to put her heart at risk, so he'd kept away from her for the longest time, until Bernhard had banished Hermann.

Hermann had intended to take Theresia with him, but that was when Gregory had finally found the courage to speak out, and he recalled the wide-eyed expression on her face to this day: wonder, awe, love, gratitude – all of that blending together in the space of a few seconds, and she'd come to him, taken his hand and stood beside him, stood against her father.

Theresia said she didn't want their daughter to have to make a choice like that, one day. She didn't want Maria to have to choose between two people she loved, like she had in her time. Gregory could understand her well. He knew all about the terrible weight of a decision like that.

Regardless, he'd written a letter to Richard of Falconaer to invite him and one of his knights, Thomas of Newburg, to his tournament, and he'd received a positive answer. He didn't know Richard personally, but he'd recently met the knight at the Electoral Prince's annual congress, where Newburg had represented Falconaer. Both the archbishop and the prince accepted his procuration, so he assumed Newburg was the rising star of Falconaer.

In fact, Gregory had reliable information that Thomas was Richard of Falconaer's illegitimate son. Richard had never married, and, lacking an heir, he'd apparently acknowledged Thomas a few years ago, Dietmar of Bartholemburg had let him know. Illegitimate or not, the entire kingdom talked about the young knight who'd proven his stealth on the French battlefields. He'd fought for the emperor and returned a hero, rumored to be invincible. His sword arm never tired, and no matter how badly he was wounded, he always stood right back up and led his men to victory.

Old wives and weary soldiers loved a good tale by the fireside, young stable boys needed someone to look up to, and Dietmar tended to inflate most of the stories he told, but observing the quiet, handsome man who'd sat opposite him at the prince's table, Gregory was inclined to believe there was a grain of truth in there somewhere. Even if half of the accounts he'd heard were exaggerated, it looked as though Thomas of Newburg had a very bright future ahead of him.

Falconaer alone was worth a fortune. Located at the other end of the kingdom, its vineyards on the steep slopes along the river Rhine produced the country's sweetest wine, and its sun-kissed spelt fields yielded harvests even Winterfield could only dream of. With what he stood to inherit, Newburg was going to be filthy rich in a few years, and

Gregory firmly believed he would be just the man for Maria, though she wouldn't hear of it, of course.

He'd hoped she'd wake up to how dense her beloved Steffen really was, but she hadn't, and short of strangling the boy in the woods, he couldn't think of how to solve the problem, so he slapped him again in his frustration.

"I gave you permission to *court* her," he snapped. "Let me explain to you what that means: it means you're allowed to flatter her with poetry and give her expensive gifts."

He paused, watching with some satisfaction as Steffen raised his hand to touch the bruise on his cheek, though it couldn't have been hurting half as much as his honor had to be.

"It means you may *occasionally* bring her flowers and tell her how pretty she is," he continued. "I did *not* give you permission to debauch her in my very own back yard on the eve of your first and probably last tournament, going by what I've been hearing about your horsemanship from my stable master."

Steffen wisely chose not to say a word in his own defense. Maybe he couldn't think of anything that would have had relevance to Gregory. The duke wasn't sure Steffen would *ever* have anything of relevance to say to him, but at least he knew when to shut up. Harald had taught his son that much. He'd been married to Celeste, after all, and he'd probably spent the better part of their marriage shutting up.

"My daughter has come to a point in her life where she should be married to a man of standing, a *man*, not kissing some milksop who can't even stay in the saddle when he's got armor on. You better shape up, laddie, or I'll send you packing with my boot so far up your ass, you won't ride a horse again, *ever*, let alone with a lance in your hand."

He looked Steffen firmly in the eye, but the young heir of Winterfield unwaveringly held his ground.

"Well?"

"Yes, Milord."

"Yes, *what,* Milord?"

"Yes, I'll shape up, Milord. And, I'll keep my fingers off your daughter."

"Good," the duke returned, but he was skeptical. "Then I'd suggest you get yourself to the stables so you won't disgrace yourself completely this evening."

Steffen made haste. Gregory turned, thinking he'd have to either withhold payment on that little maid of Maria's this week, or offer to double it. She'd have to let him know a bit sooner what his girl was up to, or he'd be the one disgraced.

Steffen of Winterfield would never be a man, and the thought of leaving his daughter and his land in his charge made Gregory's stomach churn, but there was still a chance his daughter might learn to appreciate someone with a face he didn't constantly feel the need to slap. Someone like Newburg. If she did, he thought he might even be able to sleep again at night, knowing Maria would be taken care of before the Wishmaster came to collect his price. If Blackvale didn't have a newborn heir of his blood by the time Maria had reached her twenty-first birthday, both Wildenburg and Blackvale would be Ricdon's. That was the deal.

Gregory decided he would have to get his daughter to at least speak to Newburg while he was here. A clever seating plan for the banquet after the tournament was in order, as was a walk in the park, and a ride to Wildenburg with a tour of the castle. He would have to get to work on that right now, because nothing would please him more than to send the milksop back home to Winterfield the following week with a cock-and-bull letter of recommendation to his father on his amazing horsemanship.

Seventeen

Ghosts

Tom felt the sting of loss and failure as he emerged from the water, gasping for air and empty-handed. He'd completely worn himself out searching for the young woman who'd gone off the drawbridge and into the moat. Every muscle in his body burned.

He would have gone back if he'd thought he had any hope of finding her, but he'd never in all his life seen a moat as deep and as dark and full of weeds as this.

He hadn't been able to save the girl, but she hadn't *wanted* to be saved. He knew of a number of people who'd ended their lives by drowning themselves, but it was beyond him why anyone would feel a need to harm themselves. Too many poor souls died of illness, hunger, or so others could live, and what a waste their sacrifice would be if those *others* were to throw theirs away. Life was precious.

"Hey," he shouted to one of the guards standing at the gate. "Help! Can you not see there's been an accident?"

One of the bearded men came forward on the drawbridge. He had a look of amusement about him Tom desperately wanted to slap off his face.

"Sir?" he asked simply.

Tom hauled himself out of the water. "Did you not see the girl who… fell in?"

"The only person I saw *jump* in was you," the keeper said. "Bit muddy for a swim, and we've got huge pikes with teeth on them that would take your nose right off."

Tom combed his dripping hair back out of his face with his fingers. "There was a girl – I tried to save her. She stumbled and crawled *right past* you."

The keeper's brow creased, and the smile froze on his lips. "There was no girl, sir. Only you."

"She went off the bridge *in front* of you."

The soldier's mien remained unmoved. He had to have witnessed the young woman's actions. Tom turned to the other guard a little way back. "Don't tell me *neither* of you saw that."

The guard shrugged. "Did you hit your head, sir?"

Tom let his gaze wander between the two soldiers.

A boy who'd been scrubbing moss and mildew off the windowsill above the gatehouse's entrance dropped his brush, and it fell onto the cobblestones next to the guard, breaking in two halves.

The man looked up. "Watch it, you little rat!" he yelled, but then added more mildly, "Tell us, boy, how long have you been working up there?"

The lad's cheeks reddened. "Sorry! I didn't mean to…"

"How long?"

"For a while now."

"And did you see a girl throwing herself into the moat?"

The boy's face took on the color of beetroot. "No, sir. There was no one else."

Tom did not understand what was going on, but he knew better than to force the issue. He was mortified. Had he seen a ghost? A demon? No... the girl he'd tried to help was no demon.

"Have you been in the saddle very long, sir?" the gatekeeper carefully suggested, studying him intently.

An awkward moment passed before Tom was capable of an answer. "That must be it."

The guard didn't seem entirely satisfied. "Do you want me to call someone to help you... with your horse?"

Tom shook his head. "No, thanks, I don't need any help, but I would like to be announced to the duke."

He saw the uncertainty in the keeper's eyes. His mount had remained on the other side of the bridge, and he whistled to it. It came to him immediately, and he pulled a leather satchel from the bag tied to its saddle.

The letter he took from it was addressed to his father and signed by Blackvale himself. He presented it to the guard. The man probably couldn't read, but he'd recognize his master's name and crest. There was bound to be a lot of coming and going at the moment because of the tournament. Tom was sure he'd made a fool of himself, and he didn't want to make any more of a scene. There was bound to be talk as it was.

The guard's mien relaxed when he saw the seal on the parchment. He took the letter from Tom and called to the boy. The lad seemed glad for the prospect of a break from his job, and made haste to take the letter inside. He returned a few minutes later with two squires. One led Tom's horse to the stable, the other relieved him of his traveling bag and led him into the outer courtyard.

All of the timber-framed houses that enclosed the yard looked well-kept and sound, despite the rumors of Blackvale's unfortunate financial situation. Maintenance wasn't a problem when you had manpower, and the duke *did* have manpower, it seemed, if not much else. The fields in this area were said to be quite unfertile, but Tom had seen many well-fed children on his way here, so Blackvale had to be doing something right.

Tom noticed the sundial fixed to the wall above the door to the largest building on the left. Its gnomon and the hour lines on the dial plate gleamed golden in the sun. Tom had seen a gadget similar to this before in one of the big towns he'd passed through during his time in the prince's army. He loved the idea behind it, but he wondered how having a timepiece to mark off the hours might affect the working day of the household. Would people look at it and wish the shadow moved faster on the dial plate, or would they feel hounded by its progress? He made a mental note to inquire after it.

The squire showed him to his room in the house next to the forge. There, he found towels to dry off on, and a clean cot with a pillow and thick, inviting blankets. He was stiff and tired, and he would have loved to test his bed, but he'd barely changed out of his traveling clothes when the squire returned to let him know the duke would see him now.

On his way to the keep, his gaze caught on a young woman by the well, and his heart stopped for an instant. She looked right at him, immobilizing his senses as he remembered how she'd fought him in the water, but she did not recognize him. Her eyes were different, but it was her all right, and he wanted to say something, but couldn't.

He recalled how she'd struggled in his arms, and the look of shock on her face at his intervention, her anger at being held back, and the urgency with which she'd freed herself of him. All that was gone, and what remained was a timid kind of curiosity in her glance. A small smile graced her lips, and she turned away, but he continued staring, unconscious of how utterly impolite he was being.

He knew he hadn't imagined what had happened at the moat, and again he asked himself if he was seeing a ghost, some form of apparition from a time gone by or yet to come. He forced himself to move on and keep following the steward to the main building, where he'd meet the duke who'd probably already heard all about his strange behavior.

And still... this woman was beyond pretty without the deadly weight of the misery he'd seen clinging to her earlier, dragging her under into the bottomless depths. Out here in the light, she looked as though nothing unusual had occurred that day, or *any* day before in her life. No darkness, no intent of self-harm wavered around her, and he did not wish it was so.

He did not begrudge her life and happiness, but he had the feeling there was something wrong, something *terribly* wrong with this beautiful girl who pointedly avoided looking in his direction as he walked on. He took a deep breath and tried to put her out of his mind, but he was sure he wouldn't be able to.

Eighteen

History

Back at Falconaer after his short and unsatisfying trip to Blackvale, where he had won a championship, been shown around a run-down castle somewhere in the backwoods, and had been almost completely ignored by the duke's spoiled daughter, Tom stepped through the wide doorway into what he thought of as Richard's Holy Halls. He became acutely aware of his own footfalls echoing on the polished tile floor as he tried to decide whether he felt any more at ease here than he had before his trip. He didn't.

Throughout the years, he'd called several places *home*: the little bakery in the village down below the castle walls; Sir Gernot's stables, where he'd spent most of his youth; the rooms he'd had to himself in the Electoral Prince's palace before the war, and finally the little cottage in the vineyards where he was spending the summer, learning the secrets of the estate's excellent wines. The one place where he'd never feel at home was Falconaer, in Richard's *Holy Halls*.

Entering the Great Hall, a strange thought struck him: perhaps his father felt the same. Richard traveled a lot, and he was here as rarely as Tom, it seemed, but there was hardly a way of telling. They hadn't had more than two proper conversations over the past year.

This wasn't at all what he'd expected when he'd agreed to accept his father's invitation to live at Falconaer as his son and only heir by bloodline.

It was time they talked. Tom had meant to provoke with his visit to Blackvale, since Richard had expressly informed him he did not wish him to attend Gregory's tournament. Going anyway had obviously gotten the job done, judging by the very short note Richard had sent him to the vineyards, summoning him to the castle today. It read:

Falconaer. Now.
R.

Whatever very discreet servants Richard employed had set the long banquet table for two, an odd sight, since it could easily have seated twenty on each side. Richard sat at the far end, slouched back in his chair with his hands folded over his flat stomach, waiting.

"Welcome home," the older man said without much conviction.

Tom acknowledged the greeting with a nod. He felt cold, and cast a glance at the large fireplace. A blaze raged in the hearth, but it didn't seem to carry any heat.

The food was still warm, and Tom was famished, but he ignored the smell of veal and carrots that filled the air, and instead helped himself to a cup of water before leaning back in his own chair to hear what the duke had to say.

And still, Richard waited.

"You wanted to speak to me?" Tom said.

Richard hummed, but then gesticulated at the food. "Are you not hungry?"

"I feel strange eating alone," Tom answered truthfully.

At that, Richard lifted his fork, speared a piece of meat from the platter in front of him, and dissected it on his plate. Tom waited until he'd plopped the first piece into his mouth before he did the same.

"I trust you had a pleasant trip," Richard said between bites.

"I did. I'm glad I went, actually."

"Even though I forbade you to go."

"Yes. But I'm not sorry."

"I don't require you to be."

"Blackvale mentioned that you've never met."

"Not entirely true."

Tom's eyebrows arched. "Not *entirely*?"

"He wouldn't remember, but I do. Just out of interest, what was your impression of the man?"

Tom thought about it, surprised his opinion be asked. "What was yours?"

Richard huffed a laugh, and sat back. "I believe

you've already come to understand that I don't think very highly of Gregory."

"I have. But why?" Tom knew by the look in Richard's eyes he was standing on thin ice.

"I don't owe you an explanation for that."

"No, you don't."

Richard pushed his plate away.

It always irritated Tom to find there was never a servant around when one was needed.

"Good God, Richard, you never explain anything, and there are things I might need to know. I'm happy to run your estate for you as best I can, even if I don't quite understand why you'd want that, but I can't turn down invitations like these without a reason."

Richard studied him, and he felt like a five-year-old caught with his hand in the honey jar. "I'm not asking *you* to turn down invitations like these. *I* turned it down. Actually, I'd sent a messenger, only to hear that *you* chose to intercept the man. You consciously defied me. Why?"

"Because I saw no reason *not* to go."

Richard did not twitch, though he was obviously upset.

"I had my reasons."

Tom took a deep breath. "Then tell me. Tell me because I'm *asking*. Tell me because I'm your *son*."

Richard rose, and Tom thought he was about to leave, but he didn't. He just went to stand by the window to look out, though there was nothing to see, it seemed. The night was starless. The stained glass neither showed, nor reflected anything but darkness. Not even Richard's face, Tom realized as he moved to stand beside Richard.

At first, he thought he was mistaken, and there had to be another explanation, but the longer he stared back and forth between the man and the lack of his likeness, the more certain he became that there was none. And still, he was not repelled, or shocked, or afraid. He'd heard stories of men who had no reflection. Most of them ended in horror and bloodshed, but Richard would not harm him, and he was curious. Just curious.

Richard saw the way Tom looked at the glass, and then at him. He went rigid for a second, and then turned his back on the window to face him, leaning against the frame to block his view, again, waiting for a reaction, now one of his secrets had been revealed.

"What are you, Richard?" Tom asked quietly.

Richard looked directly at him. For the first time, Tom read an emotion other than concealed irritation or grim amusement beneath the façade. He'd seen it in the eyes of many dying men on the battlefields when they'd reached out to him, asking for a merciful death, though there was nothing undignified about Richard. The duke of Falconaer was no beggar. He was just tired.

"I'm your father. That's all that's important. And, it's important that you're safe, and that you never have to fear for a child, like I did."

"Is that why you sent me away? My mother… the woman who raised me, she told me there was another boy."

Richard nodded. "Nicholas. He was your brother."

Tom had no memory of a brother. He wished he did. His childhood had not been unhappy, but he'd always felt an emptiness, a quiet space that should have been filled with something more, or *someone* more.

"Were there… were there any other children?"

"Several."

"What happened?"

"Blackvale did, and a man named Heistermann."

"Tell me."

"It's a long story."

"I have time, and I wish to hear it."

Richard spoke, and Tom listened. Richard's words evoked images so strong, Tom could feel the darkness that carried them like a sad melody.

Richard told him about the witch trials in Wildenburg. He told him of an evil butcher named Heistermann, and of the father and two sons who'd given him free hand to maim and murder in the name of God.

Tom wasn't surprised. He'd come to know a lot of people who killed in the name of God. The woman who'd raised him had taught him to believe in the

Almighty, but there had been times when he hadn't been able to believe in a god that was good anymore. Later, he'd come to realize it wasn't God who made promises only to break them. It was *men* who lied, betrayed, stole, and killed.

He listened as Richard spoke of a messenger named Peter Smith, a simple man, who'd worked for Bernhard of Blackvale. Richard told him of his wife's death, and of the children Peter had failed to take far enough out of harm's way before going back to plead for Agnes' life, and how Peter had ended up in the tower of Wildenburg himself, bargaining with Rambert Longsword.

"Rambert Longsword," Tom whispered. He knew many stories of the great king, but couldn't remember who he'd heard them from. "So it's true? He's not just a myth?"

Richard's lips turned upward in a twisted, unhappy smile, and he shifted his weight uncomfortably on his feet.

"I don't know what you've heard about him, but he is most certainly no myth."

"Longsword was married to a Black Fairy, and couldn't go to hell because an angel saved his soul." The words gushed from Tom's mouth before he'd taken a moment to think, and he instantly regretted his outburst. He sounded like a five-year-old, but legends had always fascinated him. This one in particular.

Richard cast him a cold glance. "I have no idea whom he was married to, and what angels could have had pity on him, but after eight hundred years, when he came to me, he was tired of his immortality."

Tom drew air. "You are... *were* Peter Smith, then."

Richard shrugged. "Rambert had found a means to trade his immortality for a place in heaven, if he found an unblemished soul willing to do his work, his penance here on Earth."

"And you were that soul."

The older man folded his arms across his chest, and turned away. "I would have taken on *anything* to have the kind of power he promised, and use it to save my family. All I had to do to seal the deal was choose a name for myself, a name which people could use to summon me."

"And which did you choose?"

"I chose *Ricdon*, because, like you, my father was a fool for good stories and songs of old by the fireside. When I was very small, he told me of a creature that lived in the woods near our home: Ricdin-Ricdon. Ricdin-Ricdon would make deals with anyone who'd summon him for gold and silver – or a first-born child."

Tom nodded. He knew this tale as well. "And he taught a princess to spin gold from straw."

"Along those lines, yes." Richard paused for a moment, as if his memories threatened to overwhelm him. "Well, my father loved that story so much, he never called me Peter. His name for me was Ricdon. He said that one day, if I ran his farm well, I would make gold from straw. Now, when Rambert came to me, I was as far from that farm as I could have possibly gotten, and I was the one who was trying to bargain for my children's lives, so it seemed fitting, but Rambert fooled me. He gave me hope, and took it away as soon as the deal was made. I was Ricdon, but powerless against my own fate. *You* are the last of my children. *You* are all that remains."

Tom's mouth had gone dry. He sat back down at the table, and reached for the jug to pour himself some more water, but it was empty, and there was no maid to replenish it. From the corner of his eye, he saw Richard raise a finger and move it about in a small circular motion.

The jug on the table refilled itself, as did his cup, and a decanter of wine appeared next to it. Richard seated himself beside Tom, and poured himself a generous cupful. He drank deeply, and for a moment, his eyes went black, and his face changed, not in its expression, but *completely*, taking on another shape and tone. The different skin and features layered Richard's face, flickering like heat above the ground on a hot summer's day.

Tom wondered how many faces Rambert Longsword had bequeathed Peter Smith. How much effort did it cost Ricdon to be Richard of Falconaer for him, and for the people who lived in the valley below the fortress? How did he present himself to the desperate who summoned Ricdon? Which face did he wear for a father in some dungeon cell, which for a mother who sat by her child's death bed?

"What became of Heistermann?"

Richard's fists clenched. "He's where he belongs."

"Did you… *find* him?"

Richard took another gulp of his wine, draining his cup, and poured himself some more. "What do you think?"

"I believe I would have, had I been in your position."

"Do you mean with nothing more to lose, or with the new choices my… *condition* permitted?" He paused for a moment.

Tom guessed it might have been to equal parts for both reasons.

Richard snorted a bitter laugh. "Of course I did. I would have taken pleasure in skinning that pig alive, but when I finally caught up with him, he was already on his way to hell. Bernhard had finally decided to throw him out, and he'd made it all the way to Hamburg. He'd stirred some vicious pots of hate here and there, spreading the poison from that book of his, and a merchant paid him well to work off a list of troublesome people he wanted dead."

Tom knew men of the type his father described, but not only among merchants.

"Once that was done, and all the right people were executed, Heistermann had a very unfortunate accident. I stumbled upon him in a gutter just outside the town walls. He bled badly from a nasty little gash in his stomach. I assume he hadn't been particularly popular with his new friends. It took him a while to die. I enjoyed watching." Richard wiped a hand across his mouth in disgust, and poured himself yet another cup of wine.

Tom took the decanter from his hands and followed his example. They drank in silence for a while, and Tom realized how lost the other man looked.

"You didn't go after Blackvale, or his sons."

"No. Maybe I should have."

"Why didn't you?"

He downed another cup of wine before answering. Richard didn't have any easy answers, it seemed.

"I was six when my father hanged himself in the barn after another poor harvest. Shortly afterward, my mother was tried and executed for witchery. Bernhard saved me from burning with her then. He was the only one who spoke for me. He vouched for me and took me in, and he paid his smith to raise me at Blackvale."

"You didn't think he'd let Hermann Heistermann

convict Agnes."

"Never in a thousand years." Richard leaned closer. "But you have to understand this: there are two types of man-made evil in the world, and they have nothing to do with demons or devils. One is the monster that rapes, burns, pillages, steals, and murders, and one is the monster that watches, and permits the other to do all of these things. I could have killed both, but fate took one from me, and I let the other live because I was just as weak as he was."

A small leather journal appeared on the table next to his father's arm. Richard tapped its cover, then handed it to him. "It's all in here. I wrote it down for you to read, one day."

Tom took the diary, suddenly aware of how little he'd really known or understood about the duke of Falconaer, but one thing was for sure: whatever he chose to call himself, whoever he decided to be, and whatever face he wore, his father was anything but weak.

Nineteen

Fate

Today, the little bird would fly, and tomorrow, Triumph and Falconaer would be at each other's throats.

"Are you ready to go above?" the demon asked Louisa, wearing the only face she hadn't stolen, ocean-blue eyes trained on the young woman.

Louisa nodded. "If this is how it must be."

"We can't wait any longer. William of Triumph is gathering his men, as I told you he would. He will be marching on Blackvale within the week, but we can still stop him, and rid the world of Ricdon at the same time. Your sister is ill, so she'll be out of sight, and there should be no surprises if you're careful."

"Ill?" Louisa always worried about Maria, even still.

The demon decided to tell her the truth. Or a part of it. "She miscarried her first child today, unfortunately. Your mother is forced to hide her away at Wildenburg Castle so no one will turn this against her and charge her with infidelity." Especially since she married a Winterfield, Atiram added in her mind.

Celeste's demise had left a shambles, and a pot of malicious rumors. The demon was quite satisfied with the damage done, since she'd learned of Celeste's role in giving Rambert sanctuary. The Lady of Winterfield would not be resting in peace.

Louisa remained silent for a moment. Sorrow cast shadows upon her face.

The demon didn't assume she'd feel her sister's pain anymore. Only her own helplessness, perhaps.

"Will she be all right?"

The demon smiled reassuringly. "You know I always watch over her as well as I do over you."

The more beloved sister would probably survive the potion Atiram had given Winterfield's midwife to remedy her Lady's morning sickness for good. A few drops of it in the milk the young, inexperienced dove had the expectant mother drink every morning was all it had taken to wilt the life in her womb. The midwife had been so gullible and eager to sell it as her own, she hadn't even asked what was in the mixture.

Atiram realized she'd have to look in on Maria in a bit, just to make sure the woman hadn't overdone and there wouldn't be a death announcement before Louisa accomplished her mission. The potion was fail safe, but the stupid village girl's mathematical capacity was not.

She leaned forward to look Louisa in the eye. Lies only became apparent when they weren't delivered with conviction. "No harm will come to Maria."

Louisa seemed satisfied with that answer. "And will *you* be all right here without me?"

Stunned, the demon snorted. "Of course I will."

The words came out more harshly than intended. Atiram couldn't conceive how her welfare could be a concern to the girl. Louisa's heart harbored an absurd amount of human emotion toward something so obviously *un*human.

She'd intended for this, *needed* for this to happen. She'd taken Louisa from her home at an age where other girls still played in the sunlight, and she'd had to forge a bond with the child, but the child was a woman now, and the bond irritated the demon like a pesky fly, or a flea bite in the night. This would end soon, but not soon enough.

Perhaps it had been a mistake to give Louisa the library. Yes, that was it.

She'd permitted Louisa to read so she'd acquire a basic framework of knowledge to navigate the Aboveworld beyond what she'd seen and learned at Falconaer and Bartholemburg, but she'd neglected to think about the intense quality of gratefulness her gift might evoke. That, and she hadn't considered the side effects of reading. Gifts encouraged loyalty and devotion, but books encouraged morals and dreams. She'd take the loyalty, but she did not *want* the affection that had grown in Louisa, and she could do without the rest.

Humans were never in control of the emotions their morals and dreams unlocked. Atiram knew this from experience. She felt it every time she adopted human form, so she avoided wearing a human appearance whenever Louisa wasn't near her.

Her fosterling knew what she really looked like, but the energy Atiram consisted of, the motion and velocity that only manifested itself in the givens of its surroundings, had always frightened Louisa.

Reverting to her natural appearance became harder and harder with each passing season now. It wasn't just the habituation, however: the soul fueling the demon's life force was dying. One soul's sustenance only lasted so long before it faltered and failed.

This was when they screamed the loudest, demanding to be heard. And *seen*.

Perhaps Louisa comprehended this, on some level, and didn't just feel a grateful kind of love toward her – maybe there was also pity. This, Atiram could also do well without.

Why did humans always demand things they weren't entitled to, or had willingly forfeited? Death or its immediate proximity always caused so much confusion, so much inner turmoil, even within the demon.

Atiram still felt a good portion of Agnes' burning hate and passion despite everything. It nurtured and empowered her. It made the promise she'd given the witch worth ten times what she'd gotten.

She remembered how she'd been drawn to the searing potential of Agnes' soul the night she'd gone looking for a solution to the new problem Rambert had thrown at her. She'd actually made *concessions* while bargaining with her for it in that barn near Wildenburg. This was something she wasn't accustomed to doing, but obtaining that soul had been worth *any* promise she might have given. This was something Louisa would never comprehend.

Looking at Louisa, she thought it a shame that she'd have to live with this girl's much weaker, much less aggressive energy when Agnes' life vitality was all spent. Louisa's soul wouldn't last half as long inside of her.

Marita saw Rambert from the topmost window of his castle's keep. His horse was slower than usual because it carried not only the king on its back, but also a lifeless body lying across its shoulders. She knew immediately whom it belonged to, and her heart seemed to stop beating. A solitary tear traced its silver line down her cheek.

~*~*~***~*~*~

The demon handed Louisa three letters, all of them excellent forgeries. The first parchment's seal bore the crest of Blackvale, the second had the tower of Bartholemburg on it, and the final one showed an imprint of a falcon on a mountaintop.

The young woman hesitated.

"Theresia will deny having written that letter to Bartholemburg if there is an inquest, and this could plunge Blackvale into disaster."

"That's why you should see that you get it back once Dietmar has read it, dear." She paused. "Your mother is afraid. She would have written it herself if she wasn't, believe me. With things as they are, all we're doing here is saving her – and your sister – from Triumph, and from your father's foolish pride. Do you understand that?"

Louisa hummed absently. She did not look at Atiram as she tucked the letters into a small, flat satchel, careful not to break the wax stamps.

"I asked you a question," the demon insisted.

"Yes, I understand." Her voice sounded as small as it had when she'd first come to the Underworld. Nonetheless, she hid the satchel between her undergarments and the dress she wore.

The wound her sister's happiness and her mother's words had torn hadn't gone as deep as Atiram had hoped. She'd anticipated a good measure of grim callousness after the experience, but Louisa just didn't seem capable of not caring for the woman who'd given birth to her, and she still pined for the sister who lived in the sunlight. That bothered the demon.

Louisa acted as if the people who'd abandoned her mattered, even when they played no role in her life and gave her nothing for the forgiveness they unwittingly received from her.

Hope was a plant much like ivy; it stubbornly stayed alive no matter how often you tore it out of the ground. You had to get it by the roots. Granted, Louisa's seemingly indestructible attachment to the strangers she considered her family was likely a part of the reason why she had survived childhood in the dark. But, oh, the problems too much ivy in the cracks and crevices of any foundations worth laying could create, and the extra work this was causing…

The demon knew she'd been too soft, too lenient, and too kind. Weakness was the result.

Marita had hardly reached the bottom of the stairs when Rambert entered the Great Hall. His footsteps echoed on the stone floor. He carried their son in his arms, and lay him gently down on the long table, the Hall's heart piece where they'd shared their last meal together as a family: the king, who thought his wife was a human, the Black Fairy who'd become human so he would love her, and the boy he'd given her.

Grief bent his back and etched deep lines into his face as he sat down and rested his brow on the young man's arm. His hands clutched the fabric of his boy's tunic tightly.

"How did it happen?" she asked, but her love had

already turned to loathing for him because he'd taken Nathaniel into combat.

She forced herself to look at her son. There wasn't a cut on him anywhere, no blood, and hardly a bruise. He could have been sleeping but for the pasty color of his skin.

Rambert did not lift his glance to her when he spoke hoarsely. "He fell from his horse."

"Are you sure there is no other way?"

Atiram knew what Louisa was getting at. How wonderfully naïve the girl was.

"No, dear. You know I can't use my magic like that. But Dietmar is good natured and kind. He will set things right, if you play your part convincingly. All you have to do is prevent word from reaching Ricdon so he can't intervene. He'd stop Dietmar from helping because he doesn't help anyone except when he stands to gain from it, but your father will need both Bartholemburg's *and* Falconaer's troops to defeat Triumph. You must get Dietmar to react at once, and see to it that he sends word to Ricdon's bastard, Thomas of Newburg, to get military assistance. If you fail, I'm afraid all will be lost."

"How do I recognize Thomas of Newburg when I see him?"

The demon pictured the man she'd been loosely

keeping an eye on since Celeste's death. "Don't worry about him. You won't have anything to do with him. Newburg will do as Dietmar asks. He has to prove himself worthy of the position his father has given him, and he will be very anxious to please. He'll rush right in. You won't have to do anything but intercept the letter Dietmar might be tempted to send to Ricdon. Replace it with the one I gave you."

Ricdon had hardly set foot in his castle in over a year now, so he probably wouldn't know what hit him before it was too late and his human den was all burned out. The demon had kept him busy since Celeste's death. She'd been sending him on all manner of wild goose chases, especially since he'd brought home his long-lost son as his rightful heir.

Thomas of Newburg now had control of Falconaer's army, and he'd be held responsible for the soldiers who were going to cross the border into Cologne's lands to burn and pillage, sealing both Thomas of Newburg and Richard of Falconaer's political fate.

The demon already knew which of the men riding for Thomas she could easily interest in a pact, and who among them would swear on the Holy Bible they had received their orders to do so from Newburg himself. Newburg would be dead by then, of course, and the prince of Trier would have to depose and expropriate the duke to prevent further escalations with Cologne, even after Falconaer's tragic loss.

It seemed fitting that Thomas should be slain at Wildenburg. She'd given Agnes her word not to touch the boy, and she wouldn't, but as long as men armed themselves and fought battles in this world, willing to kill and die for their cause, death was always just a heartbeat away... a single heartbeat.

William of Triumph knew a dragon could only be killed if you cut its head off. When he cut Falconaer's head off, it would win him the victory over Blackvale, whose robber barons he'd insist had brought so much suffering over Triumph and its people these past decades, and it would tear Ricdon apart. He'd lay waste to Triumph, find that he had nowhere left to go, and then he'd set out to find the man who'd cheated him out of his family and his life.

The moment he wrapped his hands around Rambert's neck, their deal would be nullified. Rambert would turn immortal once again, and Atiram would make sure to let him know it was *her* who had put him in his place, and *out* of Falconaer, the home he'd built for her and Nathaniel.

After that, Atiram would take Louisa's soul and revive her strength. She was absolutely certain Louisa would offer it freely when she realized what she'd done.

The Aboveworld would have lost *all* of its attraction to her by then, and she'd crumple under the weight of the machinery she'd set in motion. When this happened, Atiram could offer her a way to end her torments, an easy way out.

Humans *loved* easy ways out.

Marita left Rambert to his sorrow and fled the keep. She went to the stable to find her husband's squire.

Sweat-drenched and bone-weary after more than a day of hard riding behind his master, the battered-looking lad had already seen to their horses' water. He was rubbing down Rambert's trembling mare with a cloth one-handedly. His other arm hung uselessly by his side. It looked like it had been broken and badly set.

"Tell me what happened to my son," she said from behind him.

He startled and dropped the rag. Turning, he avoided her eyes. "Milady, I am sorry for your loss."

"Speak," she said firmly, resisting the urge to shake him.

"He fell off his horse, Milady." The young man trembled like an autumn leaf in the first winter storm.

"My husband already told me that. But Nathaniel was a good rider. Why would he fall off his horse?"

The squire closed his eyes and wiped his hand across his filthy face, sniffing.

"The fastenings of his saddle weren't done up well enough, Milady. I wasn't there to tie them."

Marita drew a deep breath, struggling against the urge to strike him. How dare he not be there?

"Who was?"

The squire didn't answer right away, so she repeated the question more loudly.

"Lord Wildenburg's son readied the horses, Milady. He insisted."

She couldn't believe it. She slapped the squire's face several times with all her strength. He did nothing to defend himself. Not even when she conjured a dagger and thrust its blade into his heart. He died at her feet, and she watched his soul take flight, a kaleidoscope of colors only she could see ascending from his prison of skin and bones. The vibrant blues, reds, and yellows told of his good nature and untainted conscience. The man's slate was clean, and he wasn't to blame, but she did not regret having set him free. This was her nature.

Wildenburg's brat!

None of this would have happened if Rambert hadn't felt obliged. He always felt obliged, since he'd never stopped bedding his first love, Wildenburg's wife, even after they'd each married someone else.

Wildenburg was a fool who didn't see what went on in his own house while he spent his days hunting and bickering with his neighbors over land and mining rights, water and road taxes. Wildenburg enjoyed nothing more than taunting Triumph and

Blackvale, and turning them against one another.

But Rambert might never have interfered if it hadn't been for the boy, who he assumed could be of his own blood.

The lad was two years older than Nathaniel, conceived just before Rambert and she had been married. Marita knew him as a conceited dunce with far-fetched ambitions. Perhaps he had his sights set on the throne. It didn't matter. Whether he'd taken her son's life by accident or with purpose, she was going to make sure he never got Rambert's crown, because it should have been Nathaniel's. She was going to make all of Wildenburg suffer.

Killing young Wildenburg would be too merciful, too quick a punishment... A torrent of fear and pain was what she'd unleash upon him so he would always remember, and so his children's children would never forget. He'd never be free, even at Saint Peter's Gate, because he would know she was claiming his entire bloodline, his home, and everything dear to him.

With Nathaniel gone, Marita knew Rambert would lose his soul that night. He'd bargained it away in payment for something he had not gotten. She could have told him that, had he asked her advice before making his deal with the Devil, but he hadn't cared for her counsel. His son was to be invincible in battle, but the Devil was a trickster, and perhaps he had even whispered in the dunce's ear.

She could not save Rambert, and she did not want to. She loved him deeply, perhaps too deeply despite his transgressions, but she could not forgive him for what he'd brought upon them both. She'd become human so he would love her, yet he'd gambled away their life together. Realizing this, realizing how vulnerable she'd made herself to him shook her to the core. She'd given herself to a mere human man, and this was her punishment.

She had to return to where she came from. She needed the dark refuge of the place that had born her, the underground haven no one but her kind could access.

Human women were so helpless and powerless in this world, and human men so foolish. The local nobility would be tearing each other to pieces over the throne once it had become vacant, since there was no rightful male heir now. Her only interest was to keep Rambert's bastard from claiming it, nothing more, and the darkness would give her back the strength she needed to accomplish this. It would bring back the magic she'd given up for Rambert. There would be a price to pay. There was always a price, but she had nothing to lose. Not anymore.

The only thing she could do for her son was to avenge him. Perhaps Rambert's whore would pray for him. Marita only felt contempt toward her husband, and if the Devil hadn't already held stock on him, she'd have found another way of making him sorry he'd turned his back on her and their boy.

He'd let Nathaniel die... yes: he was just as much to blame for what happened as the dunce, and as Wildenburg.

Ocean-blue eyes turned to deepest black as Marita walked away from the stable, away from the castle, and toward the woods, where no one saw her change to wind, twigs and leaves around the life force created by the same ancient powers that had made the angels.

Unfathomable dark eyes studied Louisa. Over the past centuries, Atiram had ruined Wildenburg time and again, and she'd claimed one Wildenburg child every hundred years for the son Rambert's bastard had cost her, nine in all. This was going to be the final installment, because there wouldn't be a Wildenburg or Blackvale left alive when all was said and done. Such a shame. She could have gone on playing this game forever. It had been very gratifying.

"Well? Is there anything else you want to ask me?"

Louisa shook her head.

The demon wasn't entirely convinced her little bird would accomplish her task without some minor hiccup or other, but she'd get the job done, in the end.

Atiram hated not being in complete control of the situation, but she didn't have the strength nor the time to accompany the girl in any way. She'd never gone this close to the end of one of her souls' lives before, and she couldn't risk overexerting herself, or be in two places at once.

William of Triumph needed one last push before he was ready to march on Blackvale, just one more misinformation, and she had yet to seal the bargain she'd already initiated with the knight who'd be wearing the falcon tunic when he led his men to loot Triumph while William was gutting first Wildenburg, and then Blackvale Castle.

Both William and Gregory were fools, and both believed the worst of each other, so that was exactly what they'd been getting all these past years, as had their fathers, and their fathers' fathers before them.

Finally, her hard work was about to pay off.

"Do you remember what you have to tell Dietmar?"

Louisa nodded. "Yes."

"And you're good with the timing?"

She *had* to be. Timing was the most critical element in this. Triumph and Bartholemburg had to arrive at Blackvale at the same time, and when they did, she would leave them no chance to negotiate, no choice but battle.

Again, Louisa nodded. "Yes."

Atiram handed her first a ring, and then a pebble.

"All right. Then come back to me when you're finished. If you do well, your family will be rid of Triumph, and the world rid of Ricdon." She paused, and almost considered embracing Louisa in a farewell, but then reconsidered. It was too much to take. "Come back if anything goes wrong," she finally added.

That was the contingency plan. If anything *did* go wrong, she could always claim the girl's soul before the time she'd acquired from Agnes ran out, and she'd just have to work with what she had from there.

Twenty

Snow

Winter had come to the Aboveworld early this year. Six men worked for hours at a time to keep the steep road between the village and the castle clear, but ever new layers of glistening white covered the narrow path they dug until darkness descended, and life at Bartholemburg came to a standstill.

From a hazel grove near the village, Louisa watched the laborers trudge back to their homes. She had materialized there a while ago, and tried to keep warm as she waited for dusk.

The cloaking spell proved almost unnecessary; she'd wanted to avoid having to explain herself to anyone but the local nobleman, but there was really no one about aside from the laborers, and once they'd gone, she lifted it, and got to work.

A black mare, she thought, *here and now, saddled and ready.*

There were more words, words in an old language she had acquired a basic command of, but they melded and muddled as she imagined the horse into being. No one would assume she'd come on foot, and her father bred Friesians, so the choice seemed fitting, since a carriage would never have made it here today.

An elegant mare solidified next to her, exactly as she saw it in her mind's eye. It snorted and neighed, but did not shy. The animals she conjured never showed fear. Magic was a tool, and its usefulness depended on how one wielded it, she'd learned. She loved the wonderful things it made possible.

She could not ride the horse up the slippery hill road in this weather, so she wrapped her shawl and coat more tightly around herself, and slowly led the animal up to the castle gates. Her boots sank deeper and deeper into the fresh snow as she walked. The blizzard was gaining strength by the minute, as though the leaden clouds above her fed on darkness, and the watchmen had already closed up for the night.

Tall fire baskets stood on either side of the portal, well-stocked with dry wood to fuel decent flames and provide a bit of light, but Louisa didn't think any fire would stand a chance in this.

She found the knocker on the narrow door in the right wing of the gate. The piece had been artfully crafted in the shape of a demon's head. *How fitting*, she thought as she banged it on the copper plate several times. After a moment, a guard peeked out at her through the barred spyhole. At first, she feared he would not recognize the crest on the signet ring she held up to him, but the man had a tallow lamp and good eyes. He quickly set about sliding back the iron bolts that secured the door, and let her in.

The ring she'd shown him had belonged to her uncle, and her grandfather before him. She had no idea how Atiram had gotten ahold of it, or why the demon had kept it all these years after Anton's death, but she hadn't questioned her. It didn't seem important. At least not important enough to insist on, or maybe she didn't *want* to know. She'd found out years ago that some things were better left alone.

A squire took her mount to the stable, and one of the watchmen led her to the main building of the castle.

Count Dietmar of Bartholemburg employed a steward. That steward, Walters, had attended Maria's wedding a few months ago in the count's place. Dietmar had been ill. When Walters opened the door for Louisa, he was convinced it was Maria he was seeing, as Atiram had predicted. Hastily, he invited her inside, took her dripping coat, and had a maid bring towels and wine while she waited for him to fetch his master.

Louisa looked forward to seeing the count again. It had been a while since she'd been at Bartholemburg, or anywhere else except in her library, for that matter, but she was familiar with the castle, and she felt comfortable around him. He didn't know she'd *ever* been here since the day of his own wedding, of course, and she told herself to keep that in mind when she spoke to him, any of the children, or other members of the household.

Even after his wife's death and his year away at war, he hadn't lost his happiness. She'd immersed herself in it whenever she'd visited, perhaps coming here more often than she should have, instead of going to Falconaer, or remaining there as long as she should have. She didn't feel she'd missed anything important there. Falconaer was a cold and lonely place, where a cold and lonely man resided, if you could call him that, and there was little life and no joy in its orderly wood-paneled, carpeted halls.

Bartholemburg still didn't look like its owner could pay for a proper upkeep of the estate, but Dietmar had found time to teach all three of his children to ride that dilapidated old pony nonetheless, and he made the girls dolls from straw to play with, and carved the lad a wooden sword. He'd gained a lot of weight over the past years because he enjoyed hearty meals and drank too much, but it was his only vice.

Carefully, Louisa pulled the etui containing the letters from her dress. From it, she extracted the one with her father's seal, and then slipped the etui back in its place. The count entered the Great Hall before she could even nip on her drink, and she smiled at him. He returned her smile and genuinely seemed pleased to see her, whatever events had led her to him.

She almost regretted having come here to ask him to risk his life for Blackvale, but with Maria at Wildenburg, she didn't see how she had a choice. People would die if she didn't act, and the demon had been waiting for a chance to rid the world of Ricdon for so long now. She couldn't disappoint Atiram. Atiram was depending on her, and neither of them deserved to live the way they did, all because of Ricdon's schemes. What she was doing here today would surely put an end to his sick games, and give Atiram peace. Justice would finally be served, and no one would have to live in fear of the Wishmaster trading children for wealth and land anymore, as he had done with his own.

Unexpectedly, a much younger man entered the Great Hall behind Dietmar. Her stomach lurched as she recognized the man who'd jumped into the moat after her.

There was no mistaking his soft brown eyes because she'd been seeing those eyes in her dreams night after night for months. Surely he recognized her too, but he held back while Dietmar welcomed her. He nodded politely when the count introduced him as a friend who'd fought under his command in the emperor's army.

"I am but a humble knight at your service, Milady," he mumbled.

He was a knight, a *warrior*. It didn't seem to go with the kindness in his eyes, but she could believe that he was a brave man. Brave men fought battles for the foolish ones who hid behind them.

"I think you've already had the pleasure of meeting," Dietmar said.

The other man's face remained even, and his gaze

never left hers. "Only very briefly. At a tournament in Blackvale last year."

She shivered. Had he spoken to her sister? How *brief* did he consider *briefly* to be?

Dietmar noticed her shudder, and gently guided her closer to the fireplace so she could warm up. He and Maria hadn't talked any time recently, if ever, she was sure, but by the way he treated her, she could guess his steward had spoken well of her sister, and he was oblivious to the nature of Louisa's run-in with his friend, the knight.

"What brings you to Bartholemburg at this late hour, in this weather, and unaccompanied?" the count asked when she'd downed her first cup of spiced wine much too quickly.

The drink was strong. She hadn't eaten that day, and it made her head spin in much the same way as the presence of the man she'd kicked in the gut for trying to save her from drowning.

The hurt and confusion in her heart hadn't allowed her to interpret the knight's actions until some days later. She'd kept the incident from Atiram, but she often asked herself how he'd been able to perceive her when no one else could.

Only magic had the power to undo magic, but a mere hedge witch didn't possess the kind of skill that could neutralize the cloaking spell Atiram had taught her. If her warrior could boast magic on his side, then it had to be strong, and that meant *he* was strong – or whoever instructed or protected him was.

He tried too hard not to stare at her and failed just as poorly as she did. Her cheeks felt impossibly hot. If there had been so much as a birdbath nearby that wasn't frozen, she'd have used the pebble in her pouch right at this very moment just to escape his scrutiny.

"Sensitive matters, Milord," she finally said, forcing herself to look first at Dietmar, and then directly at his companion. "For the sake of the friendship you and my father once had, I ask that we speak in private."

Dietmar hesitated. "I see." He turned to his friend and thumped him on the shoulder. "Do you mind leaving us for a little while, Tom?"

The soldier mumbled something indiscernible, but seemed glad to oblige.

Tom, she thought. The name suited him well. Simple and easy to remember. Would he be as straightforward as his name if they were ever to speak alone? What would he say to her?

A servant brought in a platter of food, but Louisa didn't feel like eating. She wanted this over with. "The House of Blackvale needs military aid," she told Dietmar.

The count's mien darkened. "What's going on? Why did your husband send you instead of a messenger, or coming himself? And why did your father allow it? The fools! The danger they allowed you to put yourself in!"

"Because *Blackvale* is in danger. My husband did not trust a messenger to bring the news, and my father wanted to speak to you himself, but he was really not up to making the trip. Neither he nor my husband are to blame. They were still debating when I begged my mother for her blessing to come to you and ask you to speak to Thomas of Newburg on our behalf. I am a good rider, and I have no need for personal protection when my family's home is in peril. It's all explained in this letter. I know my mother and you are not on good terms, but she asked me to give this to you so you'd understand."

She held the letter out to him, and he took it, but did not open it.

"I want to hear this from *you* first."

"Marauding knights wearing the red horse crest on their tunics are robbing our mills and our farms again, causing hunger and death throughout my father's lands. They're systematically bleeding us out, and Winterfield is in no position to send soldiers because Harald can barely hold his own. He can't pay his liegemen, and he is too weak to demand loyalty. As long as he lives, he will not give my husband free hand."

"Red horse crest… Is Triumph behind this?"

Louisa sighed. "I'm afraid so."

She let that sink in for a moment before she continued.

"My husband has information that William is gathering troops. He is determined to take Wildenburg and Blackvale. We need your support, and Falconaer's, to stop him."

Dietmar plopped down on a chair, his face a mask of horror. "William wouldn't dare! The bishop would have his hide... Cologne is at peace with the prince of Trier. This is an affront! We need to get word to him."

Louisa didn't like the ashen color his skin had taken on. Atiram was right. Peace was always just a temporary state, and most human leaders knew this. Dietmar knew it. He had years of experience both on the battlefield and at the negotiation table. Yet, he seemed completely terrified at the prospect of having to take up arms to stand by Blackvale against Triumph. Perhaps his memories of the war still affected him more than she'd thought.

She closed her eyes for a few seconds. "I'm so sorry to put you in this situation... I shouldn't have come."

She rose and reached for her cloak.

It took the count a few seconds to catch on to what she was doing, but when he did, he jumped up and took the damp piece from her. "I won't let you go out in that. You will be my guest tonight. I insist. And... I *do* want to know more."

Louisa hesitated, but didn't object to him ushering her back to the table to sit.

"The first thing we're going to do as soon as the weather permits, however, is inform the archbishop of what is going on. He'll surely be the first to want to speak to Triumph and try to resolve the matter before we arm ourselves."

She looked down at her hands, kneading them anxiously. She'd rehearsed this in the woods several times. "I appreciate your counsel, Milord, but the bishop of Cologne is in Rome, bartering with the pope over the Jewish quarter by the Cathedral, and the prince of Trier has no liking for my father, as you know. Von Layen would much rather have seen his cousin hold the titles and lands my grandfather claimed, and Kaspar is as stubborn as his father was."

Dietmar sighed.

It was a well-known fact that von Layen held tight to his father's grudges out of principle. He'd never lifted a finger to aid Blackvale in any way, and he pointedly ignored Gregory at any congress, just as he had Anton.

Bernhard of Wildenburg had forced his marriage to the deceased duke of Blackvale's sister, just days before von Layen would have had his nephew wed the girl, and the cousins were close even still. Bernhard had never been forgiven, nor had the new branch of the Blackvale family been properly acknowledged.

Satisfied she'd shed enough light on the conflict, Louisa studied Dietmar silently as he struggled with himself. He had a difficult time wrapping his head around her plea.

Bartholemburg was in better circumstances now than it had been at the time of his wife's death because the count had been smart enough to volunteer his services to the emperor's army when Frederick II had marched on France. Richard of Falconaer hadn't seen himself obliged to join Frederick, but he'd given Dietmar his army, and so Dietmar had led almost a thousand men to victory for Trier. Frederick had rewarded Dietmar richly, as he had all of the noblemen who'd answered his call, but his time on the killing fields seemed to have cost him dearly in other ways.

Louisa knew Gregory hadn't stayed at home because he was a coward. He probably was, to her mind, but that aside, he'd also had Triumph at his gates, and no powerful neighbor to guard his fields while he was away. Surely Dietmar would feel compelled to at least consider helping his old friend now.

Observing the count over the years, even if she'd only gotten snapshots of the burly man's life, she'd never seen him turn away anyone in need of assistance, but he needed time to think, and she could give him a little.

Small steps, she told herself.

"I came here hoping for help, but I realize now it's too much to ask. I thank you for your hospitality, and I'll be grateful for any further advice you might have for me, because I'm certain if you can't help us, Falconaer won't, either."

Dietmar's face darkened even more. "Well," he finally said, taking a big swig of wine, "there are things to be discussed, but I will help you, of course, and Falconaer will not deny me assistance, but I can understand why you wanted to speak to me alone first. All of this could take up to a fortnight, though. I'll send a message to your father tomorrow–"

"I'm sorry, Milord, but there's no time. Word is, Triumph has five hundred men, and is ready to attack Wildenburg within the next week. We don't have more than seventy able soldiers and farmers in all between Wildenburg and Blackvale. They'll have trouble defending the castle, and if Wildenburg should fall, they'll march through to Blackvale unhindered."

Dietmar squeezed his eyes shut for a second. Then, he drained his cup, giving a small wince when he set it down on the table. "William won't be doing *anything* in this weather. We have a few days to think." With that, he left the room, taking the letter with him.

Louisa waited for him to come back. She drank another mug of the spicy, sweet wine, and another one after that.

Old magic would make certain the snowfall did

not cease until she had her answer and Dietmar had contacted Ricdon's bastard. The demon had assured her that between the men Newburg and Bartholemburg had at their disposal, they'd have at least six hundred veterans from the war against France at the ready. This was just a question of patience. Dietmar and Newburg could have them armed and moving within two days once Dietmar had made his decision, and they'd be at Blackvale in another three. It would simply continue snowing in Triumph until the tower and the falcon were well underway.

An hour passed, and Dietmar did not return to the Hall. Instead, he sent a maid to take her to her quarters. She followed the girl up the narrow stairs to her room on the second floor, worried, but not frantic.

Fear wouldn't help her. Fear wouldn't get her home. She counted the stone treads that led to her room.

One

And two

And three

And four…

She had to get this done, and that was all.

The little chamber had its own cast iron oven. A surprising amount of heat radiated out from it. The maid carefully stacked more wood in the hearth, and promised Louisa she'd be back at dawn to relight it, should the fire go out during the night.

Soft cushions lay on her bed, and the servant turned down a thick, quilted cover rimmed with embroidery. The beauty of the needlework brought back recollections of the room she'd shared with her sister at Blackvale. With those recollections came the sadness and the guilt. They were bad company, and she wondered how Dietmar was doing. Was he feeling sad or guilty in any way? Enough to tell her he was ready to come to Blackvale with her? The hopeful notion came and went, and then her own troubles began taking up space again.

The maid waited for a few moments before wishing her a good night and leaving her to her own thoughts. Random images of the first years of her life floated around in Louisa's mind – her sister singing a song while playing with her rag doll in the Great Hall at Wildenburg; her mother sewing by the weak light of a candle at their kitchen table; a child lying on a bed of straw in some strange hay loft, sleeping.

Then came the pictures of the day she'd returned to Blackvale. Fragments of conversations. The memory of her sister by the water, kissing her knight. Her mother's voice and the words she'd spoken to Maria. The moat, and finally, the face of the man who'd tried to save her from herself – she, who was least of all in need of saving.

Tom.

It occurred to her she now had a name to go with his face, and that name kept echoing inside of her as the strong wine she wasn't used to worked its magic.

She felt more tired than she had in a long, long time. Her bed seemed so inviting, she decided a little rest couldn't hurt. Taking care to place her remaining letters beneath her mattress, she undressed and lay down, pulling the quilt around her. Wrapped in its warm embrace, she almost instantly fell into a restful, dreamless sleep, while snowflakes made from magic swirled down from the heavens, blanketing the land.

Twenty-One

Time

Unaccustomed noise and a chill in the air awoke Louisa the next morning. Last night's wine had left a bitter taste in her mouth.

She pulled the quilt around her and lay listening for a while. Livestock complained. Pots and pans clattered downstairs. Heavy boots thudded on the plank floor above her. Chattering voices filled the building with lively echoes.

Her room's tiny window was shuttered against the cold. She rose to open it, and the wind sent an icy gust inside. A good three feet of snow had fallen while she'd slept, and the clouds promised more to come. That was good. All was as it should be.

A servant bustled into the room, carrying a basin of warm water, and some towels across her arm. "Good morning, Milady," she said, setting down the basin and hurrying to close the window. "You'll catch your death!"

Another maid followed to lay out a clean dress and undergarments for her, while the first set about lighting the little stove.

"Compliments of the count," the woman who'd brought the dress told her. Louisa knew her name was Josephina, but she didn't recall how she'd learned it.

She might have overheard it years ago, or just yesterday.

An experienced weaver had created a fine fabric for the garment and dyed it a pretty shade of green. Lacey finishes in white decorated cuffs, collar, and hem. Holding it to her, Louisa thought it might be quite a decent fit. Then it occurred to her it might have belonged to Dietmar's deceased wife, and she didn't feel right accepting it, even if only to borrow it for a day. She put it back down on the bed. Josephina read the doubts in her eyes.

"No one has ever worn this, Milady. The countess had me sew it for a cousin of hers, but she never got round to giving it to her, God rest her soul," she said.

Louisa could accept that. "Tell his Lordship I am most grateful."

A smile lit up the servant's face, and Louisa suspected his Lordship knew nothing of his own generosity. Josephina quickly gathered up Louisa's own clothing from the foot of the bed to wash them along with the cloak.

When she'd made herself presentable, Louisa ventured down to the Great Hall, hoping to find the count in good spirits, but only the children were there – and Tom. She nearly turned back when she saw the knight standing by the fireplace, his fingers wrapped around a mug as he watched the little ones play with wooden figures shaped like animals, but it was too late.

He spun around and his gaze met hers. Again, her heart skipped a beat, as was becoming a habit whenever they met.

"Good morning," he said jovially. "Just in time for breakfast."

The children stopped their game and stared at her. She knew them all, but they had no idea who she was. Finally, the younger of the girls asked boldly, and she crossed the floor to the child.

"I'm Maria. And you must be…" She tried to make it seem as though she had to think about it. "Gerlinde?"

The girl chuckled shyly. "No. That's my sister." She pointed at Gerlinde. "I'm Mathilda."

Gerlinde joined them, and she was about to say something, but Josephina called to her to bring her brother and sister into the kitchen for a treat, and they all gladly went, taking their toys with them.

Tom put down his mug on the table, and casually pulled back a chair for her.

A meal of freshly baked bread, butter and honey had been set out for only two people, and she wondered why. Normally, the aroma of the bread alone would have been enough to make her mouth water, but she still wasn't particularly hungry. She sat down all the same, thinking it impolite if she didn't. All she wanted now was her answer from Dietmar. Where was he?

"Something to drink?" Tom asked. She was about to decline, but to her relief, he held out a pitcher of milk to her, gesturing to her cup. "It's still warm."

"I was afraid it might be more of what I had last night. I'm not used to the wine Dietmar serves."

He leaned forward to pour the milk, and she could see this was what he was having too. Who'd have thought it?

"Neither am I," he said. "In all honesty, I always ask for water whenever I'm here, and no one thinks badly of me for it. There's a good, clean well out in the yard. As there is in Blackvale."

She had no memory of the quality of the water at Blackvale, but she was willing to gamble it was drinkable, and nodded. Tom looked at her for a moment without speaking. It made her uncomfortable, so she hurried to find something to busy herself with.

The food was a blessing and a curse. The bread tasted as wonderful as it smelled and looked, and that was the blessing. Eating it in front of him was the curse. She got butter all over herself, and the honey made her hands sticky. She felt his eyes on her, as though she was the one being studied here today. It made her even clumsier, and by the time they were finished, she was glad to see Josephina arrive with a damp cloth for each of them.

"Josephina, will the count be joining us?" she asked, wiping her hands.

The servant shook her head. "No, Milady, he's not feeling well and has taken to his bed."

Louisa cast Tom a questioning glance.

He straightened in his chair and cleared his throat. "It's nothing to do with you, Milady, believe me. He didn't take the news you brought very well, but he's been having digestive problems for a time now, I'm afraid. He knows wine doesn't agree with him anymore, but he's incorrigible in that respect."

She bit her lip hard enough to draw blood. "So he's informed you about what's going on at Blackvale?"

"He has." An unexpected smirk crept across his face. "Between two cramps and the bucket."

Louisa blushed, but almost laughed, though not at the count. It was the way Tom had said it that made her face derail. Then she realized she must be embarrassing herself. These weren't the kind of things a Lady would laugh at.

"Oh no," she stuttered, "I'm sorry to hear that... I mean..."

Shut up, she ordered herself, not knowing where to direct her gaze. This was possibly going to be a very long winter storm.

Tom rose. She couldn't see the seriousness on his face, but she heard it in his voice. "No, it is I who must apologize, Milady. I didn't mean to make light of the situation." He paused, before continuing more softly, "But I like to see you smile. You should do that more often."

She looked at her hands, and forgot for one moment that his words were meant for Maria, though realizing this made them seem even more inappropriate. Whatever was he thinking? Maria was a married woman, and he was way out of line. On one hand. One the other, she wasn't Maria, and she asked herself if he and Maria had talked about the incident at the moat, and if so, what the result of their conversation might have been. Maria, oblivious to what had happened, would have denied everything, and thought him crazy.

Did he think her strange?

An awkward silence hung between them like a heavy curtain while Josephina cleared away the dishes and the leftovers.

"I was a boy last time we had this much snow," Tom said when the servant had gone. "Let me show you something."

He took her by the hand, as though it was the easiest thing in the world to do. Louisa nearly pulled back. It was so strange to feel human skin on her own.

Atiram hadn't embraced her, or held her hand in years. Not since she'd been a child. She thought she remembered warmth, but she also knew Atiram's magic had merely made it appear so. She had no body of flesh and bone, no beating heart or muscles to produce it. The demon was made of energy that only became visible through other, more perceivable things. Nothing about her seemed real up here in this world. Not right now.

Tom's touch was real. Frighteningly real.

And wonderfully warm.

He grabbed a cloak from one of the hooks by the door and wrapped it around her.

"Where are we going?"

"Wait and see."

He guided her out into the yard. Two squires relentlessly battled the white masses there, shoveling the snow into piles. The men called out to them, wishing them a good morning in the usual friendly Bartholemburg fashion, and they returned the greeting.

"How's my horse doing?" Louisa asked the one who'd taken her mare to the stable.

He smiled at her and briefly stopped what he was doing. "A fine animal, Milady, if I may say so. She's recovered remarkably well, and she's eaten."

Of course she had. Louisa felt herself blush once again, and thanked him before Tom pulled her onward to the tower left of the gatehouse.

It seemed colder inside than it was out, but the effort of climbing the steep, winding stairs warmed Louisa somewhat. They reached the topmost floor through a trap door, and when Tom opened it, she realized she'd never been up here before. Perhaps the height had scared her when she'd been younger, but it didn't frighten her now. Not one bit. Not while Tom was with her.

The room was not enclosed. Six columns bore the weight of the pointed roof, shaped much like she'd always thought a witch's hat might be. No watchman stood guard here today.

Tom helped her straighten up after she'd managed the last treads of the ladder, and once more, she became aware of how wonderful his touch felt.

"Just stand here for a moment, and don't say anything."

He didn't let go of her hand this time, as though he was afraid she'd make another attempt to escape him, and she did nothing about it.

Eyes wide open, she drank in the silent wonder of this place. High up above the roofs of Bartholemburg, snowflakes danced in a white flurry against the backdrop of the enchanted forest all around them. Houses and sheds were nothing but ghostly shapes in the haze, and fields lay in a deep slumber beneath winter's immaculate mantle.

"It's beautiful," she murmured.

"Mother Hulda must have a new apprentice girl."

"Who's Mother Hulda?"

Tom's eyes gleamed in delight. "Have you never heard of her? It's an old story my mother used to tell me about a woman who lives in the sky, though you can only get to her by jumping down a well." He paused, searching her face.

She guarded her expression well and merely raised a questioning eyebrow at him. What on earth was running through his mind when he looked at her?

"Go on."

He tilted his head mischievously. "Well, she's very rich and powerful, and she has this big, huge bed. The pillows and covers on it are filled with goose downs, and when she wakes up in the morning, she shakes them as hard as she can..." He fiercely shook an imaginary blanket. "Until those downs start billowing out." He made an effort to keep a straight face as he gestured at the sky to make the connection.

She huffed a laugh.

"What, don't you believe me? A lot of the stories the people around here tell are true, you know."

"Only a few," she said, and directed her gaze back out the window.

For a moment, the snowfall decreased to a light fluster, and the sun broke through the clouds in shafts, creating an interplay of light and shadow that made it seem as though everything was in motion.

"Truth is rare in this world, as in any other, and by far more worrying than the tales we like to tell," Tom said quietly. "As you are."

She blushed, and frowned, and held her breath, all at the same time. He had to know he was making her uncomfortable. And he was so out of line. *Again.*

"I don't think I should be a worry to you, Sir," she said firmly.

He looked at his feet, biting his lip, and then back at her. "I meant *rare and precious*. But you are also a… *concern* to me. You see, Dietmar has asked me to take his place in gathering and commanding the troops necessary to defend your father's lands, so I'll be heading out as soon as the weather will permit it."

Dietmar's confidence in this man was astonishing. A simple knight, commanding Bartholemburg's and Falconaer's army? Was she missing something?

"Without Dietmar?" She began fidgeting, but only noticed when he did. "What about Falconaer?"

"What about it? The count won't be in the position to travel anytime soon, and Dietmar has already sent word to Richard, and to your father."

Her heart stopped. This was something she should not have missed, but she had. The letters she should have traded for those already sent were underneath her mattress. Whoever Dietmar had dispatched must have been insane, and he would probably take forever to get to either place, if he got there at all, but…

Tom said something, but she wasn't paying attention.

"Pardon me?" she said absently.

"I said, I *do* think I'm fairly well suited to the task."

There was that look again. He wasn't offended. He merely seemed amused, and the remaining morsels of her confidence evaporated.

"I'm sorry, Sir," she stammered, "I have insulted

your integrity."

He laughed, and she wanted the earth to open up and swallow her. What great entertainment he must be getting from her behavior. She felt for the pouch with the pebble, just to have the assurance it stood for, but she was wearing the wrong cloak, and it wasn't there in its lining. Josephina had taken her own cloak for cleaning.

She couldn't decide what to worry about first; the fact that she was making a fool of herself in front of a man who constantly seemed to make her feel silly, or that she'd possibly lost the pebble, if Josephina threw it out with the wash water.

She was about ready to bolt, though she had no idea where to.

"Look," he said, putting himself in her way, as if he could sense her apprehension, "I understand it's Dietmar you place your trust in, and that's all right. But we really should stop apologizing to one another, don't you think?"

"You astound me!" She couldn't believe she'd said that, but the words had tumbled from her lips before she could have stopped them.

"Well, I've been told I'm full of surprises. I do tend to jump headfirst, and I fight only for what I truly believe in."

At that moment, from the corner of her eye, she spotted a man leading his horse slowly up the hill to the castle.

Tom's mien darkened, and he headed for the trap door. "That's Walters."

Walters had made it to the gate by the time they stepped out into the yard. One of the squires hurried to take his exhausted horse off his hands. The steward was near frozen, and Tom had to help the older man shed his gloves and boots once they were back inside the main building.

"It's no good," Walters told them, numb hands clumsily pulling forth the leather etui he carried inside his shirt. "I tried, but there's no way anyone will get to Falconaer or Blackvale today. *No way.*"

Tom nodded, taking the etui. "I understand. It was worth a try."

Louisa felt a weight lift off her shoulders. "It would really be a help to my father to see that army at Blackvale as soon as possible in any case."

Tom sniffed, running a hand through his hair. "I realize this. You have my word that we'll have six hundred men there as soon as we can move out." He turned back to Walters. "Send every available squire and boy to the village, and to the farms and noblemen of Bartholemburg and Falconaer the very moment the blizzard lets up. Tell them the count of Bartholemburg requires every armed man they can spare immediately."

Twenty-Two

Doubts

The view from the small open window in her room was less spectacular than from the tower, but Louisa needed to be alone. The cold didn't bother her as she watched Mother Hulda's ceaseless labors bury the earth.

Time was an odd creation. You had too much of it in the dark, and not enough in the light. But Louisa had her answer, she supposed: six hundred men would soon be underway to rescue Blackvale, under the command of a young knight who seemed willing to sacrifice them all for her cause. It was what the demon wanted, wasn't it? It was what *she* wanted.

Wasn't it?

Triumph certainly had to be stopped at any cost.

She kept asking herself why it had to be like this, why it had to come to the armed conflict the demon insisted on, and why this battle had to take place at Wildenburg. The risk seemed huge, and for what?

If she could learn to make it snow, she could send a thunderbolt from the heavens to strike down William, and Ricdon along with him. The demon's answer to that was always about how things weren't so simple, and always, there was Ricdon.

Everything the demon did was geared toward

making the evil little creature suffer. Atiram didn't just want to destroy him. She wanted to pound him into the ground and take everything from him, including his haven and his only living relative.

The more Louisa thought about it, the more it seemed to her Ricdon and Atiram had something in common, on one hand. On the other, Ricdon made all of mankind miserable, and he'd done things so terrible to the demon, even slaying him in the end might not release Atiram from the darkness. Perhaps it was this knowledge that drove her.

Pain made people do strange things. Sometimes it made them stronger, sometimes it made them lead a life in search of more pain.

Falconaer's men might have an advantage over Triumph and prevent William from taking Wildenburg, but that didn't mean there wouldn't be a lot of bloodshed. A lot of pain would have to be dealt with on both sides in the aftermath of this battle.

Maria was in pain right now, too, but how much pain would she be in if she lost Steffen? Or if either or both of their parents were killed? The demon had promised Maria would come to no harm, but what if she did all the same?

War sounded so quick and easy when it was written on the pages of a book. Strategies and losses were discussed, but not individually assessed. Even if her family survived unhurt, it might consume Rothmill, Oakwood, Mousebach, or any of the other villages in the area.

And for what?

She couldn't answer that herself, and realized how ignorant she must be. Ricdon, whatever he'd done, and bitter and malicious though he was, didn't seem worth *so much pain.*

Snow, she thought. *Snow until Mother Hulda's pillows are empty.*

She wished she was anything but human so she could find a solution to save Wildenburg and at the same time rescue the demon from her own hate. Atiram never tired of telling her how pitiable humans were, and how incapable of overcoming their weaknesses, but she was really no different herself. Louisa wondered how the demon would live on after Ricdon, and with him, her purpose was destroyed.

Snow, she thought again, but snow only delayed the problem.

Stop. She imagined how the clouds would recede, and they did.

After a while, the sun came out, and temperatures climbed steeply. Within a few hours, sheets of slush tumbled noisily from the roofs, and the pine trees in the forest lost their winter coats. Bartholemburg's courtyard turned into a pigsty, and the village road became visible before dusk.

Tom stood by his promise and dispatched every available man to get word out. Louisa hovered around Walters to keep an eye on him. She exchanged the letters he was to take to Richard of Falconaer and Blackvale while the leather etui briefly lay unattended on the table in the Great Hall. Strangely, there was no message for Newburg inside. It bothered her, and she made a mental note to ask Tom about Falconaer's new heir.

She assumed she would be meeting Newburg over the next few days. He'd be joining them, the demon had assured her, and he'd play a part in Ricdon's downfall, but Louisa didn't know the details. She didn't need to, Atiram had said, and she was to slip away quietly when her work was done.

"What strange weather you've brought us," Dietmar muttered as he carefully sat down by the fireplace after Walters had left. Josephina had to help him.

Louisa couldn't deny it, and smiled, sitting next to him. "Nature is a moody woman."

A cramp silenced Dietmar for a while, and Josephina wrapped a blanket around his sweat-drenched torso.

Louisa hoped he'd recover. If he didn't, she hoped his relatives would be kind to the children.

"Your mother is also a moody woman," he said when the pain had passed.

She hummed. "Maybe. She says things she can't take back."

Dietmar nodded. "Some people do. I'm glad she wasn't too proud to let me know your father needs help. I know he always looks for peaceful solutions, but sometimes there are none."

Louisa felt like making herself small again so her conscience would stop its agonized lamenting.

Just as Tom appeared in the door, another cramp dug its claws into the count's middle, and he and Josephina helped him back to his room.

Josephina served them dinner, and Tom and she ate their meal in polite silence. Louisa noticed he seemed as unhappy with the situation as she was. Finally, he pushed his plate aside, barely touched, as Louisa's, and asked Josephina to take it away. The maid snorted in disapproval.

"You'll starve yourself, good man," she grumbled.

An involuntary smile tugged at Louisa's lips. People catching their death and starving seemed to be the woman's answer to everything that caused her displeasure.

Tom waited until she was gone before leaning forward. "She means well."

Louisa nodded. "I know. The family is very lucky to have her." She rose. "If you'll excuse me, I'll be going to my room now."

Tom jumped to his feet and took hold of her hand. "Stay, please. Just for another while."

So inappropriate... But so warm. So wonderfully warm.

She wanted to allow herself to do as he asked,

though she had no idea what they would talk about, and every reason to believe she'd embarrass herself further than she already had.

Something inside of her told her she'd never have this moment back if she let it go.

Hesitatingly, she turned her hand in his, locking their fingers together. She did not want to look him in the eyes, but she could feel his on her.

"Are you afraid?" he asked softly. "Of the coming days, I mean?"

"No." She knew the moment she'd said it that she should have said yes. She didn't want to be, but deep down, she was. Maria would have been, and she'd have admitted it.

Tom's eyes betrayed he didn't quite believe her. "*I'm* always afraid before I go into battle."

"Fear won't help me. Fear won't get me home." She bit her tongue.

Why did she say that? She'd been saying it to herself forever, it seemed, but tonight, she would have given anything to have had a home to truly want to return to. The demon was good to her, and she had her books. She had everything she needed, didn't she? No, she didn't. When she went back, she'd miss the warmth. She'd miss the sunlight, the wind, the snow, the rain, the trees, and… *his* warmth.

He brushed a lock of hair from her forehead, and she raised her gaze to his. She saw her own reflection in soft brown earth and coal, and it made her question how he saw her, because she didn't think she was much to look at, and only loveable in her sister's place.

"You're one of the bravest people I know," he said, shocking her. Shame burned red hot on her cheeks, and she withdrew her hand. He was terribly mistaken. She was making a fool of a good man.

"You don't know me at all."

"No." He paused. "But you're right. I don't *know* you. I wish I did."

She did, too, but there was nothing she could have shared with him. Absolutely *nothing*. They lived in different worlds, and they had no common ground.

"I grew up far away from my home," he told her then. She realized he was only trying to keep the conversation going, but she was willing to indulge him, or indulge *herself*.

He took a sip of his water before continuing. "Would you believe I lived in a bakery until I was six or seven?"

Somehow, she couldn't picture him as a boy, kneading bread.

She recalled how she and Maria had loved to spend their Friday mornings in the kitchen at Wildenburg, watching their cook bake the household's supply of bread for the week. Maria had been happy to watch the cook mix fine white flour with honey and ale for the sweet cakes they'd both adored, and sometimes the cook had let her blend the coarser, darker rye flour for the hard, double-baked biscuits they stored in the pantry. Louisa hadn't liked the sticky dough on her hands, and she'd preferred to draw pictures and patterns in the flour on the tabletop with her fingers.

Tom seemed to wait for her to tell him about this, or some other story, she was sure, but she couldn't bring herself to share with him what memories she had left of that time. Not tonight. They'd only disappoint, or require more input than she could manage, and she wanted to hear more about him.

"Where did you go afterward?" she asked.

Tom blinked, but went on. "I was sent to start my apprenticeship as a squire at a castle I'd never been to before. I didn't know anyone there, and I was scared stiff, at first, but I learned to read, write, ride, and fight."

"So you had a good teacher."

"Well… not always. My teacher had a mean temper. There were days when I just wished he'd fall off his horse and break something." He chuckled, and this time Louisa saw the boy inside the man. "He was some piece of work, but he taught me two things that shaped me. One was the art of war, and the other was that peace is harder to uphold than fighting any battle."

She could have sworn she'd read something similar in one of the books from her library beneath the earth, but she didn't comment. She loved listening to him.

"Then he was a wise teacher, in any case."

"He was always afraid, deep inside, and I think this had to do with how much he stood to lose by war, just as he did by a failed peace. He had a family he was fiercely protective of, and he felt very much responsible for the other members of his household and his peasants. You have *everything* to lose over the next weeks, and you should be shaking with fear, but still you came here, on your own, insisting on Dietmar's help. I know that's brave."

She felt a crippling weight on her shoulders. An ocean of doubt threatened to sweep her away. What was she doing here? *What?* The demon had assured her they were only expediting the inevitable, making it happen their way to enable them to control the situation, but was this really what they were doing?

"Tell me honestly… does Blackvale stand a chance of surviving this?"

He drew air, but then smiled reassuringly. "With Falconaer's experienced army behind Blackvale, of course. We may not even have to fight, if we can manage to put the fear of God into William before he can attack. I do understand why your mother made haste in sending you."

"And if we don't get there in time?"

"We will. It's why we're leaving in the morning. Believe me, any- and everyone who's sworn fealty to

Blackvale and has two good hands will be here by dawn, and we'll ride like the wind."

She knew they wouldn't get there before Triumph. The dice had been cast, and the mechanisms released, like those of the drawbridge at her father's castle. There was no going back now, but the longer she sat opposite one of the soldiers who would have to fight this battle, the more wrong it all felt.

If Gregory was smart, he would surrender Wildenburg to William to prevent the carnage, but she didn't see him doing any such thing. Not even to save *the other daughter*. He hadn't given up Blackvale for her, had he, so why would he surrender Wildenburg for Maria?

Louisa wanted to talk to Atiram, but the pebble was gone. Josephina had returned the cloak to her without it, just as she'd feared.

There was that word again: *fear*.

She had no way back to the Underworld, at least not now. She had nowhere to go back to *at all*.

Tom moved all the way around the table to her, as though he sensed her inner turmoil and misinterpreted it, just like he had at the moat when he'd jumped in after her. She rose, intending to withdraw from him and hide away in her room until daybreak, but he still held her hand, and would not let go.

This was all wrong, she kept telling herself as she pressed against his body, feeling his warmth, nestling her face against his chest. She hardly dared look up at him, but when she did, she lost herself in the depths of his eyes. They searched her face, found her mouth, and then he kissed her.

She opened her lips to him, and her arms intuitively wrapped around his middle. He tasted of milk and honey, sunlight, and clean sheets. His warm touch felt like a magic she had no knowledge of, no control over. It was exciting, deliciously excruciating, alarming, and dangerous. She burned for more, and she felt that he did, too, but something made her stop. This wasn't right.

Withdrawing from him, she whispered, "I'm a married woman."

He released her at once and backed away without taking his eyes off her. She forced herself to turn away from him. She needed to keep her mind on the reason why she was here, but she wanted to follow him, hold him, kiss him senseless. What did that make her? She didn't recognize herself, but even if what she desired wasn't right – could wanting something for herself be so wrong?

Twenty-Three

Fairytale

For the umpteenth time in the past year, Tom felt like he desperately needed guidance. He didn't think his father was the right person to give it, and Dietmar suffered too much from his poor health to be troubled. Not that he could have explained to either man what he was doing. Both of them would have deemed him completely insane.

All things considered, perhaps he was.

Pacing in his small chamber by the sparse candlelight, he recalled one of the other squires at Sir Gernot's telling him to suck it up and let nature guide him when he'd fallen in love with the dairy maid. He'd confessed his feelings to the curvy blonde and bedded her in the freshly cut hay behind her father's house one night. At fourteen, all sweaty palms and giddy stomach, this had been a short and embarrassing feat, but she'd made him feel like a king and sworn he was the best she'd ever been with. A few weeks later, she'd married the cobbler's son. This hadn't caused Tom as much pain and irritation as the rash she'd given him. Irmie had six or seven children now, none of them his, and he was glad.

None of the women he'd been with over the years since then had been *ladies*, any more than Irmie, but lying with them hadn't been about being in love, or even a pretense of it. Long days and cold, restless nights made him yearn for warmth and comfort, sometimes. Every now and then, in between asking himself what exactly he was looking for and the sensible choices he should be making, he'd given in to loneliness and allowed himself a guilty pleasure. He wasn't proud of it.

But what *did* he want?

And would he have what he really needed, in the end? Would he have love?

His life had taken enough of an unsettling twist lately to keep his mind busy beyond foolish fantasies and dreams. He didn't need another ghost or immortal, witch or specter twisting his reality, but this particular ghost, or whatever she was, seemed so... *human*. He'd never met anyone who'd both bewildered and at the same time captivated him like she did.

He simply couldn't stay away from her. Good Lord, he was holding her hand at every chance since she'd arrived to Bartholemburg just to prove to himself that she was real. In return, she held his heart for ransom.

He'd always guessed there was more between heaven and Earth than the naked eye could perceive, but after he'd learned his father's secret, he no longer doubted his sanity where the incident at the moat was concerned. He hadn't imagined it, and there was a reason he'd been there.

How often had the same nightmare tormented him? The image of Lady Blackvale slipping from his grip and vanishing in the dark waters had replayed in his head for months, and he'd finally asked himself whether the war had driven him crazy after all, but he was still the same man, and his thoughts were clear.

A soldier's perception always depended on how long he'd been awake, how little he'd eaten, how much blood clung to his armor, and what he expected to see. The French battlefields had taught him to rely not only on what he thought his eyes were telling him. Whenever he was in doubt, he'd find a few seconds' inner quiet and listen to his heart, or *gut feeling*, as Dietmar called it.

In this case, his gut told him to believe in himself, and believe in her. He trusted in what his heart told him about his Lady Blackvale, and he recognized her essence from the stories his soldiers liked to share by the fireside. Ghosts *did* exist, and they came to warn the living when those they loved were in need.

He'd been able to accept and digest Richard's secret and gruesome family history without a lot of difficulty, and this wasn't much different.

The girl who'd died twenty years ago in the fire that devastated Blackvale Castle and killed Anton of Blackvale's entire family had returned. He'd heard the tale from Blackvale's stable boys.

Magic was all around, and it was not necessarily dark or detestable.

He'd often felt it. Many gruesome things happened during the war, but unlike Dietmar, he'd always felt somehow protected. For the longest time, he'd attributed this to his faith in God, but God did not shield just one man from a lethal rain of arrows that wiped out dozens of others on the same killing grounds. He did not shatter spears in mid-air before they could penetrate your skull, and He did not come at night in the shape of an old beggar bringing you a healing ointment to cure the festering wound that was about to cost you your leg.

Sitting down on his too-soft bed, Tom was aware he should have been just as dead as his brothers and sisters many times over. But perhaps he was a ghost, too. A ghost, yet breathing the same air as Louisa.

Whatever game she was a part of, whatever role she played, she was just as much a child of magic as he, but something told him she'd never felt protected in the way he did, and she had chosen him to help her. She *needed* him to protect her in this world.

He couldn't say whether she was trying to aid or damn the Blackvales, but he would surely find out. Richard would be furious, and he had every right to be, but Tom was determined to find out why she was here. He was committed to safeguarding her until she'd done what she'd come here for. Without his father's help, and without *Ricdon's* kind of intervention.

He stripped off his shirt, sat there for another moment, and then put it back on again.

He knew he shouldn't have kissed her, but he had a talent for doing things he shouldn't. In two days, he'd be leading six hundred men into a battle he had no way of predicting, and no business fighting.

For her.

Triumph was a sneaky pig with a tendency to covet his neighbor's goods, but was he really greedy and foolish enough to endanger the peace between Trier and Cologne like this without provocation? His scouts would tell him what awaited them hours before his troops got to Blackvale, but who knew what really boiled below the surface of this conflict? Numbers and position were the only things his men would convey to him, and he'd have to base his tactical decisions on those findings alone.

Did *she* know more, or was she just as much in the dark as he?

He barged to the door and yanked it open, not knowing whether he'd have the courage to knock on his *Lady's* door tonight. He'd sworn himself he'd wait until morning to confront her. Despite the circumstances, he'd placed his hope in Mother Hulda buying them a little more time together here at Bartholemburg, but nature was a moody woman.

He didn't get as far as the corridor. Louisa stood

right in his path, as though she'd been compelled by the same intentions, looking as disheveled and befuddled as he felt.

Whatever he might have said to her by daylight got lost en route between his brain and his mouth, and all he could think to do was cup her face in his hands and kiss her again. She made a small sound of protest, and he nearly let go of her, but then her arms snaked around his waist, and she held on to him like a drowning woman in the water. Like she should have in the moat.

She tasted of apples and summer wine in the vineyards, and he wanted nothing more than to hold her and feel every inch of her velvety skin beneath his hands. He gently pulled her into his room, and she followed him without releasing him, without stopping him when he gradually undressed her, and without knowledge of a man's body, he realized as he slowly guided her trembling hands.

The wonderfully soft bed embraced her slight form as he lay her down and inhaled her scent. He let his lips roam her perfect body, his fingers trace every line, and she reacted with raw desire to his touch, wrapping herself around him, moving with him, breathlessly whispering his name. The trust she gave humbled him, and her sweet sweat on his body drove any manner of question he could have asked her far from his mind.

Again and again he wanted to say her name, her

real name, but dared not for fear of what might happen then. Instead, he made love to her until the candle on the night table burned to a stump. In the early hours, she fell asleep in his arms, and he found himself wishing for snow, ever more snow, so that this night and this fairytale would last forever.

Twenty-Four

Cold

Louisa left Tom's room while he was still fast asleep. He'd told her things would quickly get busy in the morning, as soon as the first of Falconaer's liegemen arrived, and she didn't want to be seen anywhere but in her own bed when the household began stirring.

She lay awake beneath her quilt, waiting, and listening to the old stronghold breathe in the stillness of what remained of the night. Darkness had a different quality here than it did in the Underworld. The absence of light was much more noticeable when light was so readily available. Black so easily gave way to gray in this place, and gray to white…

Nothing was profoundly *dark* or *light* or black and white up here. Even love and hate gained different qualities when you had a direct comparison. The absence of love wasn't hate or indifference – it was loneliness.

For the first time she could understand Ricdon, to an extent There was nothing good in his life. Perhaps he would have lived it differently if he hadn't decided to bargain away his family for his powers.

She was almost glad the pebble was gone. She needed to see Triumph stopped so her sister would be safe, and she wanted to see Ricdon destroyed so that

Atiram would find peace, but she didn't think she wanted to go back to the Underworld when all was said and done.

Staying with Tom would be impossible, but she didn't belong in a world where love and light did not exist. Darkness had its own magic, but magic was only beautiful when it was put to use to create beauty, and humans feared it. She didn't think she belonged anywhere at all.

Eventually, she fell into an unrestful slumber thinking how wonderful things could have been, had she and Tom met under different circumstances, in another place and time. But maybe… just *maybe* she could find a way so she and Tom could be together. *Maybe* was such a gray word, after all, and didn't gray fit perfectly in this world? Somewhere?

With the first sunlight came the men Tom had promised her. The noise out in the yard woke Louisa abruptly. She got dressed, and by the time she reached the bottom of the stairs, she found the Great Hall already crowded with the knights and the other gentry who would be leading Falconaer's liegemen to Blackvale.

Tom was explaining the situation to a dozen men both younger and older than he. She did not know any of them by name from her visits to Bartholemburg, and regretted not having paid more attention in the past.

She'd preferred to spend her time there with the family rather than at the meetings Dietmar had hosted. Atiram kept telling her how important politics were, continuously preaching how vital it was to know the minds of people who could be valuable to them, but Louisa had never listened.

A few faces seemed vaguely familiar, but it was hard to tell. She wondered if one of them was Newburg, but by the way they hung on Tom's every word without interrupting him, she guessed Ricdon's bastard hadn't arrived yet.

He appeared to be very much respected by all who were present, and he filled Dietmar's place well. Instead of wearing the Tower crest on his tunic, his had the falcon embroidered on the front. It didn't surprise her to find that he was one of Newburg's noblemen. She should have asked him about the man while she'd had the chance. He'd surely know his duke's heir well.

He excused himself to speak with her when he noticed her standing on the bottom step of the staircase. For a moment, everyone seemed to stare at her. She did her best to look unmoved, and he kept an appropriate distance.

"Good morning, Milady," he said. "We're almost complete, but one important person is still underway."

She bit her lip. He probably meant Newburg. "I'm glad."

New conversations began, and the Hall reverberated with talk.

She was about to ask after the Wishmaster's son when one of the squires entered the Hall and interrupted her.

"Lord Newburg," he said to Tom, "Sir Carthouse is here. We're ready to go."

Tom patted the squire on the shoulder. "Excellent! Go get a warm drink."

Louisa's thoughts whirled as she watched the young man head straight for Josephina. The old maid was at the fireplace, doling out generous amounts of Bartholemburg's spiced wine from a crock on the hook to whoever wanted their cups filled. She was speaking too loudly. Everyone was.

All those loud words made Louisa want to cover her ears. She searched for her pebble, but did not find it, and all she could do was hold on to Tom's arm fiercely when he reached out to steady her as her world spun out of control for a few seconds.

"Are you not feeling well?" she heard him say from a great distance, and she looked up at him, tried to focus on his eyes. They betrayed his concern.

It was as if they were in the water again, but she didn't know whether she wanted him to let go of her or not. She wanted to take another swing at him, kick him, yell at him, just because he was who he was, simply for being Ricdon's bastard. How could she have been so blind?

"Lady Blackvale?"

"No… Yes…" she stuttered, letting go of him to stand against the wall. "I'm fine."

She wanted the people in the Hall gone. Every last man. All back to where they'd come from. Right at this very moment. She wanted to turn back time, and she wanted to tell Atiram she would not be a part of this. There had to be some other way…

But it was too late and she knew it. No matter what she did now, it was too late.

Tom wasn't satisfied with her answer, and she saw that he was torn. Finally, he leaned a little closer, careful not to touch her, as though he sensed that this was the last thing she would permit right now.

"Wish us well, Milady," he said into her ear. "You should rest. I'll have someone come for you as soon as we have dealt with your father's troubles."

"I'm going with you now," she mumbled barely noticing the hitch in her voice.

He hadn't heard her, or hadn't wanted to. "Pardon me?"

She straightened her shoulders. "I said, I'm going with you."

His brow creased. "No, you're not. You're staying here, where you'll be safe. It's what your mother would want."

"My family is at stake here, and you… you're risking your life to defend my home. I will be safe enough riding with you."

"We don't have time for this. I can't be sure you're properly protected."

She wanted to tell him she didn't need his protection, or anything else from him. She just wanted him to defeat Triumph. As Tom, not Thomas.

"I can look after myself."

He wanted to argue, but then he stopped short, his lips a thin line in his face. "Do as you please, Milady."

He turned to his liegemen and they fell silent.

"Mount up! We're moving out," he told them in a low voice.

When he glanced back at her briefly, she almost feared he'd have her gagged and bound to make her stay at Bartholemburg, but he left the Hall without another word. The knights filed out of the entranceway behind him. She fetched her few belongings and followed them.

Bartholemburg village teemed with the new arrivals. Carts and wagons lined the roads, some to take the men, some to transport their weaponry and supplies. Louisa followed the main body of riders on her mare, a squire Tom had assigned to her always by her side.

Sludge turned the hollow ways and paths into swamps, and that made for slow progress at first, but they halted only twice to rest the horses, and the farther they came, the less snowfall there seemed to have been, much to Louisa's surprise.

The demon had assured her the spell she cast would reach far enough to veil the entire country in white, but they managed to get within ten miles of Blackvale soon after nightfall. The carts would be there in the morning, and the foot soldiers by midday.

The ground was hardly even soggy where they made camp near a farm to rest and get fresh horses for their scouts. She didn't think it had snowed in this part of the country at all. Atiram had lied to her. Was she hoping it wouldn't matter to her? That she didn't care? What else had Atiram lied about?

The knot in her stomach made it hard to breathe, and a mixture of sadness and anger burned in her chest. She did not feel like eating the bread Tom offered her by the fireside, or the salted meat the squire handed her on a plate.

She had to see for herself what had become of Blackvale, because Triumph was bound to be there already if Atiram hadn't kept to the plan. Something told Louisa the demon hadn't, but Louisa didn't understand why.

They'd gone over this again and again to the last detail. *Timing was everything,* Atiram had insisted, but apparently, she herself had been on another schedule, and the skies over Triumph had been clear all along.

Why had the demon countered Louisa's spell? Had something gone wrong, or had she decided to change the plan without letting her know? And if so, to what intent? Surely she'd foreseen the consequences.

Blackvale could be in ruins, and Maria dead.

Louisa ached to leave horses and riders behind and use her magic to take her to Blackvale, but doing that in plain view of Tom and an entire army of god-fearing soldiers would do more damage than good, so she stayed and waited her chance.

It came while Tom was speaking to the farmer, and her squire answering a call of nature. She took the horse behind one of the buildings, out of sight for just a moment, and gone the next.

Twenty-Five

Fire

Thick smoke hung in the air. Gregory could hardly see the soldier trying to kill him as they struggled for control of the broken sword in his hand. He punched the younger man repeatedly and got as good as he gave. Finally, he managed to turn without releasing his opponent and elbow him in the belly. The knight groaned, but did not give him one inch.

Another deafening crack, and the roof of the stable collapsed right next to them, pressing the half-timbered wall outward in an explosion of dust and embers.

Both men only just got out of the way, but the distraction worked to Gregory's advantage, and he was able to regain the hilt of the weapon. With effort, he thrust the stump of its blade into the side of the other man's neck. He didn't wait to see his opponent die. Spinning around to search for a familiar face, he realized he was just one shadow of a hundred in the ruins of his childhood home. He hadn't felt comfortable here since the demon had taken his little Louisa, but today it had indisputably become hell.

Flames flicked out through the keep's broken door and the tiny windows of the first floor. He briefly considered going in to fetch a new sword from the armory anyway, but he couldn't stop coughing, and reason got the better of him. They were defeated. Outnumbered by at least five to one, he had to accept that Wildenburg was lost.

Triumph himself was probably heading for Blackvale already, and now Gregory had to make sure he didn't lose that as well, or this would be the end.

He ran for the northern section of the guards' walkway, where they'd put the horses, but before he'd reached the burning structure, it came crashing down. A few of the terrified animals and several peasants managed to free themselves from the smoldering debris and scrambled for their lives. He didn't want to guess how many people were buried beneath the rubble – there wasn't a thing he could do for them.

A panicked horse with its blanket ablaze on its back nearly trampled him. The creature bolted out through the gaping hole where the gate had been just hours before. Several of the others followed it, one carrying a corpse, the other a near-naked, screaming man, most of the skin on his torso charred beyond hope.

Another of Triumph's soldiers launched himself at Gregory. He knew the broken, bloodied blade he still held in his hand would not save him this time. He threw the useless thing in the fellow's face as hard as he could, but it only bought him a few moments.

Retreating from his assailant, he tripped over a body sprawled out on the cobble pavement. The soldier was nearly on top of him by the time he'd pried the ax from his dead steward's hand. He used the wooden grip to block the heavy blade that came hurling down toward him several times before it splintered. When it did, his enemy lost his footing and fell forward. Before he was able to recover, Gregory scrambled to his knees and swung the ax, splitting the man's skull despite the helmet he wore. The soldier toppled forward against him, knocking him over.

So, are you ready to give up? a voice whispered in his ear as he labored to get out from under the swordsman.

He hadn't heard it in a long, long time, but he remembered it all too well.

"No," he whispered back, and then yelled the word again as he rose, clenching the dripping ax in both hands. "No!"

You'll never make it to Blackvale, the voice continued, soft as a summer's breeze and ghastly as mold at the same time. *Stop fooling yourself, old man.*

He struck with deadly precision at the next opponent coming at him, and the one after that. He'd already reached the gate when he felt the pain in his chest.

Time waits for no man, the voice continued, *and war finds any man who doesn't keep the peace... eventually...*

The weight bearing down on his chest became unbearable, and it almost immobilized him as it shot into his arm like a poisoned arrow, but he stayed on his feet.

You didn't keep the peace very well, Gregory, did you?

"I did what I could," he muttered, breathing hard. "I *always* did what I could!"

None of the Blackvales were ever very good at keeping the peace. Or their word...

"What do you know? Who are you?" He blindly stumbled onward through the wreckage, telling himself he was imagining things. It was all in his head. It had to be.

Oh, you know me. And I know you. Look at me! Turn around and look at me, you sad, old failure!

He did, again and again, but there was no one to see. Presently, he thought he caught a glimpse of a woman's form through the smoke. He wanted to go after her, but a rider blocked his way. It was difficult to tell whether the man was one of his own or the enemy.

Wiping at his eyes and coughing, he tried to lift his ax, but it was too heavy. He couldn't even raise his arm to defend himself... He was indeed a sad, old failure.

The knight did nothing to harm him. He bent down, and Gregory recognized his face, but didn't recall the name that went with it. The man reached out his hand and dragged Gregory up into the saddle behind him. Gregory held on to him for dear life as the horse slid and slipped downhill, weaving through the trees, following a dozen others going in the same direction.

The iron corset around his chest loosened, somewhat. "Make haste," he stammered, thumping his liegeman's shoulder. "We have to get to Blackvale." He hoped the milksop had gotten Maria safely there by now.

"Triumph is regrouping his men at the mill, Milord," the rider said, spurring his horse and spitting out a bloody tooth. "We're cutting through the forest."

Gregory sat up as straight as he could, ignoring his pain and willing the numbness in his arm to go away. He couldn't recall the name of the man who'd just saved his neck, but the forest brought back another memory he didn't want to deal with at all. It was of the night Blackvale had been on fire. The night he'd lost Louisa. He had no use for those images right now. History had a way of repeating itself. His life was determined by smoke and ashes, and the smell of burning flesh.

You reap what you sow, the voice breathed into his ear.

He wanted to believe it was only the wind, but lying to himself at this stage of the game only made his own helplessness and incapacity all the more obvious.

Even through the veil of his agony-born haze, one thing was clear: fate was the demon that haunted him, and there was no escape. But he wouldn't surrender the other daughter without a fight, and he'd sacrifice every last man to save Blackvale – and Maria.

Twenty-Six

Grief

Every further mile on the overgrown forest trail made them slower and more reckless. A dozen men had volunteered to ride with Tom and help him search for Louisa, but he'd only taken Carthouse along. He trusted the young knight with his life – and he'd trust him with her secret, if necessary.

Tom cursed the overcast skies. He could hardly keep track of the guide riding silently ahead of them. They didn't have a hope of finding Louisa if she'd chosen any other path than this one, and they'd miss her if she deviated from it a mere twenty feet.

Or… had she even chosen a path? She'd come to Bartholemburg on a rested horse, and no one had seen her leave their camp that evening. Perhaps ghosts traveled by other means than men did, and he was nothing but a fool to attempt to follow her.

They halted on the hilltop closest to Blackvale. From there, Tom observed a weak glow in the distance. Carthouse saw it too. Something was on fire about three or four miles from where they stood. Probably Wildenburg, going by the direction and the sheer size of the aura the blaze painted into the blackness.

Tom was about to say something, but Carthouse hushed him. "Listen!"

A consistent "*heave!*" echoed in the valley below them at intervals, and then someone shouted, "*Loose!*"

A thud and a whizz followed the command. Wood moaned, and a second or two later, a loud bang ripped through the night.

Tom knew that noise. This was the worst they could have expected to find.

"They have a trebuchet," he whispered to Carthouse.

The knight nodded. "They were quick."

"They have manpower."

Carthouse rubbed his stubbly chin. "Let's get a bit closer to see just exactly how much."

Tom hummed, dismounting. "We'll split up and meet back here as soon as we can."

Handing his reins to their guide, he said, "You stay put. Keep your head down, and don't come after us, whatever happens. If we don't return well before dawn, head on back to the camp and warn Walters."

He'd promised the farmer who accommodated his troops to bring his son back unharmed, and he'd promised Walters he'd be careful.

Carthouse vanished without a sound in the darkness. Tom made his way downhill on the western side of the slope.

He managed to dodge two or three of Triumph's patrols before he got close enough to see anything but vague shadows and undefinable movement, because the little village and the area around the moat lay in complete darkness. Triumph's soldiers worked without fires or torches to give Blackvale's archers as little a target as possible to aim at.

Tom ducked behind an empty pig pen and counted five men on the winch team and siege crew that operated a fair-sized trebuchet, working hard to keep it loaded and firing at the castle. They hurled one projectile after the other across the water, and one ear-shattering crash after the other confirmed the damage done to roofs and walls, flesh and bone.

Keeping his head low, Tom tried to get a little closer. He needed an idea of how many men-at-arms they'd be dealing with in all. Some of the soldiers, perhaps as many as a hundred and fifty, would be sleeping in the abandoned houses so they could take over their shift in the morning. He could only guess a rough number of about two hundred out there on their feet.

Then, he saw something he couldn't believe. Louisa walked out in front of him, in plain sight of anyone who might happen to look her way. Several people probably did, but they did not perceive her. It was like on the day he'd jumped after her into the moat.

She stared at the trebuchet. In between sobs, she muttered strange words he did not understand. She was crying, but no one except he could hear her, and he wondered whose death the ghost only he could see was mourning. He straightened, intending to grab her and run. He couldn't leave her here.

Suddenly, two of the ropes holding the arm of the catapult came loose, and the whiplash knocked several of the men next to it over in a bloody mess. Then, the farmhouse farthest from them and its outbuildings burst into flames. Seconds later, the next house was alight, and a few moments after that, another.

The night was on fire. And still she stood there, unmoving, whimpering with grief, and within a few feet of him as she watched chaos unfold.

Keeping his head down, he made use of the bedlam and dashed out of his hiding place.

"It's just me," he told her. "It's Tom."

She glared at him in disbelief.

He took her hand, compelling her to come with him. "We have to get out of here!"

He pulled her behind the shed and uphill into the thicket, as far as she would come before she dug her heels in and started to fight him.

"What are you doing?" he asked her quietly, shaking her so she'd come to her senses.

She wouldn't look at him, and he cupped her cheeks in his hands.

"They're saying she's dead!"

"Who, dear? Who's dead?"

"My sister."

He gently wiped the tears from her face, but more came in a never-ending river.

"People say a lot of things when they're afraid. Who did you speak to?"

"No one. I heard my father say Steffen was supposed to take her to Blackvale after Wildenburg had fallen, but they never got there. He said there were dozens of bodies in the woods between Wildenburg and Blackvale, and he was sure Maria was among them…"

"But we don't know anything for a fact, *Louisa*."

Sorrow turned to shock on her face, and she struggled with him for a moment, but he held on to her.

"It's all right," he said. "It's all right. I know, and it doesn't matter. I know, and I came anyway, didn't I? Please trust me."

"Why should I? And you know nothing about me, *nothing*! Why would you trust *me*?"

He huffed, looking at his feet. "I don't know. I really don't. But I *do* know we have to get out of here and get help. You may be good at setting things on fire, but you won't defeat an entire army on your own."

Maybe she actually could, after what he'd seen, but he didn't want that on her. Taking lives changed a person inside, and he could tell she didn't have a clue what she was doing.

"I just want the killing to stop." She wept. "It *has* to stop!"

Of course she wanted the butchery to stop, but he didn't think he or anyone else could end this peacefully now. Triumph seemed determined to destroy Blackvale, and Tom imagined he might not be particularly interested in talking things over. Blackvale and Triumph had always had issues with one another, and neither Trier nor Cologne demonstrated an interest in settling the matter for them, so Triumph was doing this his way now.

Tom had no other motivation for helping Blackvale than Louisa. By being here, he was going against everything his father expected of him, but how could he make that plausible to her if he didn't fully understand it himself? Love changed a person inside, too.

"Who's there?" a voice shouted from below. "Show yourself!"

He immediately knew he'd made a mistake by not forcing Louisa farther away from the village.

Another voice drifted across to them from the left. "Could be another spy sent by Newburg…"

Tom guessed what had become of his scouts. He hoped they were still alive.

Twigs snapped and dead foliage rustled all around. Shadows moved through the trees, noisily as though the men they belonged to had nothing to lose.

"Let's get out of here," he urged Louisa, her hand in his own. She didn't object.

"I've got him," a man yelled, moving in on them with his blade in his hand and closer than he should have been.

"He's alone!" another soldier called.

Tom drew his sword, but suddenly, they were surrounded by half a dozen armed warriors. An icy shiver ran down his spine. This was bad.

He pushed Louisa out of the way, and shoved the first man down the slope while trying to keep the second at arm's length. Warm blood trickled from a wound on his shoulder where another of his opponents cut him. A kick in the back of the knee from behind brought him to fall. Someone seized his sword.

"Stand down," Carthouse's voice bellowed from somewhere nearby. "You're assaulting Lord Newburg, here to speak with William of Triumph!"

"Well then, we have just the man we've been waiting for," he heard someone say before metal hit him hard in the side. Almost immediately, he tasted his own blood.

Time seemed to slow down, and he couldn't fill his lungs with air anymore. He toppled over, face first.

Louisa screamed. A hard silence followed. It intensified to a deafening ringing in his ears. He flipped over on his back with far too much effort. For a moment, he watched the pale moon emerging from behind the clouds, and he wondered where everyone had gone. Everyone but Louisa.

She was with him. She held his hand. It felt wonderfully warm. He'd been wrong about her. She was no ghost. She was the only thing that was real to him.

He tried to stay awake, but then everything went black.

Twenty-Seven

Friend or Foe

Ricdon sat back in the weaver's best chair and grinned. The man was trying to make a fool of him by telling him he had nothing to offer in return for the help he'd received. Nothing but the length of cloth lying on the table between them. Granted, the fabric was a fine quality, but it wasn't enough.

The weaver's wife and three children slept at the other end of the house's only room. One of those children was there solely because Ricdon had found her at the bottom of a dry well. The entire village had searched for days without finding her, until everyone but her father had given up hope.

The little girl was in a bad state. Cold, dark places did things not only to the body, but also to the mind. It took a lot of innate strength to overcome darkness.

If there wasn't enough strength to heal, what remained was to forget. If a child saved by magic could not forget, sometimes a little more magic was the answer. Her father had asked for more magic, and Ricdon had brewed a potion for the girl, but now the weaver wouldn't pay him appropriately.

Who did he think he was?

This wouldn't do.

"There has to be something else you can give me for my hard work," Ricdon said, playing with one of the two vials he'd been meaning to hand over tonight.

One potion worked to take the edge off despair, and the other strengthened acceptance. Despair and acceptance were concepts children had no words for when adults impatiently demanded explanations.

The weaver looked down at the tabletop, twisting a handkerchief in his hands.

Ricdon was about to draw air and make a suggestion when a tingling sensation in his bowels alerted him to the Calling of yet another father in need.

He closed his eyes to get an image. Blackvale. Again. Tenacious as ever. Third time over the past day. This was interesting. Maybe he would finally be getting Gregory's castle and lands after all. He'd have to answer soon in any case, but not just yet.

The weaver looked like he was going to cry as he glanced around the tiny house. "I have nothing."

In another life, Ricdon might have felt sorry for him. Here and now, his gut told him the man wasn't being honest.

He sighed. "Well, then I'm afraid this is as far as we go together." He tucked the vials into his coat pocket and rose.

"No, wait!" The weaver jumped up and grabbed his arm.

Ricdon expressed his displeasure at being touched by burning his hand and donning Rambert Longsword's rotting, eight-hundred-year-old face.

Cracked lips curled back to reveal black, decaying teeth in a wide sneer, he tilted his head and watched the man squirm. Lifting the veil to get things moving in the right direction generally worked well on uncooperative peasants and noblemen alike.

"I'm sorry," the man spluttered, waking at least two of the children huddled together in the family bed. They stared wide-eyed across the room.

The weaver folded his hands as though in prayer. "She *needs* that medicine – give me a day to come up with something. *One* day…"

At that moment, a searing pain shot through Ricdon's side, biting right into his spine. It was strong enough to blur his vision. His stomach cramped, and he stumbled forward. Bile rose in his throat. He dematerialized at once with no specific goal in mind, only the rough idea of needing to find the source of his agony and confusion, and the will not to throw up in the weaver's kitchen.

Seconds later, he reappeared on his hands and knees at Peter Smith's old house near Oakwood village. He vomited in the dirt until he had nothing left, and then collapsed, lying on his back for a few moments just as the moon showed itself for the first time this overcast night. Its pale, empty face seemed to mock him, but the pain subsided.

Peering around as he got back on his feet, he saw that the cottage he'd built for his family when he'd been young and full of dreams was reduced to a smoldering frame and a heap of ashes. Only the crumbling chimney still stood. The whole of Oakwood was on fire, and there was no one around to extinguish it.

Where were all the good, righteous people of this godforsaken hole?

His heart thumped wildly, though not from empathy for Blackvale's peasants.

Blackvale certainly had something to do with this, but no father's Calling had ever brought him to his knees before. One Summons wasn't like the next, and if this particular Calling could hurt as badly as to bring him to the one place he least wanted to be, there had to be a reason more important and more personal than Blackvale himself.

His heart would not still. Finally, it dawned on him. This wasn't a father's Calling. This was a son's.

His son's.

Thomas was close by, and he was injured.

It wasn't his own heart pumping so madly, it was his boy's. He felt it because a part of Thomas' heart was shaped from his own, from Rambert's legacy.

He'd given Thomas most of the half an angel had gifted to Longsword to keep the Devil from claiming him the night after Nathaniel died.

No man should have to die before his father.

An arrow had lodged in Thomas' chest during his first days on the French frontlines, and the angel had appeared again. She'd shown Ricdon how to utilize

Rambert's legacy to save Thomas' life. He'd kept just enough for himself to make sure God and the Devil would have a hell of a time trying to decide whether he was still worth arguing over.

If he felt Thomas' pain, his son was in grave danger again now, and he needed help.

Before Ricdon could decide where to start searching, a woman appeared next to him. He sensed her magic, and prepared to fight, but she did nothing to provoke him. Blood soiled her face and hands, and desperation emanated from her every pore.

He fixed his gaze to hers, and to his astonishment, he recognized her face. Louisa of Blackvale had grown into a woman. Although he'd never seen her before, he knew her because, between one thing and another, he'd spent years observing her sister to see if they would ever trade places again, as he thought they might have the day of Celeste's death. He'd suspected all along that she was still alive… somewhere.

Fascinating, how unfinished business always came back to you in the end.

"Blackvale here, Blackvale there, Blackvale everywhere," he chanted, pressing a hand to his throbbing side. "Tell me, long-lost daughter of Gregory, to what do I owe the honor?"

"Tom needs you," Louisa said simply, her voice close to breaking. "He's hurt."

"What ties do you have to my son?"

"He's… We're… I love Thomas. I was with him.

He's hurt very badly."

How could she love his son? When had this happened, and how? Thomas knew nothing of demons or lost children, but she was here, and she seemed so serious and sincere.

"Damn you," he muttered. A new wave of agony assaulted him, doubling him over. "*Damn* you and your whole bloody family! Where is he?"

Not that it mattered. He could locate his boy without help from her. He'd *always* found him on any battlefield. *Blood always found back to itself.*

"In the woods beyond Blackvale village. Hurry!"

She offered him her hand, eyes pools of suffering in the pale moonlight. She shook like a leaf in a storm, and he could tell she was afraid of him... but she'd come anyway.

He hesitated for a second, realizing this could be a trap despite what he perceived of her, but Tom *was* hurt, whether he was walking into a set-up or not.

"It's the quickest way," she said. "*Please!* We have to hurry!"

She was right, and he believed her. Her kind of magic was learned, not inborn or gifted. Someone had taught her, perhaps the demon who'd taken her all those years ago, but that demon was not here. He'd know if it was. Louisa reeked of abandoned Fairyhill, or some other dark Underworld place, but he couldn't detect the presence of a key or any other magical item on her that would take them there instead of to

Blackvale, and she was alone. She posed no danger. Not to him.

He accepted her hand, and allowed her to pull him along through her amateurish loophole in space and time.

They emerged on a hilltop. Screams and shouts from the valley below drifted up through the trees.

His son lay on the frozen grass in a small clearing, enveloped in a peasant's coarse cloak soaked with blood. A young man sat with him, shivering in the icy wind. It was his cloak warming Thomas. The lad scurried away on all fours when he saw them, clearly terrified.

"Who did this?" Ricdon demanded, paralyzing the boy with a flick of his hand so he wouldn't run off into the woods.

"Leave him," Louisa said, kneeling down beside Tom. "He has nothing to do with this."

Turning to the lad, she said, "Find your horse and ride back to your father's farm as quickly as you can. Tell Walters we need help at Blackvale *now!*"

"Walters?" Ricdon asked, quickly hunkering down to feel his son's deathly pale brow. "What's he doing here? What's going on? *Who did this?*"

The lad fled into the night without looking back.

"Tell me!" Ricdon repeated, releasing the fastenings of his coat so he could place it under his son's head.

Louisa ignored him. She swiftly pulled up one end of the cloak covering Tom and undid the buckles of his leather breastplate to reveal his ghastly wound.

"Please help him," she repeated, tears streaming down her face. "I don't know what to do."

He had to restrain himself from slapping her.

"Light," he growled, "I need light."

She lowered her head and raised her hands. The crystalline frost on the grass around them lit up and glowed.

Ricdon stripped off his shirt to dab at the ragged gash in his son's flesh so he could see how deep it was. He wished he hadn't. Whoever had inflicted this cut knew their business.

Helpless, he rolled his shirt to a ball and pressed it against the wound. To hold it in place, he firmly pulled the peasant's cloak back around Tom and tucked the hem under him.

Rocking back on his calves, he absently wiped his bloodied hand over his mouth, trying to steady himself and sort his thoughts. His son was dying, and there was nothing he could do. Nothing, except...

There was *one* thing, but he wasn't sure it would work. Thomas was unconscious, and he needed to be awake to make a clear decision.

Again, the tingling sensation plaguing him all day returned, but amplified tenfold. Blackvale was calling him again. He willed it to stop, but it wouldn't.

Not now!

"Is there anything you can do?" Louisa asked.

"He's dying," he told her, struggling to his feet and feeling his real age.

The Calling grew stronger still, exerting a tremendous pull on him. He could barely resist. He needed room to think, but the violent fury inside of him scrambled every coherent thought in his brain. He wanted to kill first Blackvale and then Rambert for what they'd both made of him. He had everything, but in reality, he was nothing but fate's eternal laughing-stock, damned to save other men's children while he lost his own. How entertaining he must be to watch.

Hands clenched to fists against his temples, he tugged and tore at his hair as he retreated from Thomas. What he wouldn't give for just a few seconds of clarity.

He hadn't gotten more than two or three steps when a loud crunch sounded as he trod on one of the vials he'd filled for the weaver. The potion meant to be drunk dispersed in a fine fog when it touched the frosty grass, settling on the naked skin of his arms, chest, and face. Calmness and healing began, and his head uncluttered. The tingling paused. He breathed in the cold air and made his decision.

Louisa stood in front of him, unaware of what had just happened. "You can't just let him go!"

"He's not going to," a voice echoed from the trees.

Ricdon wasn't surprised.

"Go away," he shouted. "I'm not done here yet!"

The old bastard to whom the voice belonged had no business still being alive.

None.

"You do realize you have to answer that Summons," Rambert said, coming forth from the shadows and into the meadow. A thick wad of fog carried his meager form.

Peter Smith's body looked not ten, but twenty years older than when they'd last met. Time had reduced him to skin and bones, and the left side of his face was sagging.

"Wasn't it *you* who warned me to stay away from Blackvale?"

Rambert smiled indulgently, as much as his drooping mouth permitted. "Indeed... But that was then, and this is now. We had a deal, as I'm sure you'll remember."

"Go to hell!"

Rambert laughed. "That's something I've known to avoid. But *you* are well on your way, it seems." He paused, and the expression on his face changed to anger. "Heed his Call, or we'll both pay the price!"

Again, despite the potion's effect, Ricdon felt a blinding rage about to destroy his self-control. No matter what he did, he was going to lose Thomas, or lose himself, or lose both of them.

At that moment, from the corner of his eye, he saw Louisa dip down and bend over Thomas to pull something from his belt. The metal blade of his son's dagger reflected the glow from the rime for a mere fraction of a second before she flung it at Rambert. It met its mark in the middle of his chest despite the raging wind, and he crumpled to the ground. The old man didn't stand a chance.

"Save Thomas," she said decisively, but he could hardly hear her over the bitter gale that howled through the trees, and the renewed, overwhelming din of Blackvale's Summons.

"I can't," he stuttered. "It's *your* father! It's *his* fault! Then and now, *his* fault!"

Louisa placed a gentle hand on his arm, and her warmth penetrated his skin, soothed his anguish. "I'll handle it. Stay here, *please* stay... *try* to stay." With that, she was gone, and the squall abated.

Twenty-Eight

Light Magic

The fire raged like a rabid beast, roaring as it feasted on timber and flesh, while the castle lay in near silence. Only five or six of Blackvale's archers still held their ranks on the battlements. They shot at anything they saw moving around the moat by the light of the flames from the other side.

Louisa did not bother making herself invisible as she ran slalom across the rubble-littered courtyard and up the steps to the entrance of the main building, or what was left of it. Her presence could do no more damage than the trebuchet already had, she told herself, and no one gave Lady Blackvale a second glance.

She knew where to find Gregory. He couldn't have gone anywhere by himself since she'd last seen him. Three guards had carried him feet first into the Great Hall. They'd lain him on the floor with all the other injured and dying.

Theresia held his hand. He kept calling out to Ricdon, and she continuously tried to hush him.

Louisa knelt beside him.

Her mother's face lit up for a moment when she became aware of her. Then her mouth fell open. She was about to speak, but Louisa slowly shook her head, and took Gregory's hand in her own.

Whether Theresia understood or just accepted who she really was and why she'd come didn't make a difference. Maria was dead. Tom was not. He needed Ricdon, but all Gregory needed was comfort.

"You're here," Gregory said. "You're safe! He heard me!"

"He did," she replied softly, patting his hand.

Theresia let out a sob and touched Louisa's hair, then her shoulder, as though to convince herself she was real, or as real as Gregory needed her to be.

Gregory reached for his wife. "See? I told you. I told you he'd bring her back if she was alive. He can do that…"

Louisa smiled down at him as best she could. "It's going to be all right, Papa."

She wasn't sure about that. Things could hardly be any worse.

A rumbling crash shook the structure, and Louisa feared another attack. Dust billowed out and made it difficult to breathe. She heard screams and cries for help, and someone yelled that a section of the roof had caved in at the rear of the building.

"I should be there," Gregory said, panting. He tried to sit up, but she stopped him.

"No, don't do this," she told him. "Help is on the way. Bartholemburg's army is almost here. You just rest yourself."

A tear trickled down her cheek. He reached up and wiped it away with the pad of his thumb, just like he'd done when she was a child. The gesture felt awkward, but she did not withdraw from him.

She'd cried so much tonight, perhaps more than she had in her entire life before. She'd cried for Maria, for Thomas, and now she was crying for a man who'd chosen to give her away so he could have... *This?*

At least, that's what Atiram had told her. But Atiram had also made her believe Triumph would be snowed in until Bartholemburg's troops arrived, and Blackvale would suffer no harm, while politics dismantled Triumph's wealth and Ricdon's life.

Today, Wildenburg and Blackvale had been reduced to ashes, and Falconaer's troops were still miles away... and she'd gone for help to the one man they'd set out to destroy.

"He'll be leaving this world soon," the demon said from inside her head.

For a few seconds, Louisa thought she'd imagined Atiram's voice, but she scanned the crowded room just the same, wondering who, exactly, she meant. Her father? Her lover? The priest with the crushed spine lying on the bearskin rug a few feet away?

"You lied," she said out loud, hoping to see a reaction. "You lied to me."

Atiram scoffed, confirming she was there, watching her, but she did not reveal herself. "Don't tell me you're grieving a man who chose a title over his own child? Or... are you perhaps grieving for a secret lover?"

"There is much to mourn," Louisa replied, stiffly getting to her feet and motioning at the soldiers and peasants lying alongside her father; the cook who'd likely never wake up from the severe head injury she'd sustained, the knight who'd lost his right leg at the hip and bled profusely through his bandage, and the young boy who refused to let anyone touch his dead mother's body.

Louisa knew none of these people except for her parents, but they suffered because Triumph had managed to take Wildenburg and destroy Blackvale, turning the lies she'd told Dietmar into fact. Pools of blood had gathered on the tiled floor like puddles on a rainy hollow way.

All of this was on her... but it was also on Atiram.

Theresia stood up beside her. "Who are you talking to?" she asked sharply.

Atiram hummed indulgently. "There has always been death and pain in this world, child."

"But this isn't how it was supposed to be."

"Tell me who you're talking to!" Theresia demanded again, grabbing her arm.

"I *never* lied to you," the demon said. "I'm the only one who'll ever be honest with you."

Louisa spun around like a mad woman, trying to locate Atiram. "Show yourself!"

Theresia looked on in horror, unsure of what to do. Most of the other people in the room did not notice, or pretended not to. No one did, except for Gregory.

"Don't you see her?" he mumbled unexpectedly. "I see her. She's right there, by the door."

Louisa directed her gaze at the doorway. She was only vaguely familiar with the aged, wrinkled face Atiram wore tonight, but ocean-blue eyes betrayed her. They shone like eerie stars in the night.

"Who *is* that?" Theresia asked.

Suddenly, the old woman was right next to them.

"Agnes," she said quietly to Theresia. "Agnes Smith. You don't remember me, but your husband does." She hunkered down beside Gregory. "I've come to see you off, Milord. Like you came to see me off, and my children, and all those others you and your father's hellhound watched burn." Her face changed, morphing from one semblance to another liquidly. Dozens of images blended, appearing and vanishing.

Gregory's mouth worked as he recognized many of them, the memory rising from a place inside he'd thought he'd locked so well away, but he had no words, just a final dying breath, and then he was gone. Theresia lowered her head, and tears leaked from her eyes.

Ricdon carefully pulled a tiny pouch from the pocket of his coat and pinched some of the powder it contained between his thumb and first finger. He sprinkled it on Thomas' nose and bluish lips, and Thomas opened his eyes.

"Richard," he whispered, unmoving, "Where's Louisa?"

Ricdon smiled. "Don't worry. She'll be okay. She's buying us some time."

"Time for what?"

Ricdon felt shame for having woken him to so much pain, but he had no choice, and the powder would not keep him conscious for very long, whatever the outcome.

"Time for you to make a decision. You... you..." he couldn't say it to his boy's face. He'd never thought he'd have to. All had been well when he'd last seen him.

"I'm dying, aren't I?"

The sorcerer nodded, and then shook his head, trying to paste on a smile that didn't fit with how his heart bled for his son. Hearing it from Thomas was even worse than saying it himself. "But I can help you. You just have to give me permission."

"Permission for what?"

Ricdon took a deep breath. "Permission to make you immortal so you can live. You would be like me... but still yourself, of course. Only you'd have a heart that's half dark and half light, half the Devil's and half God's."

Thomas managed a small laugh. "So where's the catch?"

Ricdon placed his palm on Thomas' cold cheek and his smile widened. "Well... Only a bit of... *humanitarian work* to balance the years you'd be getting. For fairness' sake. You just have to say yes, and we can seal the deal."

"What, no scribe, no wax, no fanfare?"

Ricdon huffed. "We'll have to make do out here, I'm afraid. The real action is down at the castle. But old Walters will give you a good fanfare at dawn if you're back on your horse by then."

"Will I feel different?"

Would he *ever*. Maybe he'd hate him for it, after a few decades. Maybe he'd love it – like father, like son.

"A little," he lied. He tried to remember his life before the bargain with Longsword. Immortality had definitely been an improvement. Only... "The heartache is more intense, but the women are more worthwhile, too."

Thomas coughed, and Ricdon wiped the blood from his chin. "I've already found the one I want."

"Then live for her. Choose a name and say yes."

"A name?"

"You have to choose a new one because your old life has come to its end."

Thomas was silent for a few faltering heartbeats. "I don't want to. I like my name."

Ricdon didn't think it mattered. Not in this case. It wasn't as though he'd have a need for it. The Wishmaster had no illusions: he would trade places with his son and die in his body on this clearing tonight in Thomas' stead. That was how it worked.

He planted a kiss on his boy's brow, like he'd always done at bedtime when Thomas had been a baby. "Then just say yes. It's all right."

Thomas gave a weak nod, humming.

That was good enough. "All right," Ricdon whispered. "Close your eyes."

Thomas did.

Once she had fulfilled her obligation toward Agnes Smith's dying spirit, the demon assumed an appearance more familiar to Louisa. It did not change the way the girl looked at her; anger and disdain lined her face. Life had indeed taken an unexpected turn. How quickly a human's loyalty came to an end.

"Get away from me," Louisa shouted. "Leave this place!"

"Why should I do that, love? I've come to help you."

"You lied! You told me all you wanted was to ruin Falconaer, but you played me for a fool, and you used me! All these people. All this bloodshed!"

Her fosterling was full of surprises. She had been from the very beginning. Who would have thought she'd have it in her to kill, but Louisa had killed a king. For *love*. Things had gone so well until then – right down to the troop of soldiers wearing the falcon on their tunics underway to Triumph for a bit of pillaging.

But Atiram would not be defeated by a little girl. "Yes… bloodshed *you* had a part in, dear." She gestured around them. "You have their blood all over you."

Louisa paled even further. "I didn't want this…"

"No, you didn't. But I didn't ask for it, either. Fate is a cruel regent."

"Why? Tell me *why* this is how it had to be!"

Atiram drew air, reveling in the coppery scent of devastation, despite the gnawing deterioration of her corporeality and the waning of her strength. "You would never understand."

She took another step toward her prey. Within seconds, her face aged by decades until the parchment-like skin peeled off the skull. Toxic, yellow eyes shone in the gloom, dissected by serpentine slits of ocean blue.

"Do you have any idea who you murdered in the woods tonight, *dear*?" She flung a stream of icy air at Louisa and watched her crumple and shudder.

Of course she didn't know. How would she? The

look on her face was priceless.

The demon was about to pitch another freezing gust at her when Louisa made herself invisible.

"You're not afraid of me, sweetheart?" Atiram crooned, hiding her irritation.

She didn't have time for games and regretted not having seized her while she'd had the chance.

"No," Louisa answered, her voice strong and loud as her form reappeared in several places at once. "Not afraid. Just evening out the odds a bit."

"You're no match for me, Louisa."

She'd learned a lot, Atiram had to admit, but a projection didn't shake or bleed. A few well-aimed, jagged pieces of debris quickly shattered the four images the girl had created of herself, while the real Louisa sent the razor-sharp rock hurling back at her. It lodged in the demon's middle, and it took a moment for it to spill back out, releasing a swarm of black crows that lunged at Theresia and the dead and injured who still lay on the floor. The birds began tearing into them, all wings, claws, and beaks. Flapping and cawing filled the Hall. Anyone who could still crawl fled, and those who could not screamed.

Louisa immediately mumbled a counterspell. Her words turned the ravens into the delicate petals of the tiny golden daisies that covered the fields and meadows of Wildenburg in early summer. They rained down on the writhing and thrashing bodies, while the first light of day stole in through the broken windows on the east side of the building.

Atiram knew Falconaer's horsemen would be arriving any time now, followed by foot soldiers. Agnes' dwindling life force sapped her. She had to put an end to this. *Now.*

"I see that I taught you well," she told Louisa, bringing the chandelier from the ceiling down on her.

Louisa jumped out of the way, but the iron candleholder struck her shoulder and ripped into her back. Still, she managed to get back on her feet, and levitated every tool and weapon in the room, pointing at Atiram.

"Last chance. Leave!"

Atiram had no intention of doing that. She twisted the knives, arrows, daggers, and files around in Louisa's direction.

"Come on, stop this. You don't belong here," she said, but the words had barely left her mouth when a man faded into sight, blocking Louisa from her view.

"You're right," he said, clapping his hands once. "She doesn't." He clapped again, and the deadly arms vanished.

Anger blurred Atiram's vision. She couldn't see his face very clearly, but she recognized the old magic that clung to his essence and the scarred heart that beat in his chest. She'd been connected to its fate for so long, she would have recognized it anywhere, and the brief moment of hope it evoked distracted her.

But Rambert was dead, and she loathed herself for her weakness.

"What did your father get from this bargain?" she asked the much-changed Thomas of Newburg, slinking around him, a skeletal cat on the prowl.

Good instincts prompted him to mirror her steps, shielding Louisa. She sensed his devotion to the girl. It had been strong enough to bring him straight here from the meadow where the remains of his body lay. She'd underestimated Ricdon in his will to keep his son alive, and the price he'd pay. Perhaps Agnes had, too.

Her powers were failing, but she kept circling Louisa and Newburg. His calm stare enraged her.

"He used light magic," he finally replied. "The kind that comes naturally to humans. You're not familiar with it. It's called *love*. Love gives without expecting. It doesn't take choices away, but creates them. Where there is love, there is hope. Where there is hope, there is a way. Hope is a matter of free decision, not fate."

She scoffed, looking down at her legs and feet. They had begun to evaporate. She didn't feel pain – just numb, just *nothingness*.

"*Love!* What do you know of love? You haven't lived more than a day, and you speak of it as though you had experienced it and felt its consequences. You do realize you damned your father to hell with that *free decision* you made, or did he not tell you that?"

Newburg's face went blank for an instant, and she used the opening his inner turmoil gave her. He had not grasped the extent of the *love and hope* Ricdon had been willing to invest in him. She gathered all her remaining strength, became wind and echoes, dust and debris from the floor, and launched herself at Louisa.

Louisa ducked into Newburg's embrace, and together they tried to fight her off, but neither the girl nor her lover had a real means of defense against the hurricane she'd become to retrieve her own hope and obtain Louisa's soul. Louisa was hers by right. Blackvale himself had made the free decision to sacrifice her. For *love*.

Newburg held on to Louisa fiercely, and at first she thought it was his proximity protecting her, but there was more to it... She concentrated all her energy on separating the girl's spirit from her body, but she could not. A second soul depended on Louisa's. Her fosterling was with child, and the child's innocence rendered its mother untouchable.

Atiram knew her time was almost up. She stormed and raged against fate, and did not see Newburg reach into a pocket in his cloak to pull forth the pebble she'd given the girl.

Pushing Louisa away, Thomas cast it into the wet blood on the floor. Almost at once, a tunnel of deepest crimson opened, swirling and eating its way into the Underworld. The demon felt its pull too late, and before she could prevent it, she slipped into the vortex it created. It drew her like nothing ever had, and she fell and fell, too drained to stop her plunge into the darkness.

After the tunnel closed, swallowing Atiram, Louisa reluctantly disentangled herself from Tom's embrace. She was not repelled by his appearance or his new form of existence, having taken it into account when she'd left him with Ricdon. She'd been looking at this face for years, and it would take some getting used to that Tom was behind it now instead of the sorcerer.

Glancing around, she had no idea where they'd go from here. The only thing she knew for certain was that they would go together.

Outside, swords and axes rhythmically clattered against shields and armor, first a few, then many. Louisa didn't know how to interpret that until she heard the soldiers on the battlements shouting and cheering.

"Falconaer is here," Tom said in a low voice.

She should have been relieved. She turned to where her father lay. Her mother still cowered beside his body.

"This is all my fault," she said. "I'm so sorry!"

"No." Theresia shook her head, rose, and stood as close to her as she dared. "I don't believe that. We all make our choices the best we know how, and then we have to live with them."

A squire called from the yard, "Steffen of Winterfield has been sighted riding with Falconaer's army. Lady Blackvale is with him!"

Theresia looked at her. Louisa noticed the hope in her eyes and shared it.

"What are you going to do now?" her mother asked.

Louisa's breath caught. Blackvale was not her home, but they all knew that.

"Tell Maria I always thought of her," she said.

Theresia cautiously touched her arm. "She never stopped talking about you, and we never stopped thinking of you."

Louisa nodded. She wanted to wrap her arms around Theresia, but she couldn't. Instead, she reached for Tom's hand and pressed her face against his chest.

"We have to leave before they arrive," she whispered.

Theresia wiped a tear from her cheek. "I know."

"Ready?" Tom asked.

She hummed and closed her eyes. She felt a small jerk, and then the cold morning air on her face. The sun warmed her skin, and although winter was by no means over, she had confidence that there would be ever so much light in her life from now on.

If you enjoyed Trading Darkness, sign up at

www.lisahofmann.net

to receive the author's newsletter and get a free short story from the Dies Irae Series, as well as some other goodies delivered straight to your inbox.

Check out the first book of the Dies Irae Series,
a Writer's Digest top-rated medieval fantasy novel:

Stealing the Light – *Dies Irae Book One*

The gravedigger's daughter has high ambitions. She also has a secret, no control over her magic, and she is about to make a fatal mistake.

Catherine lives in a world where sorcery is forbidden under penalty of death.

When she finds out she is descended from *tainted* nobility, she is determined to learn more and escape the misery of her father's home.

Then she steals from a dangerous stranger, and tragedy strikes.

Haunted by repression, murder, and betrayal, Catherine learns to survive as her powers unfold – but they are dangerous even to her own kind.

Can she find her place and gain control over her *talents*, or will she plunge headlong into the darkness that is consuming the realm?

If you enjoyed Stealing the Light, you might also like

Into the Dark – Dies Irae Book Two

When trust is betrayed, the gravedigger's daughter doesn't get mad. She gets even.

With blood on her hands and the steward's soldiers at her heels, Catherine is running for her life. When she encounters a troupe of traveling harlots and the madam saves her life, offering protection, she sees no other choice than to join them.

Rejected by The Fair – at Lorcan's call – her dream of the easy life promised to her by the madam goes up in smoke. Once the ladies reach the port of St Aeden, she realizes that there are much more dangerous places for a woman alone than the Northern Forest or the trading roads.

Catherine must fight to survive, but just surviving is not enough when she has nothing left to lose and is hell-bent on getting revenge.

Find out if Catherine can manage to turn the tables!

Also available for e-book readers and in paperback:

Gates of Eventide – Dies Irae Book Three

Like action-packed, character-driven raven, phoenix, fox, and dragon shapeshifter stories that will leave you guessing right until the end? Then you'll love

Tales from the Midnight Forest
The Shapeshifter Collection

The Midnight Forest is a place where curses are cast... but also broken. Follow five unusual women shifters into the mysterious woods of Midnight in medieval Ireland, Germany, France, and 19th century England as they discover the power of their Gifts and learn to shape their own destinies in the face of dragons, sieges, and evil sorcerers!

Available for e-book readers and in paperback.